Of
BRIGHTER
DAYS

HEARTS OF EIRE

Of

RACHEL NICKLE

SWEETWATER BOOKS
An imprint of Cedar Fort, Inc.
Springville, Utah

ISBN 13: 978-1-4621-4290-3

Published by Sweetwater Books, an imprint of Cedar Fort, Inc.
2373 W. 700 S., Springville, UT 84663
Distributed by Cedar Fort, Inc., www.cedarfort.com

Library of Congress Control Number: 2022937924

Cover design by Shawnda T. Craig
Cover design © 2022 Cedar Fort, Inc.
Substantive by Rachel Hathcock
Edited and typeset by Valene Wood

Printed in the United States of America

10 9 8 7 6 5 4 3 2 1

Printed on acid-free paper

For Cameron

Even when times get tough
and everything seems impossible,
you can still make me smile.

Books by Rachel Nickle

Hearts of Eire series:

Distant Shores
Of Brighter Days

ACKNOWLEDGMENTS

A big thank you to my beta readers and critique partners, Ruth Willardson, Roxanna Peterson, Rosilynn Babble, Laura Clark, and Kailey Greenwood. Their input and questions helped strengthen this story and gave me the means to shape it into something so much better than the original idea I'd had in my head. I so appreciate the support you all have given me, whether it be cheering me on while I wrote my first draft or by asking the hard questions that made me rethink entire sections of the story. You've made me a better writer.

Thanks to Susy McLellan for all of the rich information she shared with me about Catholic weddings and the myriad of questions she answered. I've tried so hard to do everything I've learned the justice it deserves.

Thank you to Cedar Fort for taking the chance on and seeing the potential in another one of my stories. Their patience with my questions and eagerness to see my story make its way to the hands of my readers is so appreciated.

My little family has been so patient and supportive of my writing. My amazing husband, Cameron, has listened with patience to my story ideas when he would probably rather have been sleeping. Although I never "kill off" half the people he thinks I should, he is my first sounding board for all my crazy plot ideas and takes it like a champ.

CHAPTER ONE

27 December 1845, Liverpool, England

Norah McGowan jumped at the sound of a knock at the door. The needle she held in her hand stabbed her finger, and she yelped in surprise. She nursed her wound, preparing to unleash her displeasures upon whoever stood on the other side of the door. When her friend, Órla Boyd[1], moved forward to let her brother-in-law, Finnegan, inside, Norah's frown deepened. What had been a passing moment of pain and irritation mere seconds before settled into permanent annoyance.

She didn't know if she would go so far as to say that she hated Finnegan Boyd. It wasn't quite that—she tried not to apply any overly strong emotion when it came to him. Though, if pressed, she was prepared to say that it was more a general disdain. But she wasn't pleased to see him, and she certainly wasn't happy that he was the Boyd brother Órla had chosen as their confidant and co-conspirator in their plans for Bridget's wedding dress.

As if sensing Norah's thoughts, Finnegan glanced up at her. She both saw and heard him swallow thickly as he nodded in greeting,

---

1. Pronunciations and translations of Irish names and terms can be found at the back of the book.

his expression guarded behind those same blue eyes she had come to associate with all of the natural-born Boyds.

"Did you get it?" Órla asked him, eyeing the brown paper package Finnegan held securely under his arm.

"Aye," said Finnegan, glancing at Norah again as he relinquished the package.

Órla practically jumped up and down with excitement as she pulled back the paper. When she saw the brown material, her enthusiasm drained from her face.

"Oh," said Órla. She pushed a strand of golden hair from in front of her eyes before speaking again. "It's rather plain, 'tisn't it?"

"'Twas the best they would sell to me with the money you gave me," said Finnegan, his mouth pulling to the side.

Norah suppressed the urge to roll her eyes and snorted softly instead. Finnegan glanced at her out of the corner of his eye but said nothing.

"I suppose it will have to do, then," said Órla long-sufferingly. "And anything is better than the stained rags she is wearing now."

"I should have gone myself," said Norah. She had suggested it to Órla, but the lass had insisted that Finnegan would keep their secret. Why Órla had such faith in him, Norah wasn't sure. Trust, it seemed, came easier to some than others. "Like I said. 'Twas my money anyway. I could have bartered for something better."

"No," said Finnegan sternly. The word was said with such conviction that Norah's eyebrows shot up into her hairline. After the initial shock and the immediate blush which crept up Finnegan's neck, Norah shook her head in disbelief.

"Well, this ought to be good, like," she said. "Let's hear why I'm not fit to spend my own coin."

"Norah," Finnegan began, and her name sounded like a growl on his lips. "You're always putting words in my mouth. It has nothing to do with being fit to do anything. The man who owns the shop hates the Irish, as you well know. I didn't think you would be wanting to be abused, is all."

"Finn was just looking out for us," said Órla, calmly laying a hand on Norah's arm. She smiled so brightly that Norah couldn't help feeling calmed by it. Then, turning back to Finnegan, Órla asked, "Was he very awful to you?"

Finnegan shrugged, smiling wanly. He pulled off his cap and ran a hand through his honey-blond hair. "'Tisn't anything I haven't heard before nor anything I'm not likely to hear again."

"I'm sorry," said Órla. "I would have sent Torin, but you know he can't keep a secret from Daniel to save his life. And Daniel is even worse when it comes to 'his Bridget.'"

"Not a bit of it," said Finnegan. "But will you be able to get the dress done in time for the wedding?"

"Are you questioning our abilities, now?" Norah asked, arching an eyebrow but not looking up from her sewing. She wouldn't dignify him in that way. He did love to rile her, after all. And, if she was honest, she rather enjoyed her ability to fluster the man.

"No," said Finnegan, long and slowly.

Órla smiled weakly, obviously not identifying Finnegan's response as sarcastic. But Norah saw it for what it was.

"Off with you now," said Órla to Finnegan after glancing uneasily between the two. "We have our work cut out for us, and no mistake. We have a whole dress to sew between the two of us and only a handful of days to do it in."

"And you have your work and all. And Colum," Finnegan reminded her as the babe began to fuss from the basket where he lay near his mother's feet. "Are you sure you don't want me to say anything to Catriona for you? She might be able to help."

Órla shook her head at the mention of her sister-in-law, "Catriona has her hands full with her own children as it is—as does Ma Boyd. No, Norah and I will be grand, won't we, Norah?"

"Grand altogether, like," Norah muttered, not looking up until she heard the door close behind Finnegan. Órla situated herself in her chair, taking up the simple skirts meant to replace Bridget's current petticoats. However, Norah had serious doubts that Bridget had ever owned petticoats.

Órla didn't say anything for several moments, and Norah began to hope that she might be spared the conversation that inevitably occurred after every one of her encounters with that insufferable man.

"Finn means no harm, you know," said Órla lightly, never looking up from her sewing. Her hands moved with a swift confidence which Norah could only dream of possessing with a needle. Órla's stitches were so small and close together they could have been created by one of those machines Norah had heard tell about during her time at the textile factory in Cork.

"I've nothing against him specifically, like, as I've said," said Norah. "But don't think you will change my mind that there is something about his approach that leaves much to be desired. The same could be said of most of your menfolk, to be honest. They are so brash and boisterous. Just standing in the same room as them gives me a headache, like."

"I'll give you the Boyd boys are a loud lot when they are together," said Órla with a smile. "But Finnegan is the quietest by miles."

"That's half of the problem," said Norah with a little frown, knowing that her words sounded contradictory. "It's the quiet ones you have to watch out for, like—they're the ones who surprise you. Take Alastar, for example."

"Oh, please no," said Órla with a conspiratorial laugh. It went without being said that Alastar Boyd, the eldest of the Boyd brothers, was the loudest of them all.

"The man is as brash as they come. But what you see is what you get. There are no surprises there."

Órla laughed, then nodded thoughtfully. "I don't know if 'tis as simple as that. I think any man might be capable of being loud or quiet, or good or evil if he chose it. I've seen more than one side to Alastar, though he is loud and merry most of the time, to be sure. But what did you mean when you said the quiet ones are the ones to watch out for? Watch out for what, Norah?"

Norah set down her sewing carefully and picked up the package of fabric Finnegan had brought, inspecting it closely.

"The quality isn't so bad," said Norah. "The weave is quite close together. I think this should last her some years yet."

Órla only hummed, watching Norah closely. Norah knew the conversation was far from over, especially if Órla should choose to bring the subject up in Bridget's presence.

Bridget was Finnegan's younger sister—the only girl amongst five boys—and one of the few people Norah considered to be a true friend. The lass had a fire in her, which reminded Norah of her younger self, though at twenty-three, Norah was only four years older than Bridget. And although Bridget had seen her fair share of trials, the past months especially, she still held out hope for a brighter future. Heavens knew Norah missed the ability to be so positive.

But Bridget was bent on figuring Norah out, and Norah wished more than anything that she wouldn't. Norah wasn't a puzzle to be solved, and some stones were best left unturned. All her past could do was turn her friends against her, and there was no way Norah wanted to do that. Not when she was finally beginning to feel there might be a place where she belonged again.

*   *   *

FINN WALKED AWAY FROM ALASTAR AND CATRIONA'S RENTED ROOM with a shake of his head. Why did the lass have to be so . . . Well, he couldn't quite place his finger on what she was, but whatever it was left him feeling out of sorts—like his heart was going to beat out of his chest from frustration. It made him want to shout and laugh at the same time, which was just madness, plain and simple. That was it. Being near Norah McGowan made him lose his head, and he wanted none of that nonsense if he could help it.

Finnegan Boyd prided himself on being the sensible one among the Boyd lot. He had never been quite so loud or hotheaded as Alastar, Michael, or even Torin was wont to be. Conner, Finn's youngest brother, was still coming into his own, so it remained to be seen where the boy would rank amongst the brothers. But based on an altercation the lad had experienced with a particularly unruly merchant just the day before, Finn didn't hold out much hope.

Conner had become increasingly discontent with the way the Irish were treated by the locals. The Boyds had grown up under the oppression of an English landlord back home in Ireland, but this was something else entirely. They were unwelcome in a number of shops, spit upon, called names, and more else besides as soon as they opened their mouths to speak. For Finn and Conner, it often interfered with them completing their deliveries in a timely manner. The whole situation was enough to throw the best of them off-kilter.

As the self-proclaimed reasonable brother, Finn tried his best to avoid anything or anyone who would throw him off-balance. He had fought hard for his sense of inner peace, after all. But Bridget and now Órla insisted that Norah was an honorary member of the Boyd clan. And that, more than anything else he had faced of late, didn't bode well for Finn.

"After all," Bridget had said. "It's our fault she's here in the first place."

Finn knew Bridget referred to the incident which had cost Norah her long-standing job at a textile factory in Cork back home in Ireland. From what Finn understood, all it had taken for his sister, mother, sister-in-law, and Norah to be fired from the factory was dropping a bit of linen in a puddle. The overseer of the dyebath had seen it as a grievous error, to be sure, but Finn wasn't sure that the punishment fit the crime. Nor that he should be punished along with them by having to endure Norah's censure for no reason that Finn could fathom.

At their insistence that she should save her money, Bridget and Órla and, to Finn's dismay, even his own mother had insisted Norah board with them. Luckily she stayed with Alastar's family and Daniel and Aunt Aileen for the time being, where they rented a room several streets over from the rest of the Boyds. After the wedding, Norah would switch boarding houses so that Bridget could be with Daniel, and then Finn would have no reprieve. If only Daniel had been able to find a small place to rent as he had initially planned, Norah could stay precisely where she was. But even that wasn't far enough away for Finn's liking, especially if the lass was bent on hating him for no reason.

"Life isn't meant to be fair," Gran would say if Finn were to voice his thoughts on the matter. It was a saying he was as well-acquainted with as its meaning.

No, life wasn't fair. It certainly hadn't been to Finn as of yet. But that didn't stop him from trying his best to live every day the way the good Lord would have him do. If only the lass would leave him be and stop scrutinizing every word from his mouth and every move he made, maybe he and Norah McGowan could actually be friends. Besides, Finn wasn't entirely sure what he had done to deserve being the object of her scrutiny in the first place. Surely she couldn't still hold their first encounter against him?

One Month Earlier

Alastar laughed loudly at his own joke and Michael and Conner followed suit. Despite the crowded docks and the shouts of sailors, the sound of laughter reverberated back to them. Finn only smiled and shook his head at his brothers' antics. They were a loud bunch, there was no doubt about that. But the levity did help the tasks feel lighter and the workday to go by quicker, and he would be the last person to complain about that.

"Is that the last of them?" Finn asked as he helped Conner readjust the heavy crates in the back of the delivery cart. This was the first of many deliveries he and Conner would make throughout the day, and Finn wanted to get a move on. He was new to carting and he didn't want to waste this opportunity to prove himself. After all, the wage was a bit higher than a "lumper," the name given to men who did regular dock work. And the change in task allowed him to see more of the city and its people.

"Now it is," said Alastar, lifting the last crate into the cart by himself with a grunt.

In his haste to get started, Finn almost bumped into Conner as Finn turned back around to tell his younger brother that they had best begin the deliveries, but he stopped short. Conner's entire body had gone rigid and he had turned away from Finn. A glance at Alastar and Michael told Finn that they had all seen something off to the side of the docks to distract them.

There was no mistaking the small group of people making their way towards them on the causeway. Finn would have known his mother's fair head from a mile away, though it had been months now since he and Conner had left Shancloch for Cork and then journeyed on to Liverpool for better employment.

Beside his mother, Finn could just make out Da's form, followed by Torin and Órla, the latter who held a little bundle that could only be their new babe. Finn didn't look beyond that, as he was too busy rushing to scoop his dear mother into his arms.

Overcome with joy and relief so profound he couldn't contain it, Finn twirled her about, his laughter rivaling even Alastar's in volume as he allowed his relief to pour out of him. When there had been no reply to the dozens of letters Daniel had sent home to Ireland, Finn had begun to wonder if the worst might have befallen the remainder of his family. To be reunited once more filled Finn with an overwhelming sense of gratitude and wholeness.

"I can't tell you how good it is to see your blessed face again," Finn said on a laugh.

Ma was laughing and crying, clinging to Finn just as enthusiastically. But their moment of joy was interrupted when Finn felt his side connect with something, which gave way with a yelp. He quickly released his mother to discover a young woman lying in a heap at his feet. He moved to help her up, but she shifted away from him, moving to wipe her hands against her skirt.

"I'm so sorry, miss," said Finn, his hands hovering in the air, waiting to render aid. But her silent glare made her brown eyes almost black, and Finn could easily see that she held his blunder against him. He hadn't the foggiest idea of who she was or why she had been standing so close to his family, but there was something about the way she held herself that told Finn she wasn't simply a passerby. Even so, they hadn't even been introduced, and this lass was already spitting daggers at him!

"Norah," Ma began, putting an arm around the young woman with a smile. "This is my son, Finnegan. Finn, this is Norah McGowan. She's our good friend from Cork. We're so glad she agreed to come with us."

Finn smiled weakly and nodded. He muttered out several more apologies, but Norah only nodded curtly in reply, and, eventually, the words died on his lips.

"Do you—" Finn tried once more, determined to make things right. A glance down at her hands confirmed that she had cut them when she fell. "Are your hands all right? Do you need to wrap them?"

"I'm grand," Norah bit out between clenched teeth.

But it was obvious, even to a flustered Finn, that she was anything but fine.

Even now, after having known her for almost a month, Finn knew that Norah McGowan had plenty of spirit but not much else that he could see. Bridget maintained that Norah was a sweet young woman, always helpful and so good with the children, though a bit on the closed side. Excepting the part about being closed, it was a sight Finn had never had the pleasure of seeing. Every time he so much as looked at Norah, she was scowling at him. After the first few weeks, he had all but given up trying to win her favor.

Unfortunately for Norah, and no doubt to Finn's detriment, Finn wasn't one to give up so easily, even when he probably should. Simply giving up when there might still be an inkling of hope—no matter how small—was something he had long ago promised himself he would never do again. He refused to live with any more regrets than those that already lay heavy upon his heart.

But the hope of Norah reversing whatever poor opinion of Finn she had formed seemed rather a dim thing. Wracking his brain yet again for something that could be done to change Norah's mind was the last thing Finn wanted to be doing as he returned to the delivery wagon and a waiting Conner, but here he was.

"Oh, good," said Conner, speaking thickly, his mouth full of bread. They had used this time as a brief break of sorts, and Conner never missed an opportunity to eat if there was food to be had. He examined the list of deliveries as he spoke. "I was about to go looking for you. We'll have to hurry if we're going to make it back to the docks in time. You know how the captain has been lately."

Finn nodded glumly. They had stopped off between deliveries so that Finn could drop off the material he had purchased for Órla. He could have and perhaps should have waited until they had finished for the day and given it to her then, but Finn had hoped that by surprising them with the fabric early, Norah might have noticed . . . what exactly? That Finn was willing to risk employment to run a silly errand? That he would be Norah's lapdog if it meant she would see him as a human being instead of whatever villain she had conjured in that pretty little head of hers?

It was pointless, and Finn knew it. He had almost resolved to give up altogether and not spend so much of his mental energy on the scheme when the door to Alastar's boarding house burst open, and Norah hurried out. She turned back to say goodbye to Órla and kiss little Colum's cheeks as he cooed in his mother's arms. It was a touching gesture, proving to Finn that Norah was capable of feeling and had made a connection with the babe.

"Morning, Norah," Conner called pleasantly when Norah turned towards the street and their wagon.

Finn paused, his hand still on the wagon as if he would pull himself up. He knew he should climb in and hurry them away before Conner was his usual friendly self and offered Norah a ride with them. But Finn found himself hesitating, though he couldn't say why.

Norah approached them slowly, turning to Conner with a small smile. "Where are you headed now, like?" she asked. "Only, I'm working a half-day today; otherwise, I would have been at work already. I'm afraid I'm running a little late, like."

Finn tried not to smile at Norah's random use of the word "like" at the end or sometimes in the middle of a thought. He had heard the word used thus from time to time growing up in Shancloch, but it had been a prevalent part of speech in and around Cork City especially.

Norah was dressed in the black dress she always wore to work, and the dark color made the rosy flush on her cheeks stand out against her pale skin. Finn had to shake his head to dispel that last thought, wondering why he had even noticed.

Both Norah and Finn's sister Bridget were employed as scullery maids in a house on the opposite end of the city. The work must have been difficult because Bridget always came home exhausted, her hands near to bleeding from scrubbing and working all day long. A glance at Norah's hands confirmed that she suffered the same fate. Somehow sensing Finn's gaze, she pulled her shawl closer about her against the cold December air, hiding her hands beneath the folds.

"We have a few deliveries to make before we head back to the docks," said Conner. "But we might be able to take you a few streets over. That would get you a head start, at least."

Finn opened his mouth to protest, then closed it quickly. He couldn't decide if he had been about to suggest they take Norah all the way to Vincent Street or if he had been against her coming with them at all.

He moved forward without a thought and offered Norah a hand up into the wagon. She accepted it, as there was no other way for her to climb up beside Conner while retaining a sense of decorum. But the curious way Norah looked at Finn made him snort in confusion as if that was the only reaction his mind could settle on. She glowered then, pursing her lips in displeasure.

He hurriedly climbed into the back of the wagon with the crates, glad to have that small separation. He didn't know why Norah was so closed towards him, especially when she was so ready with a smile for Conner. What was it about the lad that put all the lasses at ease? Why, even their friend Mary Wilcox wasn't entirely immune to the lad's charms, and she was a good five or six years his senior.

Not that Finn wanted to go charming Norah or any lass for that matter. He had long ago learned that, if one wanted to be sensible, the last thing they should do was spend their time thinking about love and all the complications that came with it. No, it was much better to keep your head than to lose your heart.

CHAPTER TWO

There was nothing like a wedding to keep you busy and run you ragged enough that you had no time to think about your own troubles. It was precisely the kind of distraction Finn wanted—no, needed right now. So, when Ma had requested that he pick out the goose for the groom's dinner, he had readily agreed.

"I don't really like goose," Conner said as they made their way to the butcher that evening.

The coins Ma had given them jingled in Finn's pocket, and he shoved a hand inside to silence them. It made him nervous to be walking around with so much money, although reasonably, he knew it wasn't even that much. But the shops that would willingly cater to the Irish were not usually located in the most respectable neighborhoods. This was why Da had instructed Finn to take Conner with him after they had finished delivering their last load for the day. Better not to be alone in any part of the city. Finn had his suspicions that Captain Mahoney's choice of employing two carters instead of one stemmed from more than practicality or speed.

"'Tisn't about liking it," said Finn distractedly, keeping a wary eye out as they crossed a busy road. The streets here were more crowded than those in Cork, requiring him to watch closely where he walked. Although most members of his family had been able to scrounge up old shoes or create something close to them, Finn had yet to have been so lucky. He was the tallest brother by barely an inch over Alastar, but his feet were unfortunately large and, as such, a challenge to find a fit for in the parish charity bins.

"What's the point in spending money on something I don't even like?" Conner grumbled.

"You know how important the tradition is to Ma," said Finn. "How do you expect us to tease Daniel properly if we can't say, 'You can't back out now, the goose has been cooked and all'?"

Conner rolled his eyes at Finn's overdramatic tone. "I don't remember a goose at Torin and Órla's wedding."

Finn looked at his younger brother with mock concern. "Then your memory has turned because that was less than two years ago."

"I remember Michael's wedding, though," Conner countered. "I remember how Niamh fussed over that goose. But I think the goose at Alastar's wedding dinner was bigger."

Finnegan absently nodded as they approached the butcher's shop, not allowing memories to distract him from the task at hand.

"What can I be doin' you for?" the butcher asked as Finn and Conner entered. The burly man took in their appearance in an instant and attempted a weak smile. Finn quickly removed his hand from his pocket, allowing the coins there to clink together as he stepped further into the shop. The man's smile stuck more firmly in place at the sound. Just as Finn had suspected, the butcher had been afraid they had no coin to spend. Although his initial reaction was annoyance, Finn didn't think it was an altogether unfair assumption for the butcher to have made, given Finn's decided lack of shoes.

"We need a goose," said Finn brightly, ignoring Conner's quiet groan.

"A goose is it?" The butcher's smile widened knowingly. "Which one of you lads should I wish happy?"

Conner snorted loudly, and the butcher's smile faltered.

"Sorry," said the man. "It's just that I don't generally sell many geese after Christmas unless it's for a special occasion."

"'Tis our sister who is to be married," said Finn quickly. "We shall pass on your congratulations. May we see what you have?"

Finnegan spent the next several minutes haggling over the price as Conner wandered idly about the small shop, reading the signs and looking at the meat on display with a dissatisfied expression. Finn watched Conner out of the corner of his eye, his feelings of concern for the lad deepening.

When they had first arrived in Liverpool, there had been a fire lit beneath Conner. Formerly the laziest member of the Boyd family by miles, Conner had worked hard to improve his English, and Daniel had raved about how good he was with the customers, as long as he was able to keep his temper in check. But Finn had seen a change in the lad in the last month; Conner was becoming increasingly discontented. And Finn couldn't say that he necessarily blamed him.

The more time they spent in Liverpool, the more apparent it became that they weren't welcome here. The Boyd clan did their best to stick to the predominantly Irish neighborhoods if they could, but venturing out to their places of employment tended to put them on edge. It was a completely different city than Cork, despite the similarities in industry. And, try as they might, there was just no replacing the feeling of home and belonging. Perhaps Conner was beginning to feel the pull Finn had from the moment he had stepped foot on the ship bound to England. The pull to home was powerful and could mess with your head and heart if you let it. It was yet another thing Finn worked hard to suppress.

"That goose is too small for the number of people I'll be feeding," said Finn to the butcher, eyeing the bird the man presented to him. "Why, it'd be no more than a mouthful for each of us. My mother would never live down the shame."

"I do have another," said the man slowly, moving to grab the bird in question, "but I'm afraid those are the only two. I had plenty last week, but Christmas cleaned me out."

Finn frowned, looking at the size of the goose the butcher held up to him. With the size of the fireplaces in either Catriona's or Ma's kitchens, there would be no way to cook the bird, never mind the price. After inquiring, the butcher confirmed that it was indeed more money than Finn currently carried.

"A small goose is better than no goose," the butcher insisted.

Finn begrudgingly agreed and waited while the man wrapped the bird in brown paper for him.

"Did you buy a chicken?" Conner asked as they exited the shop. Either he hadn't been paying attention to the conversation between Finn and the butcher, or he didn't notice Finn's dark mood as they made their way across the busy street.

"It's just small," said Finn, his tone clipped. "We'll have to make up for it in veg if we can manage it. But since you don't like goose anyway, maybe you can forgo your bite."

Conner shrugged noncommittally. "Maybe we could get a chicken. Either way, there will also be the wedding breakfast that Mary is putting together."

"I must say I'm a bit surprised Mary offered to host a breakfast at all," said Finn. "I'd thought for a time that she might fancy Daniel, so to support him and Bridget like that is awfully good of her."

"Mary is as good as they come," said Conner with pride.

"Despite being English and all?" Finn teased, nudging his younger brother with his elbow.

"We've almost as much English blood as she does," said Conner, his expression souring. "Ma's gran and grandad were English, remember?"

Finn nodded. He remembered well the tales of England his grandad Denton had used to tell of visiting Southport as a child, the town Finn's great-grandparents had moved from when they left England for Ireland. The town was several hours to the north of Liverpool, so Finn doubted he would ever have the chance to see the place.

"Hold up," said Finn, recalling Conner's words. "I'm not an expert with arithmetic, but I know enough to say that having English great-grandparents is not the same as having one Irish parent. 'Tisn't even close to the same amount."

"It's closer than not," said Conner. His tone had the false casual quality Finn had come to recognize as the one Conner used whenever he spoke of Mary Wilcox. Finn guessed Conner was trying to throw their brothers off the scent but that the lad still hadn't gotten over his feelings for the lass. It was an interesting predicament for Conner to be in—nursing feelings for an English lass while allowing his hatred of the English to fester and grow.

Finn felt for the lad, but in Finn's experience, his brothers were usually far too busy with their own troubles to notice that one of their lot fancied a lass unless you were obvious about it. That had been Daniel O'Callaghan's fatal error, and he'd been teased mercilessly for it. He'd always had a bit of a soft spot for Finn's sister, Bridget, and had never been good at hiding it. Only Bridget's complete obliviousness had kept her from noticing as long as she did.

Struck by a sudden thought, Finn turned to his younger brother, a smirk already playing on his lips. "Doesn't Mary have a younger sister?"

Conner's nose scrunched up in distaste, and he guffawed loudly. "Katie is thirteen."

"Ah, well," sighed Finn dramatically. "I suppose if you're bent on finding an English wife, then you had better look elsewhere. It appears as though the Wilcox girls are all wrong for you."

"I'm not looking for a wife," said an annoyed Conner. "I'm still sixteen, remember. I wouldn't have a way to provide for one, anyway."

"Aye," Finn agreed. It was a difficult thing to want to provide for a family but not have the means. He wondered how Daniel was feeling just now, knowing that all the dreams of the life he'd wanted to share with Bridget would have to be set aside or changed entirely. But at least they had each other. That was far more than Finn could boast.

"What about you, though?" Conner asked teasingly. "As Gran always says, 'You aren't getting any younger.'"

Finn rolled his eyes and sighed long-sufferingly. At twenty-six, Finn was one of only two of the Boyd clan who had never been married or didn't currently have a sweetheart, the other being Conner, who was ten years his junior. Finn knew that, to others, it might appear as though he hadn't been able to find the right lass or that perhaps he just hadn't started looking. But it was more complicated than that. They didn't know the whole of it. And they never would.

"What's this here then?" a voice called.

Finn's head whipped up from where he had been watching his feet, trying not to step in any muck. Up ahead, a group of four or five men loitered outside what looked like a pub. By the way one of them ambled about, they had already been in the drink for some time.

Finn placed a hand on Conner's arm and indicated with a nod of his head that they should cross the street. Conner didn't hesitate, his mouth already pressed into a hard line. As much as their brothers might disagree, Finn knew it was better to avoid confrontation, especially if not all the parties involved had full control of their faculties.

They were halfway across the street when Finnegan chanced a glance behind him. The group of men was just beginning to cross the road, one man leading the rest. And he looked irritated.

"Where are you runnin' off to?" the man asked, his speech slurred.

Despite being noticeably drunk, the men were able to overtake Finn and Conner, stepping in front of them in the next moment. As ridiculous as he would have felt, and as much as it would have wounded his pride, Finn regretted not running full out when he'd had the chance. Now he was surrounded by a group of Englishman who, as soon as their suspicions were confirmed, would take great pleasure in antagonizing Finn and Conner about their country of birth.

"Where are you goin' la's?" the first man asked, the smell of drink and body odor so strong on him that it made Finn's stomach churn.

"Just goin' home, la's," said Conner in such a clear impression of the Liverpool accent they often heard on the docks that, had Finn not been his brother, he might not have known that Conner hadn't been born and bred in Liverpool.

"Is that so?" the man asked, closing one eye and squinting as if to examine them better.

Finn only nodded in agreement, knowing that any word from his mouth would derail Conner's story.

"Wha's wrong wit' you?" the man asked, getting so close to Finn's face that he could see each one of the man's yellowing teeth.

Conner looked at Finn quickly, his eyes flashing in warning, then turned back to the men.

"He's feeling poorly," said Conner. "That's why we're hurryin' home and all. Good evenin' to you, gents."

Conner made as though to walk around the men in front of them, but the man grabbed at Conner's arm, his face still scrunched up. "Why don't you have a drink with us before you go."

"Ta'," Conner said with enthusiasm. "But I'm afraid we really must be going. Perhaps another time, la's."

After flashing them all a beaming smile, Conner managed to extricate himself from the man's grasp, and Finn followed him quickly, not looking back to see if the men would follow.

When they had crossed several streets, Finn finally let out the breath he had been holding, smiling as it formed a bark of laughter.

"Where did you learn to do that?" he asked Conner in amazement.

Conner smiled, shaking his dark head to move the fringe of hair that had fallen into his eyes. "I haven't. To be honest, I wasn't sure if it would work. But you know things wouldn't have gone well if a handful of Englishman decided to make an example of us."

Finnegan nodded in agreement. Although there had been a steady stream of Irish workers arriving in Liverpool since the potato blight, it did little to ease the tension between the English and Irish. In fact, over the past month, there had only been an increase in altercations between the two groups. It was just the sort of thing that could throw a man off-balance if he let it. And Finn refused to allow it.

* * *

THEY HELD DANIEL'S GROOM'S DINNER THE NEXT EVENING AT THE larger of the two rooms the families rented. Mary Wilcox had offered her father's home up for the celebration, but considering that she was throwing the wedding breakfast the next day, Ma had insisted that she get to play hostess.

"'Tis tradition, after all, for the bride's family to throw the dinner," Ma had said with pride. "And seeing as I have only one daughter, I want to do it right. Never mind that the goose is a bit small; it shall be a grand celebration and all."

And grand it was, Finn had to agree. Though the meal itself left something to be desired, they made up for it in company and joviality. They reminisced of home—of *céilithe* past, neighbors and friends they missed, and shared and treasured memories—for what felt like ages before Ma and Da announced a wedding present to the happy couple.

"Mrs. Martin," said Ma, referring to their landlady, "told us about another room she was letting in the building next door. The rent is more reasonable, as it's a smaller room, if you can imagine it. The perfect size for newlyweds, I think."

Bridget looked to Daniel, both of them beaming as Bridget wiped her eyes.

"But, Ma, the expense—" Bridget began before Da quickly cut her off.

"You wanted a space of your own," said Da. "And never mind the money. The first month has already been paid, so if we decide that it simply can't be managed after that, we'll let you know."

Shortly thereafter, Ma insisted that they all get to bed, as they would need their rest for the following day's festivities. Everyone had managed to get at least the morning off of work for the wedding and breakfast. It would be a Wednesday wedding because, as the old saying went, Wednesday was "the best day of all" to be married.

"We have a surprise for Daniel," said Alastar, clasping Daniel's shoulder, his eyes full of mirth.

Daniel's shoulder immediately tensed as both Alastar and Michael chuckled knowingly.

"I don't know that I like the sound of that," said Daniel warily.

"You can't get married without a proper stag do," Michael said with a laugh.

Bridget groaned loudly from beside Daniel. "Don't you go taking him about and getting into trouble."

"I wouldn't dream of it," said Alastar. He held a hand to his heart and solemnly bowed his head.

"I don't trust you as far as I can throw you, Alastar Boyd," said Bridget. "See that he makes it back in one piece. *Sober.*" She poked Alastar accusingly to accentuate the last word.

"Yes, Ma," said Alastar mockingly as he ushered the menfolk out of the house.

"You boys be safe now," said Da, who insisted he was too old to go a-roving with the lads.

The Boyd brothers and Daniel escorted Catriona and the rest back to their room before they changed directions. They headed south towards the area of the city where Finn and Conner had been the day before. Finn caught Conner's eye as they realized they were headed to the same pub where they had tried to avoid the group of Englishman. Conner said nothing, but he looked about him quickly, as if the same men had spent the last day just waiting for their return.

"A pub?" Daniel asked flatly as he stood looking up at the sign. Finn followed his gaze. He was still working on reading, as he had mostly focused on his spoken English. The only word he understood was "lamp," but he wasn't entirely sure what that had to do with drink.

"You boys do remember I don't drink, don't you?" Daniel looked around at the group, and Finn moved to put a reassuring hand on his arm. Daniel had long ago sworn he would never touch a drop of ale. He had vowed that he would be nothing like his own father, who had been such a useless alcoholic that he had dropped Daniel at the feet of his uncle without a second thought.

"I'm sure Alastar remembered," said Finn with a pointed look at his brother.

Alastar grinned sheepishly. "There's more to do at a pub than drink."

"Though completely ignoring its primary purpose seems a bit nonsensical," Daniel muttered just loud enough that all the brothers heard him.

"On the bright side," said Michael. "We can be sure to bring you back sober, so Bridget won't have to murder Alastar."

"More's the pity," said Daniel, following the eldest Boyd boys with the air of one walking to his doom.

"I've never been in a real pub before," said Conner, looking about the room with wide eyes.

"Don't tell Ma," said Michael, slinging his arms around both Conner's and Finn's shoulders. "She'd skin us alive if she knew. You'd probably better not have anything—just to be on the safe side."

"I'm sixteen," Conner reminded him with a dark look. "I'm not a boy anymore, you know. And I make more money than you do as a lumper."

"Now, now, lads," said Alastar, ushering them all to a table in the corner of the room. "No need to get testy. I'll go get us a round, and you settle in and enjoy the entertainment."

As the others took in the room with its limited décor and simple furniture, Finn shot Daniel a sympathetic look. The lad was beginning to look a little pale, although that might have been the dim lighting.

"We'll get you home soon enough," Finn promised. "The music is merry, though."

Though "merry" was probably a bit of a stretch. There were only two musicians—a man playing the piano and the other a fiddle which sounded a little out of tune to Finn's ears. He didn't purport to be a musician himself, so he supposed he might have been wrong.

"Merry as a dying cat," said Michael, mouth open in disbelief. "The man needs to adjust his strings. It's starting to sound like Alastar when he was first learning to play."

Finn laughed, taking a little too much delight in the feeling of being right.

"He's probably too drunk to do it himself," said Daniel a little bitterly. He rapped his fingers on the table, his eyes darting about the pub.

"Perhaps you should do something about those strings, Alastar," said Finn when Alastar returned with their drinks. Finn would never have suggested it, but Daniel looked so uncomfortable Finn hoped it would be a welcome distraction for the lad. Finn determined then and there to make sure the evening wasn't a total disaster. A man only got married once, after all. And the final night of "freedom," as some might call it, shouldn't be marked with the anxiety and discomfort which was written all over Daniel O'Callaghan's face.

Alaster laughed off Finn's comment, insisting that it wasn't his place to fix another man's instrument. But it only took Alastar a few more moments of listening to work up his nerve. The boys all laughed as they watched the fiddler hand over his instrument with a bemused expression. A few moments of plucking and Alastar's steady bow to string proved he had done the job right. They were too far away to hear what Alastar said to the musician next, but the fiddler stepped back with a short nod, folding his arms across his chest as Alastar raised the fiddle to his own shoulder with a grin.

A lilting tune filled the air, rising and falling in such quick succession that Finn found his palm beating time against their table without having thought about it. The others soon joined in, smiles upon their faces as they listened to the familiar tune. Even Daniel had begun to relax. It was a tune Finn could remember Alastar playing dozens of times throughout the years. It was an original composition with no words, or else Finnegan would have been tempted to sing along.

Too soon, the song was over. The other patrons of the pub clapped and cheered and called for another. Alastar looked to the owner of the fiddle, who Finn noted for the first time was a young lad no older than Conner. The boy's face had transformed as he listened to Alastar play; no longer irritated, he was enraptured.

Alastar played another, and this time, Finn knew all his brothers and Daniel would know the words by heart. Before anyone could think about how an Irish song might go over in the middle of an English pub, Conner had already begun singing in their native tongue. There was nothing to be done about it; the tune called to Finn, bursting forth from his lungs only a moment before the other lads joined in, five voices and a fiddle cutting through the cool night air, which drifted in from the open door.

Finn had always felt that this is what they were built for, the Irish. If they didn't have a bit of music and lighthearted laughter, how would they survive their oppressors?

He didn't have another thought on how their little party would be received until they finished singing, and Alastar had handed the fiddle back to its owner with sincere thanks. Again, there was a spattering of applause, but it was unmistakably less enthusiastic than it had been the first time around.

As Alastar returned to sit with them, Finn happened to glance up and meet the eye of a fellow sitting at the bar on the other side of the pub. The man was looking at Finn with such concentration that Finn felt himself return the expression. Both men recognized the other at the same time.

Finn stiffened, reaching out blindly to Conner, who sat beside him, laughing at something Torin had just said.

"What's wrong?" Conner asked sharply once he saw Finn's rigid posture and look of panic. He looked in the direction of Finn's gaze and sputtered. "What do we do?"

"Well, your impression certainly won't be convincing anyone now," Finn said out of the corner of his mouth.

Daniel was watching them, the mirth slowly draining from his eyes. "What is it?"

"You'll see soon enough," said Finn as the man approached them, a sneer on his face.

"I knew there was something funny about you," he said, pointing an accusing finger at Finn. "I told the lads you were some of those Irish they've been sending over in droves, but they weren't so sure after that one"—he motioned to Conner with his thumb—"opened his lying mouth. I knew I was right."

"What's he talking about?" Alastar asked in confusion, further irritating the man by posing the question to his brothers in Irish.

The man pounded his fist on their table, his face turning red in anger. The other men at the bar started at the noise. They spun around and were making their way towards Finn and the others before another word could be spoken. A glance at Conner told Finn that he recognized them as the first man's companions.

One of them spoke to the first man so fast and low that Finn didn't have time to translate the meaning in his head.

Daniel quickly held his hands up in front of him in a mollifying manner. "We don't want any trouble, lads. We're just here to celebrate a bit before my wedding and all."

"I'll not fall for any more of your lies," said the man, slurring his words.

"Come on, Robbie," said one of his companions, laying a tentative hand on his arm. "Let's just go have another drink."

Robbie ripped his arm from his friend's grip, his bloodshot eyes flashing with anger.

"Not 'til these boys pay for what they did to me."

"We haven't done anything to you," said Conner defensively.

"You have!" Robbie shouted, causing the remainder of the pub's patrons to turn and watch the exchange. "You and your kind lost me my job! And now there's no more work to be had on the docks, and I've just spent my last pennies on ale to wash away my worries. But it didn't work because here you are in my pub—"

"We have as much right to be here as anyone," said Conner, standing abruptly. His movement caused a chain reaction as Alastar, Michael, and Torin rose in unison, their feet planted firmly, ready to stand their ground. Daniel shot Finn a pleading look as they both tried to pull the brothers back down to their seats.

"This isn't your home," said Robbie, whose friends mirrored his actions with their clenched fists and jaws.

"You took my home," said Conner, his face going red. "And now there's nothing to go back to."

"Just like a paddy to blame all of his cares on someone else," said one of Robbie's companions with a sneer.

"Aye," said Robbie. "Instead of his own lazy, papist bones."

Conner bristled beside Finn, who was quick to shoot a hand out in case he needed to hold his brother back. Conner's movements ceased, but it was too late. Robbie and his cronies had rushed forward, their actions chaotic but quick. Finn was the first to duck as he was closest to them as a fist came swinging towards his face. He dodged in time to avoid a blackened eye, but Robbie's fist connected with his ear, causing Finn to cry out in pain.

He stumbled back, clutching his ear while the three men pressed forward. It didn't seem to matter that they were outnumbered and drunk; the Boyds struggled to hold them back at first. Eventually, a fist was slung on their side, although Finn couldn't have said which of his brothers had done it.

One of Robbie's companions had a particularly powerful right hook, as Alastar was sporting what was sure to be a black eye, and Michael had a cut on his jaw. Daniel, who was perhaps the best fighter amongst them, but avoided confrontation on principle, watched the fist aimed at his face with silent resignation. At the last second, Torin stepped in front of Daniel, taking the blow for him. Torin stumbled back, his lip bleeding from the impact.

The next moment, Robbie dropped to the ground, smashing his head on the table on the way down. He groaned, and the sound slowly brought everyone to their senses. Then he stilled.

Still nursing his throbbing ear, Finn looked up to find the barman standing over them, his face hard as stone.

"Out," he said. His deep voice reverberated throughout the pub. "And don't come back."

The brothers scurried out, not waiting to see if their antagonists were asked to leave as well, though Finn doubted it.

"Ach," Alastar moaned, placing a hand over his eye. "I'll be feeling this in the morning."

Torin spat out a mouthful of blood before pressing his shirtsleeve against his lip. "Aye, and likely beyond."

"You didn't have to do that, you know," said Daniel, referring to Torin jumping in to take the blow for Daniel.

"Oh, but I did," said Torin, swinging his arm over his friend's shoulder as they made their way down the road. "You've never really been on the end of Bridget's fury yet, but you'll see in time that if it can be avoided, it should be at all costs."

Daniel laughed loudly but smiled at the image Torin's words created.

"How was that for a stag do, Danny?" Michael asked, gingerly touching the cut on his jaw.

"A little too exciting for my blood, if I'm honest," said Daniel.

Alastar clapped Daniel on the back with the hand he wasn't using to cover his eye. "But you won't likely forget it."

Daniel laughed derisively. "No, not likely."

"I don't mean to be a pain, lads," said Finn tightly, interrupting their banter. "But could we find a place to sit down for a bit? My feet are killing me from all this walking."

"We've barely walked anywhere," said Conner with a roll of his eyes as he indicated the pub only a little ways behind them.

"I know," said Finn. The dull ache in his right foot turned to sharp pain with the next step he took. Looking down, Finn quickly closed his eyes against the sight. "But I'm bleeding something fierce."

CHAPTER THREE

The needle froze in Norah's hand, and she stilled, waiting for the owners of the voices near the door to pass on. Occupying rooms on the first floor of the building, she was used to hearing snippets of laughter and conversation as people passed by, but it never ceased to put her on edge. The volume of the voices only increased until Norah could distinguish at least three or four separate voices among them. She forced herself not to jump at the inevitable knock, not wanting to stick herself with the needle again. She only had a few more stitches to make until she was done with Bridget's dress, and not a moment too soon, what with Bridget and Daniel's wedding taking place in the morning.

"It's us!" The voice behind the door was muffled but unmistakably Alastar Boyd's.

Norah hurried to place her sewing back into the basket, mindful of where she put the needle so she wouldn't have to search for it in the dim firelight later. She moved to unlatch the door as quietly as possible so Alastar and Daniel's entrance wouldn't wake anyone, especially the children whom Catriona had taken great pains to get to sleep after the excitement of the groom's dinner.

Alastar and Daniel entered the room, but to Norah's surprise, the rest of the Boyd brothers followed them in. They were all in varying states of disarray, and Norah gasped louder than she would have liked when she realized that most of them were sporting some kind of wound.

Norah hushed Alastar as he groaned softly, holding his eye. "You don't want to wake your poor wife, who only just got the baby to sleep, Alastar. Now, tell me what's happened to you."

"There were some English lads who weren't overly fond of Irish music," said Michael with a grin. He winced, then relaxed his face with no little effort. There was a cut on his jaw that had opened up again when he smiled. Looking to the others, Norah noted Alastar's swollen eye, Torin's cut lip, and Finnegan's red ear. Remarkably, Conner and Daniel appeared to have made it through unscathed, though a second glance at Conner revealed a torn shirtsleeve.

Norah tutted, shaking her head. "And that was worth fighting over?"

"We didn't really have a choice," said Finnegan, hopping over to the chair closest to the fire.

Norah moved to help steady him before he could topple over but quickly pulled back, her eyes flashing. "You've been drinking."

Finnegan looked up with a grimace. "I barely had time for a sip before all this began. I'd hardly call that drinking."

"What rich lies you tell, like," said Norah, folding her arms across her chest and fixing the lot of them with a look that she hoped rivaled that of their own mother. "You smell like you've been swimming in the drink."

"Close enough," said Finnegan. "I think my drink was used against me, as my shirt is covered in it, and I've glass in my foot and all."

Norah wasn't sure how she had missed that fact during her initial assessment of the men. Someone had tied a dirty rag around his foot, but the blood had long ago soaked through it. Even by the dim light, Norah could see the bloody footprints leading from the door to the chair and the pool of blood accumulating beneath Finnegan Boyd's foot.

"We hoped you'd be able to help," Alastar explained.

Norah remained silent, biting her lip to keep from saying what she was thinking and waking the children in the process. She instructed the lads to get her a bowl of water as she dug in the bottom of her sewing basket for some lengths of unused fabric. She was careful to move Bridget's dress far away from both the fire and Finnegan's bloody foot, knowing that it would be just her luck for it to either be stained or turned to ash because of Finnegan's carelessness.

With a frown firmly in place, Norah settled herself on the floor and carefully untied the makeshift bandage from Finnegan's foot. "Saints," she hissed, quickly covering the wound back up. She took in a calming breath before giving her instructions to the men. "I'm going to need a knife, Alastar. And if you've a drop of whiskey or the like to clean it with—"

"I don't," said Alastar. His eyes were wide as he stared at Finnegan's foot.

"Stick it in the fire, then," said Norah. "And get some water boiling. I'm going to need to clean some thread and a needle."

"Clean it?" Finnegan asked. His pallor was only accentuated by his already fair complexion. Norah had never seen his hair look so red before, and the sight of his white lips made Norah's stomach flip uncomfortably. She grit her teeth against the sensation.

"Hurry," she harshly whispered as she continued to bark orders at the men. Norah turned back to answer Finnegan's question. "Yes, I need to clean the needle to prevent infection. But don't worry, all that drink you've had will help stave off some of the pain."

"Yes, I'll just let it soak through my skin," he said with a roll of his eyes. "That should do the trick."

"You would know better than I," said Norah tightly, ignoring Finnegan's sigh of annoyance.

When the men had gathered all of her supplies, Norah instructed them to help Finnegan lay near the fire and hold him down, as she needed him to be as still as possible.

Norah hoped Finnegan felt ridiculous with his foot in a lass's lap as she attempted to dig all the shards of glass from his foot. She knew she certainly did. Maybe next time, though she doubted it if she knew men at all, Finnegan would think twice about spending his hard-earned money so frivolously.

It took her longer than she would have liked to be certain she'd gotten all of the glass out, but Norah stitched quickly. It was a good thing, too, as Finnegan required all four of his brothers to hold him still enough for Norah to finish and Daniel to place a rag to his mouth so Finnegan didn't wake the whole neighborhood with his shouted curses. When she was satisfied with her work, Norah wrapped Finnegan's foot securely, ensuring that the bandage covered enough area to keep it clean.

"You don't have any shoes, like," said Norah. She looked to the feet around her to confirm that Finnegan was the only one of the present Boyd clan without them.

"Oh? I hadn't noticed," said Finnegan dryly.

Norah frowned and pulled the last knot in the bandage a little tighter than necessary. "You're not quite so agreeable when you're drunk, are you?"

"I'm not drunk," said Finnegan sharply, sitting up to get a better look at his foot. His eyebrows rose as he looked at it, seemingly impressed with Norah's handiwork. "I'm just tired. I'm sorry if I sounded cross. And for cursing when you started stitching me up."

Norah frowned. His words sounded sincere, but experience told her that words were empty more often than not.

"Thank you," said Finnegan with a small smile.

Norah only nodded, avoiding his steady gaze. "It wouldn't have been fair to Bridget to have to postpone her wedding for your funeral."

Finnegan had the nerve to guffaw loudly, causing Cuán to stir where he and his mother and sisters huddled together in sleep.

"Torin, Michael—" Norah whispered harshly at the brothers, who were attempting to clean their own wounds over a basin near the small kitchen table. "You had best get your brother home, like."

Norah only dared truly breathe again once they had all hobbled out, and Alastar and Daniel had bolted the door behind them, whispering their repeated thanks for Norah's help before they hurried off to bed themselves.

The smell of drink and blood lingered on Norah's hands, and she scrubbed and scrubbed in the washing basin until the lye in the soap she used began to burn her hands. She continued scrubbing until she couldn't handle the pain. And even then, she thought she could still smell it in the air, though she couldn't be entirely sure if it was real or just a haunted memory.

* * *

WHEN AT LAST THE REST OF BOYD BROTHERS ARRIVED BACK AT THEIR room, everyone else had long ago settled in for the night. Everyone, that was, except for Bridget, who still sat before the small fireplace, her silhouette barely visible in the dim firelight. She gave them all questioning looks at their appearance, but said nothing as Michael, Torin, and Conner hurried to their cots with sheepish grins.

"Shouldn't you be abed?" Finn whispered in Bridget's ear from behind, smiling softly so that Bridget would know he wasn't truly scolding her.

"Do I want to know?" Bridget asked as Finnegan dropped down into a chair beside her, wincing at the tugging in his foot as he did so.

"No," he said with a quick grin. "But know that your Danny is unscathed and currently getting his beauty rest."

Bridget hummed softly in response, satisfied with his answer. Her gaze locked on the dying embers in front of them.

Finn readjusted himself in his chair, careful not to let it scrape against the floor and wake Colum. The boy had a pair of lungs on him that could rival any banshee.

"You look worried," he said when Bridget didn't reply.

"I'm always worried," she said mildly.

"You're not having second thoughts, are you?"

Bridget finally looked up at him, her lips pursed in annoyance. "Did you come over here just to tease me?"

Finn chuckled, enjoying the way it was so easy to get a reaction from her.

"It goes both ways, Finnegan Boyd." Her voice was full of warning. "I can tease you as well as the lot of them once your time comes."

"I don't doubt it," said Finn softly, his eyes gleaming from the joy of banter.

"Do you—" Bridget hesitated and returned her gaze to the fire. "Do you want to get married?"

The air left Finn's lungs in a whoosh as his mind scrambled to come up with a response that would quickly pacify her. "Doesn't everyone want to get married?"

"No," said Bridget, drawing out the word. "I think Keegan Sloan would be content to flirt with lasses and never commit for the rest of his days. But do *you* want to get married, Finn?"

Unable to deflect her direct question, he took a breath to steel himself. "I did once."

She was watching him closely—too closely for comfort, as if she was trying to figure him out. "What changed?"

Finn ran a hand over his tired face, silently willing his sister not to force him to dredge up old memories. "I did, I suppose. Or my expectations did, at least."

Bridget nodded in understanding and sat back in her chair. She smiled wearily. "My life hasn't gone at all how I expected it to when I was a child."

"Would you change it if you could?"

Bridget cocked her head to the side, her dark hair flowing down the back of her chair as she considered his question. "If I could, I'd be back home, sitting in front of a turf fire, dreaming of marrying Daniel O'Callaghan tomorrow. All the most important things have stayed the same, I think."

Finn reflected on how far Bridget had come since summertime when she had wanted nothing to do with Daniel's advances or with the life of a farmer. Life had a way of turning everything on its head. At least in this case, it had worked out in Bridget's favor. Very few people could say they were as lucky.

Bridget turned to him, her eyes wide and curious in a way that made him smile uneasily. "What would you change, Finn?"

Aye, but the lass had a way of cutting to the quick of it. "I don't think I'd have the heart to change anything. Changing something for me would hurt someone I love. 'Tis too great a price to pay for something that would have ended badly anyway."

He knew he'd said too much when Bridget turned to inspect him again. He was glad that the fire had almost died—at least she couldn't see his burning ears. He tended to look redder than most of his siblings when he blushed, save Alastar, the only other Boyd who had inherited Ma's fair-colored hair. But Alaster's hair was more gold than Finnegan's honey. Coloring so obvious made it challenging for Finn to hide his emotions and made him an easy target for teasing, which he tried to avoid at all costs, despite being fond of being on the giving end of it.

"We should get to bed," said Finn, rubbing his arms against the chill of the night air. "You've a big day tomorrow, lass."

Thankfully, Bridget hummed her agreement, and no more was said about the past and Finn's regrets.

CHAPTER FOUR

31 December 1845, Liverpool, England

Norah McGowan hadn't always hated weddings. She had a memory of at least one wedding she had attended with her parents as a child that she had thoroughly enjoyed. The memories were a bit hazy in her mind with the passing of time, but the emotions remained sharp and aching. It had been spring, and the cottage where the celebration after the ceremony had taken place was overrun with wildflowers. The bride's hair had been covered in them like a fairy crown, and she had held such a bouquet that Norah could recall remarking to her mother that she would never marry in a month where she couldn't be showered in wildflowers.

Norah wondered if Bridget had any such expectations about her own wedding. She must have, as no bride would have dreamed of getting married in a strange city in the middle of winter with none of the bridal softness one would expect. There were no flowers in sight, but Norah supposed that the intricate details in the stained-glass windows might make up for it to some degree.

But what the wedding lacked in decoration, it attempted to make up for in company. The Boyds had made few friends during their time in Liverpool, and Norah had made none. But the Wilcoxes, a family Norah understood to boast half-Irish blood, sat proudly beside the

Boyds in the chapel as they listened to the priest give the Mass. A few other men whom Daniel had once introduced as men from their village back in Ireland also sat among them with their heads bowed piously as they listened to the priest.

Moving about as quietly as possible, Norah struggled to sit comfortably. She felt as though she were sitting on a handful of nails with each word from the priest's mouth. Her soul felt heavy, and the words of her mother came back to her, vague, like all of her memories from before, but nonetheless real.

"Catholics confuse God with ritual."

There was certainly plenty of ritual to the ceremony, but Norah could see God too, she supposed. Or at least what she imagined God to be like when she allowed herself to think on Him. She saw Him, she thought, especially in the way Bridget and Daniel had looked at one another as they knelt at the altar and spoke their promises. But Norah admitted to herself with a twinge of regret that she didn't know enough about God to be entirely sure.

As Norah watched them, Bridget leaned in to whisper something to Daniel, which caused him to smile from ear to ear. From everything Norah had seen of Daniel O'Callaghan, she believed he at least intended to take care of her friend. Theirs was a love match, after all. And that was something.

There was a sharp intake of breath from beside Norah as Finnegan adjusted himself. How she had ended up sitting between him and one of the fellows from their village was still a bit of a mystery to Norah. She had thought she'd come in late enough to sit in the back and avoid the awkwardness of having to explain that she couldn't receive the Eucharist because she was, apparently, the only non-Catholic present. As Norah had entered, Órla had motioned her over, gushing about how perfect Bridget looked in her new dress and what a splendid job Norah had done on the finishing touches. In the commotion, Norah had been forced to sit hurriedly as the others filed in around her.

But the dreaded moment of having to declare her faith never came. When it was time for the congregation to receive the Eucharist, they lined up in the aisle. Before he stood to go, Finnegan turned to smile warmly at Norah and carefully stepped past her. As he did so, Norah felt his fingers clutch her own for the briefest of moments, where they lay gripping the seat of her bench. The pressure was slight, but the message was unmistakable. He had meant the gesture to be reassuring, perhaps even a way of thanking her for her help the night before. Norah immediately bit her lip and closed her eyes to prevent herself from outright glaring in the middle of a church. She reminded herself that Finnegan was far too preoccupied anyway, so the point of letting him know that his actions were not only unnecessary but unwelcomed would have been lost.

She was relieved when the guests returned, and that Finnegan ended up in a different place than before. She was also relieved to find that the wedding itself was almost over. She could not remember having ever attended a wedding that lasted so long. It had been several years since the last wedding. However, that had been *quite* a different ceremony altogether.

When at last Bridget and Daniel led the wedding party and guests out into the late December air, Norah had expected to feel relieved. The rush of relief she expected never came, and she was left feeling wound as tight as a spring.

The party began its procession to the Wilcoxes', which Norah understood to be in another neighborhood of town. The walk was not too taxing, just incredibly slow given the party's size. During their walk, several of the men from the Boyds' village said their goodbyes, explaining that they had to go back to work. Alastar, Michael, and Torin joined them, as there was a shipment expected that they would need to help unload. They all promised to return for a merry dinner later in the evening, which Norah took to mean that she would have no time for quiet the whole day long. Living with Alastar Boyd and his three lovely but extremely loud children grated on one's nerves after a time.

The Wilcoxes' home was small but inviting. There was a warm fire crackling in the hearth, and all other furniture had been moved to accommodate several smaller tables pushed together. Mismatched chairs surrounded the tables, and the party was quick to file in as Mary Wilcox and the Boyd women hurried to bring out the dishes which had been prepared earlier. Norah offered to help, but she was ushered out of the kitchen and instructed to relax and enjoy herself.

She seated herself in the chair closest to the kitchen in case someone should need her. It also happened to be the chair farthest away from where the other members of the family had sat down. It wasn't that Norah disliked the majority of the Boyds, but she was nursing a headache from lack of sleep and didn't feel like making it worse by engaging in a conversation.

"I don't believe we've met," said a young man with a lightly freckled face as he eased into the empty chair beside Norah. He spoke in the lilting tones of Cork, and Norah smiled in spite of herself. "I'm Keegan Sloan."

"Norah McGowan," said Norah with a nod of acknowledgment.

"A proper Irish name," said Keegan approvingly.

Norah raised an eyebrow, not bothering to question what name wouldn't constitute "proper Irish," as the young man's tone hinted that this line was a practiced one.

"I believe you're from the Boyds' village, like," said Norah. She attempted a small smile, but she feared it might have come across as more of a grimace.

"And you're from Cork," he said confidently.

"Close enough, I suppose," said Norah.

She was saved from any further conversation as Mrs. Boyd called for everyone's attention. Grace was said, and a delicious breakfast was enjoyed by all, culminating in the worst headache Norah had ever experienced. By the time the family and guests had finished eating, Norah was struggling not to shake.

Keegan was staring at her with concern as the family began moving chairs to help return the room to what must have been its original layout. "You look very pale, Norah."

"I'm grand, like," said Norah. But her voice sounded weak even to her ears.

"I'd offer to walk you home," said Keegan. "But I have to get to work if I have any hopes of celebrating with you all tonight."

Tonight? Norah thought, the panic rising. *Surely the Boyds don't mean to hold yet another party tonight! Merciful heavens, will the gatherings never cease?*

But then she remembered she had already known about the planned dinner and worked hard to plaster a weak smile on her face.

Norah had never before considered herself a recluse by choice, but she was beginning to wonder if befriending Bridget Boyd—Bridget O'Callaghan, she supposed she was now—had been pure folly on her part. Norah hadn't been so very lonely, after all. Had she?

As soon as she thought it, she knew it was a falsehood of the most atrocious kind. For the past four years, Norah had been engulfed by the darkness every night as she blew out her candle, alone in her little boardinghouse. At first, the solitude had been a welcomed contrast to the loud, unpredictable life which had been thrust upon her. But, over time, the refugee begins to feel alone, even in their own skin.

Allowing herself to be Bridget's friend had come as naturally as breathing once Norah had permitted herself to admit that that was what she wanted to do. At the time, Norah had no way of knowing that Bridget came with such a large group of kin. Said kin were currently saying their goodbyes to the Wilcoxes and various family members who had to hurry off to shifts at the docks, dress shops, and, for Norah, the house where she worked as a scullery maid.

Back home, a wedding would have been a day worth setting aside all but the essential chores. But when there was rent to pay and so many mouths to feed, and when taking an additional day off may have meant the loss of employment, it wasn't worth the risk.

"Keegan was right," Mrs. Boyd tsked as she took Norah's arm. "You do look very pale. Do you think your employer might allow you the day off for illness?"

"No," said Norah grimly, holding her head as still as possible. "Bridget had a hard enough time convincing Mrs. Whitaker to give her the day off for her wedding and giving me the morning off to attend. She's quite the strict and proper housekeeper, so I'll need to work hard to finish both of our work before the end of the day."

Mrs. Boyd shook her head sadly as she led Norah into the late morning air. Norah was grateful the day was cloudy—although the warmth of the sun would have been appreciated, given the chill of December— but it would have only made her headache worse. Surprisingly she longed for the dark kitchen downstairs where she scrubbed and washed and was barked at by the cook, Mrs. Williams. Though, if she could get by without any yelling today, she would much prefer it.

* * *

IT WAS WELL PAST DARK WHEN NORAH FINALLY MADE IT TO THE Boyds' rented room. Her hands stung from how raw they were, so much so that the numbness brought on by the cold was actually welcome. She only wished it were effective in relieving headaches as well. From the sound of things, while she had been a block away, the celebration was still in full swing. There was singing, clapping, and Norah was fairly certain someone was playing the flute.

"Norah!" Bridget merrily called when Norah walked through the door, feeling small and out of place amongst so lively a throng. The men from Shancloch had returned, as had all of Bridget's brothers, Norah acknowledged with a frown. "You're back! I hope Mrs. Williams didn't rail you too harshly."

"No, not too harshly," called Norah over the din. She pushed her way through the little crowd until she finally found the blazing hearth where Bridget's gran slept soundly. Norah held her hands out to the flames for want of something to do, but the heat brought feeling back into her cracked hands, and she instantly regretted the action.

"I wondered if I'd see you again," said a voice nearby.

Keegan Sloan stood just behind Norah, a winning smile on his face. Norah fought the urge not to laugh at how practiced even his smile was to her. The lad must have been very popular with the lasses back home. He was rather handsome, after all, with his sharp jaw and smiling eyes. But his efforts were wasted on her, and the sooner he knew it, the better.

"I'm afraid you're barking up the wrong tree, like," said Norah, figuring that honesty was the best policy in this situation.

"And I'm afraid I don't know what you mean, Norah m'dear," said Keegan, his smile never faltering. There were no extra chairs by the fire, so Keegan was obliged to lean casually on the mantle beside Norah. It might have been a striking image to any other lass.

"I'm not the lass for you," said Norah slowly, as if that were the only way her point could be made.

Keegan stumbled, holding his hand to his heart dramatically. "What you're after doing to me, Norah."

Norah pursed her lips at the Irish turn of phrase meant to bemoan someone's actions, but she didn't believe him to be sincere for even a moment. "I've a suspicion you'll survive just fine, like."

"Can't a lad just talk pretty with a lass for a while without any fuss?"

Norah turned her gaze to the fire, effectively done with the conversation and hoping Keegan would recognize her desire to be alone. "Not with this lass, I'm afraid."

CHAPTER FIVE

Finn laughed and clapped in time with the others as Michael finished the latest tune on his flute, and everyone paused for refreshment before he would inevitably strike up another one. Finn sat off to the side of the room with his back to the fire and his snoring gran. His little nieces had been begging him to get up and dance with them, but they'd had to settle for dancing with their Uncle Conner. Finn's foot was smarting after such a long day, despite having spent much of it sitting in the wagon, allowing Conner to make deliveries whenever possible.

As his family and friends reassembled, Finn watched Keegan Sloan make his way to the fire, where Finn was surprised to see Norah. He hadn't noticed her come in, but she didn't appear to have been there for long, as her nose was still red from the cold.

Finn suppressed the urge to talk to her, to strike up a casual conversation so that they might get past whatever was preventing them from being on friendly terms. After all, she had saved his life the night before. But then, Finn reminded himself, he wasn't the one who had been cold and distant all this time.

Whatever her reasons, Norah preferred to keep Finn at arm's length. He wasn't sure why she would sit there talking genially to Keegan Sloan, of all people, nor what made Finn so repulsive to her.

But Finn didn't have to dwell on Norah McGowan's complexities very long before he bore witness to a scene that allowed him insight into her thoughts.

Keegan Sloan was his usual self, flirting with any lass who so much as smiled at him. Only Norah wasn't smiling. Finn wasn't sure how to feel when he heard Norah inform Keegan that he would do better to find another girl to give his attention to. Was it vindication? If not, it was something very close to it.

Before Finn knew what he was doing, he was walking past Keegan, who threw Finn a look as if to say, "good luck with that one." Pulling up the two chairs he'd brought with him, Finn sat down and offered Norah the second chair, mindful to give her enough space. Although he tried not to, he was still grinning at his new theory. He was almost sure that Norah didn't dislike him in particular, but perhaps she had something against men in general. Although that made his chances slimmer of convincing her he was a decent fellow, and that she shouldn't hate him for something out of his control, it was a comfort to know that he wasn't the only one who might never earn her favor.

He opened his mouth to speak, to say something clever now that he felt he better understood why Norah had been treating him the way she had, but Norah was determinedly *not* looking at him, her gaze locked on the fire. Her hair, usually a dark copper, glowed red in the firelight, her dark eyes sparkling.

His mouth still open, Finn stopped short as his breath caught in his throat, and he blinked rapidly to correct his vision. But the image remained, and he feared he would never unsee it. How had no one else noticed the similarities? How had *he* not noticed? For the briefest of moments, as Norah's normally copper hair burned a fiery red, the resemblance was uncanny. So much so that Finnegan almost threw himself at her feet, taking her in his arms with the intention of never letting her go.

But the next instant, the phantom image had passed, leaving him empty and cold and grateful he had been prudent enough to sit still. When Norah finally looked up at him, her expression was pained, and the thoughts warring within Finn's mind quieted as he focused on only her.

She was pale, as she had been during the wedding breakfast. Ma had said something about a headache, and Finn wondered if she had been dealing with it all day. Her hands were raw, cracked, and bleeding in some places. He had the inexplicable desire to help her, to lighten her burdens if he could. Never mind that she might hate him, nor that he now couldn't look at her without seeing the ghosts of his past. Finn *needed* to help her.

Those ghosts had stirred up old feelings he had almost thought extinct within him and with them came a need to prevent history from repeating itself. He couldn't stand idly by. Not again.

He moved to the mantle where he knew Bridget kept the hand salve she and Ma had recently replenished. He turned back towards Norah on one foot, concentrating on keeping his balance and putting as little pressure on his injured foot as possible. But it proved to be too much, and Finn overcorrected, tumbling unceremoniously at Norah's feet. He looked up at her look of surprise, knowing full-well that he wore a matching expression. Then he felt the color rising until his ears were burning. Again, he cursed the trait he had inherited from his fair-haired mother. Alastar and Michael had teased him mercilessly about it growing up.

"You look like a *fear dearg* when you go all red," Alastar had used to say with a laugh, referring to the mischievous faerie who was purported to dress all in red and go about wreaking havoc. As the sensible brother, even then, it had bothered Finn to be compared to a malevolent mischief-maker. He had since learned to hide his displeasure when around his brothers, knowing that it would only give them more fuel for the fire if he let on that it bothered him. But he couldn't deny that there was something to the comparison. He did tend to go all red in moments such as these.

"Are you all right?" Norah asked after a long moment of silence between them. Finn tried to correct himself, to pull himself up and reclaim what was left of his dignity, but the stitches in his foot pinched and pulled painfully.

"Oh, I'm grand," he finally answered, sounding more strained than he would have liked. "I just thought I'd take a little nap down here, is all."

Norah's lips twitched and then pulled down. She was trying not to smile. *Saints.* Was it just the pain, or were even their lips similar? At that thought, Finn forced himself to look away. The last thing he wanted was for Norah to catch him staring at her mouth. He knew he would never live down that level of humiliation.

"Is it your foot, like?" Her lips twitched again, and she brought a red hand up to cover them with a little cough that did not sound genuine. She was laughing at him!

Finn grunted in assent as he was finally able to pull himself up and return to his chair, which he pulled closer under the guise of reaching it faster. He now sat mere inches from Norah. Eyes closed, Finn took several long, calming breaths as he waited for the pain in his foot and the redness in his face to subside. When he finally opened his eyes again, he met Norah's curious gaze. She looked away quickly, but she raised her eyebrows, daring him to question her.

"What is that?" Norah asked, gesturing towards the tin of salve Finn was still holding.

"'Tis for your hands," said Finn, handing it to her without further explanation. His little tumble had left him feeling dizzy and unsteady in more ways than one; he was left looking a fool while Norah had the upper hand. Again.

She opened the tin, testing the salve gingerly with one finger. After a moment of contemplation, during which she glanced at Finn out of the corner of her eye more than once, Norah finally applied a liberal amount of salve to her hands. The tightness about her ears and jaw relaxed by degrees, and Finn smiled in relief. He didn't want her to suffer, after all. Even if they weren't friends. Though, admittedly, that instinct to eliminate her suffering had increased one hundredfold in the last few minutes. Blast those ghosts.

"Do you happen to know what's in it, like?" Norah asked, bringing the tin to her nose and lightly sniffing. The movement of her short nose reminded him of a rabbit, and it was his turn to hide his amusement with a cough.

"I'm afraid not," said Finn. "Ma is the herb expert. I find it best to leave the healing to the womenfolk in my family."

Norah turned to look at him slowly and her dark brow raised dangerously. "And yet men are the only ones seen fit to be doctors, like. Isn't that interesting?"

Finn's brow furrowed as her words registered. "Interesting," he agreed, although he admitted to nothing more. He wasn't sure what his opinion was on the matter, and he wasn't about to say something foolish and give Norah yet another reason for disliking him—not when he had just gotten a clue about her character. Then again, this line of thought did seem to fall in line with his theory that she had something against men.

"Do you think women would make better doctors, then?" he asked, keeping his tone as neutral as possible.

Norah continued to look at him, her expression guarded. She did that a lot—watching and listening without giving much of anything away. It was maddening. Finn was beginning to understand why his family sometimes grumbled about how quiet he tended to be. Were they driven as mad by not knowing what he was thinking as Finn was by wishing he could see inside Norah's head?

"You did fix up my foot," said Finn with a nod to the foot he had propped up between them. "Ma has helped me clean the dressings twice already, and she says these are some of the finest stitches she's seen on a body."

"Has your ma seen her fair share of stitches, like?" She wasn't looking at him, but she had spoken—had contributed to the conversation, and that was something.

"She's done more than her fair share of the stitching if there wasn't anybody better available to do it," said Finn with a shrug. "She has five boys, after all." He hesitated before asking a question he'd heard Bridget wonder aloud once, but Finn wasn't sure of the answer. "Do you have any brothers or sisters?"

Norah looked at him sharply, her brows pulling together as she observed him for a moment before shaking her head. It was more information about herself than she had ever been willing to admit to Finn before, and he took it as a personal victory, though he did his best not to let his triumph show.

"Where did you learn to doctor so well, if you don't mind my asking?"

"I do," said Norah shortly.

Finn sat back in his chair with a sigh. He knew he shouldn't feel so frustrated that she had closed herself off again, effectively ending their conversation much the same as she had done with Keegan. But Finn knew something Keegan Sloan didn't. He knew that, at least to Bridget and Órla, to Finn's parents, and to the children, Norah was pleasant. Why, she even seemed to enjoy Alastar's company better than Finn's and possibly Keegan Sloan's. So, Finn concluded with a wry smile, it wasn't men she disliked, then, but perhaps just a certain kind of person.

Finn had never before been placed into the same category as Keegan Sloan, but he was positive he had an issue with the comparison. Aside from the fact that they had both grown up in the same village, the two men were as different as could be. Finn considered himself the thoughtful sort, never hasty, and loyal to a fault. Whereas Keegan had a reputation as the village flirt back home in Shancloch and had been known to have stolen more than a few kisses in his short twenty years. That was something Finn could not compete with. The only kissing he'd done had been welcomed. Or so he had believed at the time.

A banging sound broke through the noise of music, dancing, and chatter as everyone turned to the source of the sound—the front door.

Daniel, who held his bride in his arms where they had stilled their dance, looked about the room in confusion. "Did we forget to invite someone?"

"More than likely, someone complained about the noise," said Catriona. "'Tis getting a little late."

Da moved to the door and opened it. He immediately threw his shoulders back, a movement Finn knew meant his da was startled.

"Are you a Mr. Boyd?" a voice boomed about the room, making Norah visibly start. Without thinking, Finn grabbed her hand, squeezing it gently in his own.

"I am," said Da slowly. "I'm sorry, sir. Were we making too much noise? Only it's my daughter's wedding day and all. We're normally a quiet lot."

"That remains to be seen," the man's voice boomed again.

Norah's hand flinched under Finn's, but she didn't pull away, keeping her eyes locked intently on the fire. Her eyes and jaw looked tense again.

"I'm looking for a bunch of Irish lads were seen in a pub yesterday evening about this time. One of them was to be married today, which fits the description you've just given me."

"What are you needing them for?" Da asked. Although Finn could not see the man who stood in the doorway, he could see that his father took a half step towards him, pulling the door with him to shield the room from view.

"There was a man who was attacked by those Irish lads who wishes to press charges against them for his injuries," said the thunderous voice. "I'll be needing to bring them in for questioning."

"Tonight?"

"I wouldn't be standing here in the cold if it were any other night, Mr. Boyd."

Da took another half step towards the doorway, continuing to pull the door with him. "But couldn't you come back tomorrow night? We aren't going anywhere, you have my word. Only, let the lads enjoy the rest of the wedding. 'Twould be a terrible thing to spend one's wedding night in such a way."

Bridget pulled herself from Daniel's side and ducked under Da's arm on the door. Finn heard her muttering, but she was too quiet to be heard from across the room. He could only guess that she was pleading with the man.

There was silence for a moment before the man spoke again, his voice only slightly muffled by the partially closed door. "I can allow it—but only because I'm assigned to this area tonight. I'll see any comings and goings, you can be sure."

"God bless you, sir," said Da. "Thank you."

He wasted no time in closing the door behind him as he turned back to the group, his beard positively quivering.

"I've not asked details about your little night outing," said Da, surveying the room before him as he found each of his sons. His voice was dangerously low as he spoke. "Nor your mysterious collection of injuries. But if this family is torn apart because of some fool scheme you lads pulled while drinking, so help me—"

"'Twasn't like that at all, Simon," said Daniel, holding Bridget, who had returned to his side, a little tighter. She looked up at him in desperation. By all appearances, she was scared half out of her wits at the presence of what Finn assumed had been a policeman at her wedding celebration. "There was a group of English men who attacked us—we defended ourselves in the end and left straight away. It was as simple as that."

"'Tis it true?" Da asked. For some reason, his eyes turned to find Finn's, who nodded, gulping under his father's intense scrutiny. Finn couldn't remember the last time he had seen his father so angry.

"'Tis just as Danny said, Da," Finn answered.

"You'll all be here tomorrow night to answer the policeman's questions," said Da. "And I think it would be wise to steer clear of any alehouses in future."

"Hear, hear," Norah muttered.

Finn looked back at her, only just remembering his hand on her own. She hadn't tried to reclaim hers, despite the policeman's retreat. But perhaps she had been too preoccupied with staring at the hearth to have noticed. Finn slowly pulled away, but the movement brought Norah's attention to him. She was staring at Finn as if he had two heads, and he squirmed, smiling as best he could, though he could already feel the heat starting at the tips of his ears.

Norah stood, and, in one swift movement, she walked around their chairs and towards the center of the room. The mood of the party had shifted, and the guests immediately began to disperse.

Finn watched as Norah helped Catriona ready the children to return home. Since Daniel and Bridget would have their own room, at least for a time, Norah would continue to stay with Alastar's family. Finn hadn't expected to feel the twinge of disappointment that he did as Norah walked out the door. But he hadn't expected a lot of things about her.

When Finn finally turned back around towards the fire, he jumped in surprise. Gran, who had been lightly snoring throughout the noise of the party, had awoken. She was looking at Finn in that way of hers that made him feel like she was staring into his very soul.

When Finn could no longer stand her penetrating stare, he finally asked, "What is it, Gran?"

"It would never work, lad," said Gran softly, almost pityingly, Finn thought.

He scratched his head and shifted in his chair, trying to ignore the pain in his foot and focus on her. "What's that, Gran?"

"She's a Protestant, you know," said Gran, leaning in and whispering as if she were sharing some juicy bit of gossip. "It would never work. Best not to tangle your heart, lad."

"I don't think there's any danger of that, Gran," said Finn with a chuckle. "To start with, she hates me."

Gran only hummed thoughtfully and gave him a pointed look. But she was right, of course. Finn shouldn't tangle his heart. Not when it wasn't his to give, not really. Tonight had been a painful reminder of the fact that he'd given his heart away long ago. And the heart was a thing that wasn't meant to be given twice. He believed that as firmly as he believed the sun would rise, and he knew that if he started doubting even the most basic of truths, his entire façade of steady and sure threatened to crumble into pieces.

CHAPTER SIX

Norah was avoiding Finnegan Boyd as though her life depended on it. And perhaps it did. It had been two days since Bridget's wedding and the "unfortunate incident," as Norah was now calling it in her mind. It had been a lapse of judgment not to pull away the moment Finnegan's hand had touched hers. She knew she shouldn't have even talked to him, so she included that in her list of regrets about that night as well. She wouldn't make the same mistake again. To be sure of it, she had avoided the entirety of the Boyd clan, saving those with whom she lived. She hadn't seen either Bridget or Órla, and they had yet to seek her out, for which she was grateful. She needed time to gather her thoughts and to make plans.

Of course, there was no avoiding the children, as she was obliged to help Aileen Sullivan watch them. Norah couldn't even complain because Aunt Aileen, Daniel's aunt, was one of the sweetest women Norah had ever met. She had insisted that Norah call her "aunt," noting with a smile that everyone else did, and it would just make things easier. So Aunt Aileen and Norah looked after the children in the evenings when Norah was able to finish work at a decent time until Alastar and Catriona were through working, and often later if they would need to search out something for dinner.

"Oona's too loud," said six-year-old Roisin, Alastar and Catriona's eldest. "Can I sit with you?"

Norah looked up from her mending into Roisin's wide, green eyes with a smile. She couldn't deny having a soft spot for the girl. Unlike her sister, Oona, who was a whirlwind of motion and sound, Roisin was quiet and even-tempered. Norah thought perhaps it was a rare quality for a child so young, and she loved the girl all the more for it.

"You're always welcome to sit with me," said Norah. "You can even practice your stitching on this scrap of cloth if you like."

Roisin positively beamed at the proposition, taking the short length of material in her hands and helping Norah thread a second needle. They sat in companionable silence as Oona and Cuán ran around the kitchen table, squealing happily.

Norah looked up at the sound of the front door opening and cursed quietly. She had thought she had bolted the door. But it was Conner's dark head that poked around the door, meeting Norah's eyes and smiling timidly.

"Is Alastar at home?" he asked, stepping inside.

"No, he and Catriona planned to go to the market after work," said Norah, pausing her stitching to examine the lad. His eyes kept darting about the room and there was a thin layer of sweat on his brow, despite the cold air outside. "Are you all right, Conner?"

Conner's eyes shifted to Aunt Aileen, but her back was to them as she fussed over little Cuán and Oona who had collided and injured themselves.

"Yes," said Conner. The word sounded more like a question.

"Is it something I can be helping you with?" The way Conner was twisting his cap in his hands with the muscle in his jaw so defined made Norah's heart hurt for the lad. Try as she might to fight it, she had never been very good at watching others suffer. It had gotten her in trouble more than once, and she only hoped this wouldn't be another one of those times.

"I need to talk to Alastar," said Conner.

"You can sit and wait for him to come back," said Norah. "Roisin and I are only working on our stitching, like. Isn't that right, Roisin?"

Roisin looked up at Norah with a little frown. "Can I be done? I don't think I like stitching very much."

Norah laughed quietly at the way the girl's eyes got wider as she begged to go. Norah nodded, and Roisin hurried away to rejoin her siblings as they resumed their game.

"There's a seat for you here," said Norah, indicating the place Roisin had just vacated.

Conner looked to the door as if he might escape that way but thought better of it. He was silent as he sat beside Norah, still twisting his cap in his hands.

"You are upset," said Norah calmly. "Is this something Alastar can help you with?"

"I don't know," Conner said, his brows knitting together. "I hope so."

"I'm very good at keeping secrets, like, if you're needing a body to practice your words on."

He looked up, his expression almost hopeful. "Finn says you're a vault of secrets."

Norah snorted. "I'm just very good at not speaking every thought that comes to mind, like. Your brother might try it sometime."

Conner chuckled, but it sounded hollow. He sat quietly, watching Norah pull the needle through the fabric again and again. He opened his mouth to speak several times but closed it again. Norah waited patiently, knowing that the lad might need time to think things through.

"I'm the one who hit the man," Conner blurted out when Norah had been almost convinced that he would sit there in silence until kingdom come. He looked up to Aunt Aileen to see if she had heard him, but the older woman was still busy with the children.

Norah watched him closely, trying to understand his meaning. "The man in the pub?"

Conner nodded. "I was so angry we were being abused for the mere fact that we sang a song, Norah. Well, not just for singing. But for *being*. They hate us for the land of our birth, and it makes no sense to me."

"Aye," said Norah. "But I don't think hate is meant to make sense. Did you tell the officer when you talked to him last night?"

Conner shook his head. "None of us took credit for the blow. They are saying the man might have permanent damage to his head, but I didn't think I hit him that hard. He hit his head on the table on the way down."

Norah stilled at the image his words created in her mind, and she shuddered, trying not to let it mingle with images of the past. The ghostly odor of blood and tears wafted before her and she shut her eyes against it, taking a calming breath before responding. "'Twas self-defense, Conner."

"That's what Da said when he heard the whole story—minus the part I just told you," he said. "But Daniel said he isn't convinced they wouldn't try and lock us all away for disturbing the peace and, again, for being Irish."

"They can't just lock you away for being Irish or their jails and workhouses would be overrun, like."

Conner shrugged. "That's just what Daniel said, anyway."

"And you want to ask Alastar's opinion on what, exactly?"

Conner was looking at his feet, but Norah could see the tears gathering in the corners of his eyes. "Should I come forward and say 'twas me?"

"I think you know what Alastar will tell you," she said.

Conner hesitated but finally nodded, his dark hair falling into his eyes. "I know. He'd tell me to be smart and keep my gob shut." Conner said it with a derisive laugh, and Norah could tell that the lad was grappling with lightening the mood but couldn't quite achieve it.

"Do you think you can live with that, given what they told you about the man you hit, like?"

"I'm not sure," he said after a moment. "But what other choice do I have? If I come forward, they might send me to prison. That would break Ma's heart. I don't think Gran could survive such a shock . . ."

Norah pursed her lips to keep herself from saying more. The lad needed to work through things on his own, and the questions floating through her head weren't going to help him with that.

"I don't know what you should do," said Norah. "But I do know that a person's past can only stay hidden for so long before it comes back to haunt them."

It was one of those rare moments of revelation for Norah, for as soon as she'd said the words, she felt them to her core. It was only a matter of time before her past caught up with her. She'd tried not to put down roots or to let anyone get close to her for this very reason. Her heart couldn't handle any more rejection than it already had. With a sigh, she let herself think the words she had grown to despise. *It's time to move on.*

* * *

"WOULD YOU CHECK ON THE SOUP FOR ME, FINNEGAN?" MA ASKED as she hurried to set the table. There were never enough chairs nor enough places for all of the Boyds to sit down for a full meal together, but they were rarely all home at the same time, anyway. It would just be Finnegan, Conner, Ma, and Gran tonight, as the other men were still working on loading a shipment. They would be along presently, so Finn would need to hurry through his meal if he wanted to sit while eating.

"Looks fine to me," said Finn, gingerly stirring the vegetables in the pot and breathing in their pleasant aroma. There was seldom enough food to feel truly full, but it was enough to stave off the hunger pangs. And it wasn't only potatoes.

Echoes from the past filled his mind at this thought. He could recall several times his being reprimanded for his lack of appreciation for the crop which had sustained his family's life, but one time in particular was recalled with perfect clarity.

Six Years Earlier

The morning had started nice enough, but by the afternoon it was spitting rain so hard that it made working the fields nearly impossible. Adding it to the wind blowing in, Finn found it difficult to see more than a few feet ahead of him, let alone the spade in his hands. So when Da had suggested someone go to check how Ma was fairing, Finn had been quick to volunteer. Anything for a short reprieve!

He made his way as quickly as he could up to the main cottage. The mud was slick and clung to his feet, making them heavy and slowing his progress. By the time Finn finally made it to the cottage, several inches of his trousers were thick with mud and he spent more time than he would have liked in his attempt to clean them off on a patch of grass. He knew how hard Ma tried to keep the dirt floor of the cottage as dry as she could, and he didn't want to see her eyes flash at him if he were to enter in his present state, tracking muddy water everywhere.

When he finally scurried inside the front door, Finn took a moment to breathe a deep sigh of relief at just how warm and dry the place was. That was until he felt the steady stream of water dripping down the back of his neck.

"You're standing in the way of the pot," someone laughed from the side of the room. Niamh, Michael's new bride, bent down near the washbasin with a bowl in her hands. It only took Finn a moment to see that she was holding the bowl under yet another stream of water. She righted herself the next moment and, humming softly, made her way towards him with an additional pan.

"I think you and your Da need to fix the thatching on this roof," she said, her eyes darting up to squint at the offending ceiling.

Finn only nodded and quickly moved out of her way. She picked up the almost-full bowl of water and quickly dumped it outside into the rain before replacing it beneath the leaking roof. Her hair was all but drenched in the process, as the leak was quickly increasing in size. But Niamh didn't seem to notice, and the contented smile on her face never faltered as she absently wiped away the fiery locks that clung to her forehead. She then moved to empty the rest of the pots and bowls scattered about the floor.

"Where's Ma?" Finn asked, moving to look into the nearest bowl for something to do.

"She went to gather all the bowls and pans from Michael's and my cottage," said Niamh. Her tone was as light as ever, but Finn didn't miss the almost nervous glance she gave him out of the corner of her eye. "Our roof is quite new, and all, and our bowls would do much better here for now."

Finn nodded, his eyes fixed on the water filling up the bowl nearest to him. "I suppose you won't need them for cooking supper, then."

Niamh laughed quietly as she continued about her work. "No, I'll simply bake our potatoes tonight if this rain keeps up."

Finn meant to make a noise of agreement, but his wet clothes clung to him and it was becoming more difficult to stand there amidst the chaos of a leaking roof, the incessant pounding of the pouring rain, and Niamh's oblivious humming, and find something to feel positive about. Not when this entire scene felt like the last straw to him. He was that bit of thatch on the roof, clinging, clinging—about to give way and allow all the thoughts and emotions he had kept bottled up for the past months to tumble to the floor in a muddy mess.

The sound which he emitted was more of a grunt, and he immediately regretted it as soon as he saw Niamh's head whip around in his direction.

"Is there something wrong with that?" she asked innocently, but Finn had known her long enough to tell when she was about to lecture him about something. Ever positive, Niamh had struggled with Finn's poor mood of late. He could tell that, despite her humming and smiles, even her patience with him was wearing thin.

But Finn's mood had darkened almost the moment he had stepped inside, and he wasn't entirely sure how to remedy it. So he leaned into it, allowing the disappointments and hurt feelings he had kept inside him to trickle out.

"Oh, no," he said, his words more acrid than he knew was reasonable in this situation. "There's absolutely nothing wrong with eating plain potatoes for every meal. Why would you suggest otherwise?"

"We all eat the potatoes," said Niamh matter-of-factly. "And we try not to complain because those potatoes are what keep us alive, Finn. 'Tis the way of things."

"But that isn't quite true, is it?" Finn asked, not really caring to hear her answer. "We don't all suffer the same at the end of the day."

Slowly, Niamh stood from her place. She considered him for several long, uncomfortable moments, during which Finn struggled not to squirm under her disapproving eye. She kept her pink lips pursed and her arms folded as a trickle of water pulled a strand of her red hair loose, plastering it to the side of her face.

"Bitterness doesn't suit you," she said, her voice full of reproach.

"They're just potatoes," he said. "I'm sure I'll get over it soon enough."

Niamh's terse expression softened as she opened her mouth to respond. "Will you? It's been six months, Finnegan. You know this isn't about 'just potatoes—'"

Finn was quick to cut her off, not liking the direction this conversation was going. "It was never about potatoes. You and I both know it and there isn't any point in rehashing things. What's done is done," he said with an air of finality.

He didn't need a lecture—especially from Michael's little bride. He had already heard enough from Ma about his mood of late, and he knew himself well enough to know he was nearing his breaking point.

Niamh had no time to think up a reply, although Finn could see the wheels turning in her mind. Just then, Ma and Conner burst through the door, fully drenched, their feet and several inches of their clothes caked in mud. Their arms were full of bowls and pans.

"Would you believe me if I told you I think 'tis letting up?" Ma asked with a burst of laughter. In spite of her disheveled appearance, she looked almost merry.

It took Finn too long to relax his features and move to the window to assess Ma's claim. If Ma noticed the anger which had been apparent only moments before, she said nothing about it. Instead, she addressed Finn with that same happy tone as before.

"When the rain lets up, why don't you and Conner go get some water from the stream so I can begin preparing supper."

Finn spread his arms wide to indicate the dishes filled with water dotted about the floor. "Don't you think we have enough water?" he asked incredulously.

"I'd prefer water from the stream, thank you," said Ma. Her pointed look told him that was the end of the conversation.

"Besides," said Niamh so quietly that only Finn could hear as she moved to empty the dish closest to him. "A bit of fresh air might do you good."

*Finn had to bite his tongue to prevent himself from informing
her that she hadn't the slightest idea what would do him good—
that it wasn't fair for her to presume to know that she ever could.*

In the present, Finn could admit that Niamh had been right about
one thing. Bitterness didn't suit him, and he examined his feelings to
ensure that none of the cynicism of the past bled through his memories into the present. It took several calming breaths and at least two
silent prayers before Finn was sure he was in control of his emotions
once more.

"Pull it off the fire, then," said Ma, pulling Finn back to the here
and now and the boiling pot of soup before him. "And go check the
door, please."

Finn did as he was told, though he hadn't heard a knock. He stuck
his head into the frigid night air, shivering slightly against the cold
and near blackness. But there was no one there. He turned to tell Ma
as much, but in doing so, he glanced down. Something was before the
door in the gathering dark, and he opened the door more thoroughly
to examine it.

"What's that?" Conner asked from his place at the table.

Finn picked up a small wooden box, turning it to look for any let-
tering that might indicate its contents. There was a small slip of paper
wedged between two of the wood panels, and he pulled it out, turning
it over until he found, written in a tiny, flowing script, one word.

Finnegan

It was for him.

Ma, Gran, and Conner all watched as he placed the box down
on the table and worked at the nails on the top of the box until they
finally gave way with a screech.

"Shoes?" Conner asked, sitting back in his chair with a roll of his
eyes. "That's a little disappointing."

"You didn't buy these?" Ma asked, pulling the shoes out and examining them. They were clearly new—there were no creases towards the
toes and no scuffs. They even smelled new. Or how Finn had imagined new shoes to smell, anyway.

"I wouldn't have had the money for something so grand," said
Finn bemusedly, turning the shoes over in his hands.

"Do they fit?" Gran asked, her usually shaky hands positively trembling with excitement. Her eyes shone in anticipation, and Finn let out a little laugh at her enthusiasm. Gran always did love a good surprise.

Finn sat down and carefully removed the shoes from the box, pulling at the laces until they were loose enough. He placed his uninjured foot into the shoe and sat back in amazement.

"Like a glove," Finn breathed in wonder.

"Then why don't you look happy?" Ma asked, leaning down slightly to examine his features. "You've never had such fine a pair of shoes in your life."

"Ma," said Finn carefully, not wanting to cast blame with his words. "I've never had a pair of shoes."

Ma stared off into the distance for a time, and Finn knew she was trying to recall a time when he had indeed had a pair of shoes. But he knew that any memory she conjured would have been false. By the time Alastar's or Michael's shoes were able to be passed down, either they were so worn out as to be useless, or Finn had already outgrown them, and they were passed on to Torin.

"Well, you have a grand pair now," said Gran with a nod of approval.

"But how?" asked Finn, not expecting an answer. "And why?"

"Perhaps you have a secret admirer," Conner said with a snort of laughter. Finn glared at him but didn't have time to retort before the door burst open, and Bridget tumbled inside. Her eyes were red, and her cheeks were glistening with tears.

"What's wrong, child?" Gran asked even as Ma rushed to Bridget's side.

Bridget's sobs were coming too quickly for her to get a word in, and they had to wait what felt like an eternity for her to be calm enough to speak.

"A policeman came 'round the house while Norah and I were finishing up work tonight," she said between hiccups. "He was asking Norah and me all sorts of questions about the boys and Daniel. Mrs. Whitaker got word of it and said there would be no scandal while she managed the house. She sacked us then and there—said she could find a hundred more Irish girls just like us without a second thought."

"That's ridiculous," said Conner. His face was red with anger, and he was shaking his head in disbelief.

"She wasn't wrong," said Bridget. "We are as dispensable here as we were in Cork. I came straight home, but Daniel isn't back from Runcorn yet—Captain Mahoney sent him to inspect a possible shipment, you see—and I wasn't sure what to do."

Bridget dissolved into another fit of sobs as Ma gently stroked her hair, whispering reassurances, though Finn wasn't sure what she could say that would make it better. He had hoped that the brothers' testimony to the policeman would be enough for them to see that the Boyds weren't at fault. But if the police were still questioning people, then this was far from over.

The uncertainty of what that meant put Finn on edge. If all the Boyd men were under the scrutinizing eye of English law, this could only end one way. Not even the leather smell of his new shoes could bring a smile to Finn's face now.

CHAPTER SEVEN

Norah was beginning to wonder if the Boyds were bad luck. After all, she'd spent four years employed at the dyebaths in Cork before she had been let go for something that wasn't her fault. That had been only a few months after Norah had befriended Bridget Boyd, an idea that had, at the time, seemed a harmless solution to her loneliness. And now Norah sat in Mr. and Mrs. Boyd's little home with the other Boyds gathered about. She watched helplessly as Bridget struggled to explain what had happened when the policeman had come to question them and how Mrs. Whitaker, the housekeeper, had sent them both away as soon as she had gotten word of it.

"We won't be able to afford the extra room next month," Daniel was saying. "But 'tisn't the end of the world, *mo chroí.*"

"There will likely be a formal inquisition, like," said Norah quietly. The family turned to her, listening intently. "Especially if the Englishman . . .doesn't recover."

She tried not to let her eyes wander towards Conner. She wanted to keep his confidence, to assure him that she was worthy of doing so. But even out of the corner of her eye, she could see how still he sat and how his knuckles were white as he squeezed his hands together in his lap.

"We could try to find work in another city. Manchester has a booming textile industry," said Torin.

"And an influx of unskilled workers, no doubt," Michael said grimly.

"Do you have a better idea?" Torin asked, one eyebrow raised in challenge at his brother.

Michael folded his arms across his chest in answer to the challenge. He answered firmly and without hesitation. "Return to Ireland."

No one seemed as surprised as Norah was at Michael's suggestion. For a moment, she had forgotten that Michael had left a sweetheart back home. But the plan still startled her. Of course, there was nothing for her there, certainly, but that didn't mean the Boyds wouldn't return someday. As well they should—if they could. Their family had owned land for generations before the English had taken Ireland as its own. They had more of a right to return home than just about any Irishman or woman she knew.

Norah had only recently resolved to take her leave of them anyway, and their returning home would admittedly be much easier than her having to find a new city in which to start anew. But . . .then why did the idea leave her feeling so empty? Why was her mind already searching for a solution to their problem as if it were her own?

"There's nothing left for us there," said Daniel sadly. "Save Michael, of course. And I think we all know it. We've no money for land. Our only hope would be for a good crop next season, but there's no guarantee of that."

"Danny's right," said Finn thoughtfully. He looked hesitant to voice his thoughts on the matter and paused for several moments before finishing. "I think we should try for America."

There was a gasp, and Norah only realized it had come from her when every head turned in her direction. She instantly reddened and smiled wanly at those around her before fixing her gaze on her hands in her lap. It wasn't a solution she had considered.

Daniel, who had just opened his mouth to speak, waited for Norah to say something as Norah's face continued to burn in embarrassment. He must have realized that she had nothing to add because he nodded before saying, "It's a bigger country. They have many cities which are booming with industry, much like Manchester—New York and Boston especially. We've never had a war with America, so there can't be that same animosity between us. I think we should think on it, at least."

Mr. Boyd was shaking his head. "There's no money for passage. There are eighteen of us, Daniel. There's no way we could save enough money—not in ten years."

Eighteen. So they included her in their number in this scheme to start a new life across the ocean. Norah's breath caught in her throat at the realization that they were not planning to abandon her. Not like she had been planning to do to them. Her heart lurched, and she bit her lip to stamp down the excess of emotion.

"We have to do something," said Mrs. Boyd, speaking up for the first time. She had been sitting in silence, a grim expression on her lightly lined face. She spoke with fervor, her voice quivering with emotion. "I thought I lost my boys once before. I don't think I could do it again."

Norah recalled all too well the way Mrs. Boyd had fretted over not knowing where her sons had disappeared to when the Boyds had arrived in Cork, thinking she would be reunited with her sons. Bridget had thought her family too busy with their own cares to go traipsing about the city in search of the lost men. But even from their first meeting, that had not rung true to Norah. Mrs. Boyd was the motherly type if there ever was one. She had embraced Norah as one of their clan from almost the first moment she had met her on the steps of that church in Cork. That kind of person, warm and kind, could never be too busy to worry about any of her children. Which made the thought of the Boyds having to separate all the more unbearable.

"What do we do?" Alastar asked. "Split our family up in order to improve our chances of more steady employment?"

"Bite your tongue, Alastar Boyd," said Bridget fiercely. She was glaring at him with glistening eyes as she held her husband's hand tightly.

"We can't stay here," said Conner, his voice hollow as he stared at a fixed point on the wall opposite him. "If we do, we'll end up in prison at some point or another. And if the English truly are out for Irish blood, 'tis only a matter of time before this family is ripped to tatters."

Conner wasn't looking at anyone, so he didn't see the concerned glances the members of his family sent to one another at his words.

They were all scared, and fear made people desperate. Norah was all too familiar with that particular emotion and the chaos that came with it. And she wouldn't wish it on her worst enemy, let alone the people who were the closest thing she'd had to family since she was thirteen years old. Never mind that she had been prepared to leave them for her own preservation. The Boyds deserved better than to be separated. Norah rolled her eyes at what she was about to do and say. She had always had too soft a heart for her own good, but how had they so easily broken her resolve?

"I'll pay your passage to America," said Norah. "If you're wanting to go, like."

The silence in the room was deafening. Even the children, who had been playing quietly in the corner while the adults discussed their options, quieted as if sensing the significance of the words spoken.

"*You?*" Finnegan was the first to break the silence. Even from across the room, she could see the way he was searching her face for answers she knew she could never fully give. Norah looked away quickly and nodded.

"With what money?" Finnegan Boyd *would* be the one brash enough to ask.

"I've put some money aside, like," said Norah defensively.

"Surely not enough to pay passage for *eighteen* people, Norah," he countered quickly.

Norah huffed in annoyance. Couldn't the man just accept help when it was offered to him without demanding to know the source of it?

"I'd not have offered if I didn't have the means to," Norah replied, fixing to stare the man down but having to look away again far sooner than she'd intended. He was looking at her as if seeing her in a new light—he was putting some puzzle together in his mind. It was exactly the opposite of what she had planned only the night before. Instead of leaving to protect herself, she was offering to stay and potentially burst herself wide open for the viewing of all. Disconcerted did not even come close to describing Norah's level of discomfort. Her skin was positively crawling, screaming at her to get out while she still could.

"But how?" Bridget asked. She had an expression almost identical to that of her older brother. She was attempting to solve the puzzle too. Her question indicated more than curiosity that Norah was in possession of enough money to pay passage for so many people and how Norah could have kept such a secret. And why she had continued to stay with Alastar's family in his cramped hovel when she could have easily gotten one of her own.

Norah schooled her features, not wanting any of the Boyds to see how their questions were unsettling both her and her resolve. "I inherited it."

"How much?" Conner asked.

"Conner!" Mrs. Boyd said sharply. "That's none of your business."

"Enough," said Norah tightly.

A severe look from Mrs. Boyd quieted her sons on the matter. And that, it seemed, was that.

*   *   *

"WHAT DOES IT MATTER WHERE SHE GOT THE MONEY?" MICHAEL sighed at Finn. "That's her business."

"Aren't you curious at all?" Finn asked as he waited for Michael to help him pick up the other end of the crate they were loading into the back of the delivery wagon. The horse started at the sound of the heavy box scraping against the bed of the wagon, and Conner, who sat at the front, pulled gently to rein in the beast.

"I got the impression the lass doesn't want to talk about it," said Michael with a pointed look. "And if she can get me back to my Aoife, I'm happy to let her keep her secrets. Besides, I rather like the way it seems to be driving you mad. We should have concocted some secret for you to solve long ago. I don't remember the last time I've seen you so flustered."

"I'm not flustered," said Finn. He turned his back to Michael under the pretense of wiping sweat from his brow, not wanting Michael to see the way his ears were already starting to redden. Of all his siblings, Finn had spent the most time with Michael, especially in the last few years. In a way, they were the closest of the siblings, but if anyone could get under Finn's skin or irritate him to no end, it was Michael. There was not necessarily a rivalry between them, but neither were they close because of any particular similarities in temperament, either. Sheer willpower on Finn's part, a stubbornness his mother said was "a Boyd trait and no mistake," was the true reason for their friendship. It was something Finn had taken a hint of pride from in the past. But, at the moment, he was struggling to remember why he put in so much effort to get along with someone who could be completely insufferable.

"Gran was right," said Michael with a laugh, patting Finn on the back good-naturedly. "You might just be a little too interested in the comings and goings of that lass."

Finn turned, fixing Michael with a sour expression. "Is that what Gran says now?"

Michael nodded with another laugh, ignoring the way Conner pointedly cleared his throat from above them.

"It's so nice to know that everyone has an opinion on who I'm allowed to talk to or about," Finn grumbled, moving to carry another crate to the wagon.

"Don't be like that, now," said Michael, following him with his own crate. "Everyone wants to see you happy, is all."

"Not all of us are lucky enough to be with the ones we love, Michael," said Finn with a bit more venom than he had intended. "Let alone *twice*."

Michael's smile immediately disappeared as he searched Finn's face. "What's that supposed to mean?"

"Nothing," said Finn, lifting the last crate into the wagon by himself. He ignored Conner's questioning glance between the two older brothers, not feeling like continuing the conversation.

"No," said Michael. He put a hand on Finn's chest, which Finn instinctively pushed away. "Explain what you meant by that."

"Let it go," said Finn, taking a step back. "I didn't mean it anyway. I'm just tired of everyone telling me what I should be doing, is all."

Michael shook his head in disbelief, his dark brows pulling together as he studied Finn's face. "Does this have something to do with Aoife? You've known I was interested in her since last winter, and you never said a word about it then. Why now?"

"This has absolutely nothing to do with Aoife Reilly," said Finn. "As I said, just forget it."

But Michael wouldn't let it go. It was a testament to his stubborn nature—that same nature that had caused him and Finn to butt heads more times than Finn could count. Yet they had always found a way to make things right in the end.

"You don't think I deserve to be happy again, Finnegan." The hurt was audible in Michael's voice.

"I never said that," said Finn. "Why does everyone insist on putting words in my mouth?"

"Because you won't tell us what you're thinking," Conner mumbled but quickly snapped his jaw shut when both his brothers glared at him.

"You don't want to know what I'm thinking, Michael," Finn warned. "Believe me. Just let it go."

Michael made the mistake of placing a hand on Finn's arm. It was meant as a pleading gesture, likely Michael's attempt to encourage Finn to open up to him. But he would get far more than he bargained for. Finn's blood boiled as words long-suppressed—words that should never have been spoken—tumbled out of his mouth.

"Fine!" Finn barked. "If you must know, I think you're awfully lucky to have found love twice—"

"So you said," said Michael, frowning.

"You're awfully lucky to be able to just move on after losing your wife and child."

Silence rang deafeningly between them.

After several long moments, Michael bristled at Finn's words. "You think I'm unfaithful to their memory."

"As you said," said Finn with a growl. "But what do I know?"

"Absolutely nothing," said Michael. He was clenching and unclenching his fists, aching to land a blow to Finn's jaw. Finn almost wished he would. If nothing else, it would bring a quick end to the conversation. "If you think allowing myself to open my heart again was an easy thing to do, Finn, you've lost all reason. Clearly, you don't know anything about my heart or Niamh's wishes. You weren't there in the end; you don't know what we said to each other when she knew she wouldn't make it."

Finn was seeing red and he knew if he didn't retreat now, there would be no turning back, no fixing this. "We need to go," said Finn, abruptly moving towards the wagon and climbing in. "Let's *go*, Conner."

Conner hesitated, his hands on the reins as he looked between the brothers. Michael was glaring at Finn, and Finn was carefully avoiding his gaze, his teeth clenched together to keep himself from saying anything more.

The wagon lurched forward, moving them away from the docks and the still glowering Michael. When they were a reasonable distance away, Conner let out a low whistle.

"I don't know what that was about," said Conner. "But I've never seen Michael so angry in my life. He looked like he wanted to kill you."

Finn grunted. "I don't know how we even got on the subject."

"I believe you were talking about Norah," said Conner. "And then you weren't."

"Yes," said Finn. But he wasn't so sure.

CHAPTER EIGHT

When Norah offered to pay their passage to America, she had fully expected the Boyds' prodding questions—especially from the ever-inquisitive Bridget—to know where she came into so much money. But, to Norah's surprise, no one said a word after Finn's initial questioning. Norah thought Mrs. Boyd must have said something to the family, as no one mentioned it again aside from discussing which ship they might sail on and the best time to depart. And, of course, the awkward conversation, thankfully held in private, in which Mr. Boyd haltingly insisted he would pay Norah back someday.

Having some experience with sailing, given their employment in Cork and Liverpool, the Boyd men insisted that waiting until spring would have been preferable. But then the officer in charge of investigating the pub fight came to the docks to question Mr. Boyd further. The officer had even talked to Captain Mahoney, who was more than a little cross that, as Bridget relayed it, "some of his best workers had gotten mixed up in such nonsense."

"Daniel had explained the situation as best he could, but when it came out that there was talk of us traveling to America, the captain was quite upset," said Bridget one evening several days after Norah's offer to pay their passage. "I think the captain was happy with Daniel's work as his scrivener and is angry he will have to find another man to do his business for him. Not everyone is willing to work for so low a wage, especially ones that can both read and write."

Bridget said the last bit with such pride that Norah was afraid her friend might burst with it. Bridget had been so closed lipped about her sweetheart when Norah had first met her, but the difference now was night and day. Daniel O'Callaghan could do no wrong in his wife's eyes, and, if appearances were to be believed, he would try desperately to keep it that way. He was a good sort of fellow, Norah thought approvingly. Just the kind of man her friend deserved.

"There are so many things to be done before we go," Bridget said with a sigh as she readjusted Torin and Órla's baby, Colum, in her lap and planted a sloppy kiss on his cheek. Aunt Aileen had gone to visit Bridget's gran, so Norah and Bridget were in charge of watching the children while the two women visited in peace and the rest of the family worked.

"I would like to have all of the children's clothes mended," Bridget said.

"You mean you would like Órla and me to mend the children's clothes, like," said Norah with a smirk.

Bridget smiled sheepishly. "You're so much better at it than I am. But you don't have to, of course. Órla and I can manage when she gets home from work. You're already doing too much."

Norah cleared her throat loudly.

"And that's my piece said," said Bridget. "I won't say another word about it."

Norah smiled appreciatively. She had forbidden Bridget from thanking her any more than the lass already had. Each time that someone mentioned that confounded money, Norah was cut down a little more than before. She hated that she had depended on the funds when she had first received them—so much so that she had barely touched them in the years since. Honestly, it would be a relief to be free from them. Norah could almost regret not spending the lump sum years ago, but then she saw the look of relief in her friend's eyes and couldn't bring herself to feel any such thing.

"Bridget?" a familiar voice called at the same moment there was a knock on the door. Bridget smiled widely and popped up from her chair. She hurried to the door, the brown skirts of the dress Norah and Órla had made for her wedding swishing prettily behind her.

"I've been looking for you everywhere," said Daniel as he stepped inside, Conner and Finnegan in tow.

"Well, you've found me," said Bridget smiling. She bounced slightly and hurried to close the door behind them as Colum began to fuss in her arms. "You weren't worried, were you?"

"No," said Daniel. He nodded to Norah in greeting with a strained smile. Of course he had been worried. Mr. Boyd had all but forbade any of the family to move about the city alone unless they couldn't avoid it. That explained the addition of Conner and Finnegan's presence, at least.

Bridget smiled up at him dubiously. "I'll just get Colum's basket, and you can walk us home."

"We'll be back in a while to bring Aunt Aileen home," Conner said to Norah as Bridget and Daniel situated the baby and basket between them.

They turned to go—all except Finnegan, who was frowning.

"Coming, Finn?" Bridget asked, looking between him and Norah curiously.

Norah made sure her expression showed all the surprise she felt at Finnegan's reluctance to follow them. She didn't need her friend to get any funny ideas.

"I'll catch you up," said Finnegan. Conner smirked and snorted as Finnegan pushed him out the door and closed it soundly behind him, ignoring Bridget's whispered comment that Conner really should stay as a chaperone. So much for avoiding any funny ideas.

Finn turned back to face Norah slowly, and she no longer needed to over-emphasize her surprise. His expression was serious, but there was something troubled about it, which caused Norah's fear to slowly inch into concern.

"What do you want, like?" Norah asked, standing up slowly and stepping behind her chair in a pitiful attempt to put some space between them. He watched her movements with curiosity.

"Uncle Finn!" Oona shrilly cried, noticing his presence at last. The next moment she was talking a mile a minute, and Finnegan listened patiently, though his eyes never left Norah's face. For her part, Norah found it difficult to look at him for any length of time. After several awkward moments, Finnegan was able to convince Oona to return to her siblings and their game. Norah waited for him to speak.

"I wanted to thank you," said Finnegan slowly. "For the shoes."

Heat crept up Norah's neck. She took a calming breath, then another before she spoke.

"I don't know what you mean, like," she said lightly.

"Oh, I think you do," he said, taking a step towards her, his knees bumping up against the chair between them. She clung to the chair's back a little harder than before, wondering if it would be too obvious for her to cross the room and stand behind the table instead. "I don't know why you did it, nor why you chose to keep it a secret, but my feet and I thank you all the same."

Norah searched for a place on the door behind him on which to focus, but her eyes kept flitting to his face. His eyelashes were a decided ginger, far darker than his hair, and she briefly wondered how such a thing could be possible. She forced herself to walk to the table—a far safer action than the one she had been engaged in—and began wiping invisible crumbs with her fingers.

But Finnegan followed. Thankfully, he stopped a few feet away, quietly observing her. When Norah was satisfied with the cleanliness of the table, she turned about to engage the children in their game, hoping Finnegan would understand that she had nothing more to say to him. But he had moved, and, when she turned, she found herself impeded by his broad chest. She was able to stop just before she ran into him, but the surprise left her trembling. She clasped her hands together to hide the shaking, then allowed the anger to creep in. It was, after all, a powerful weapon when used correctly.

"Why are you always about, like?" she asked hotly.

The rest of her planned rebuke died on her lips when Finnegan Boyd took her hand in his own. He held it gingerly, but his expression was all business.

"Your hands look better," he said, turning her hand over and over before his face. After several moments, he gave a satisfied nod and dropped her hand.

Norah immediately took a step back, unconsciously holding both hands behind her.

"I'm glad to see the salve helped."

"Yes, and they're healing grand-like now that I'm not using them for anything useful." She didn't know why she said it. She should have ignored him or asked him to go, but instead, she had given him yet another opportunity to further their conversation.

"You're far from useless, Norah," said Finnegan matter-of-factly. "I don't know where you got that notion from."

"I never said I was useless, *Finnegan*," she said, emphasizing his name with what she hoped was the proper amount of cheek. "Only that I'm unused to being idle. Speaking of which, I need to get dinner on for the *wean* before they're near starved, like."

Finnegan moved aside, and Norah busied herself with washing and cleaning the vegetables she had bought at the market earlier in the day. Once again, she had hoped that by showing Finnegan that she was far too busy to talk, he would make himself scarce. But he just continued to watch her as she cut the turnips and tried desperately not to slice herself in the process. Honestly, did the man have no sense of social decorum? Couldn't he tell he wasn't wanted?

She wanted to be blunt and tell him to head on home; then she remembered that this was technically his brother's home. He had more of a right to be here than Norah did. But there was a glass-like quality to his eyes as he watched her that suggested he wasn't actually seeing her at all. It was a small reprieve, but she accepted it gladly.

"Norah," he began suddenly, taking off his cap as he took a step towards her. He stopped to put a hand on the table beside them.

Norah moved back with the knife still clutched in her hand between them. Finnegan glanced down at it with an exaggerated look of shock and fear, and he took a purposeful step back.

"What?" Norah asked quietly, hoping he wouldn't hear the quivering of her voice when his teasing smile disappeared once more.

His blue eyes were searching her face. "Do you believe in second chances?"

Whatever she had thought he was about to say, it wasn't that. "What do you mean by second chances, like?" Norah asked. She returned to cutting vegetables, replaying his question over in her mind. She didn't understand it, but it was clearly troubling him. "Do I believe there is such a thing? Or that people are deserving of them?"

"I'm not sure yet," Finnegan said.

"Then what are you asking me for?" Norah asked testily, keeping her eyes on her hands as she continued preparations for the meal.

"I-I'm not sure," he repeated slowly. He looked at her steadily, for much longer than would have been acceptable among general acquaintances and perhaps even friends. Only they weren't friends, and she was beginning to believe that Finnegan Boyd needed a reminder of that.

"I'm quite busy, like," said Norah, moving around Finnegan with an exasperated sigh. "I think it's time for you to head home."

Finnegan nodded and replaced his cap on his head. He didn't appear offended by Norah's brusqueness, which was a shame. She would have to try a little harder to make her point known, lest the man come seeking her out again for one of these uncomfortably listless conversations.

"You might ask Michael to help Conner escort Aunt Aileen home," said Norah.

"Why?" Finnegan asked sharply. His reaction was unexpected, but Norah recovered quickly. She had wanted to put some distance between them, and if Michael Boyd were the way to do that, she would not be the one to look a gift horse in the mouth.

"Michael's a touch more agreeable than you," said Norah. And much safer.

Finnegan's eyes flashed, and his open mouth snapped shut. She wondered if she had laid it on thick, but after a moment of consideration, Norah concluded that there must be something more to it that she didn't understand. Perhaps the brothers didn't get on as well as they appeared to, or there was some rivalry Norah wasn't privy to. She couldn't help feeling a little guilty at the way Finn's jaw tightened and she found herself grasping for something else to say.

"And you really should be resting your foot like," she said a little more softly. She didn't want to provoke him or even to hurt him, only to give him a reason to leave her be. "You wouldn't want whoever spent money on those shoes of yours to be disappointed when your foot rots off."

Finnegan opened and closed his mouth several times before he settled on his reply. "You still refuse to admit 'twas you. Why?"

Norah remained silent, leaning down to pat Cuán's head affectionately as he toddled by, babbling the whole way.

When she did not answer, Finn huffed out, "You're the most exasperating woman I think I've ever met."

Norah snorted. "Doesn't that make it easier, like? You know we could never be friends, Finnegan Boyd."

"So I'm beginning to see." He didn't bother saying goodbye to her or the children before he left. It was just as well because there was no way that Norah could survive such close quarters on a months-long voyage to America with Finnegan Boyd. Especially not if he were going to continue to stare at her as he'd just done. It was clear as day he hadn't the smallest notion the effect he had on her. And she had every mind to keep it that way.

* * *

"I'M NOT COMING WITH YOU," MICHAEL ANNOUNCED TO THE FAMILY as they finished their supper on Sunday evening after service. They had just finalized plans for their passage and departure date and had been discussing what might still need to be done before they boarded a ship bound for America the following week.

His announcement didn't come as a great surprise to Finn, but their mother immediately burst into tears.

"You know why, Ma," Michael said as he took his mother in his arms. "I promised Aoife I'd return. And you've taught me always to keep my promises."

"Will you promise to join us?" Ma asked, clinging to her grown son. "Promise to come when you can."

"When we can," said Michael, sending his siblings a pleading look. "We'll join you as soon as we can."

Finn rolled his eyes at how easily persuaded he could be to come to his brother's aid, even after their argument and resulting days of silence. "There you have it, Ma," he said. "You know Michael is good for his word. We'll all be together again soon enough."

Michael's dark brows pulled together remorsefully as he mouthed a "thank you" to his younger brother. Finn only nodded and looked away, not wanting to give his brother the false impression that all was healed between them.

74

But it would need to be, Finn realized. If they were to part ways, shouldn't it be as friends, as brothers should be? As they always had done, despite it all? Heaven only knew how long Michael would be in Ireland, nor how long it would take him to return with Aoife. That was if Mr. Reilly would even bless their union. Aoife's father had been reluctant about the relationship between his daughter and a poor farmer to begin with. Finn had doubts that Mr. Reilly would be keen on Michael whisking her away to America anytime soon. Then again, Michael could be quite charming and persuasive when he wanted to be. It was a quality that Finn didn't possess himself, so he was unsure just how easy it would be to charm the merchant into letting go of his eldest child.

"I don't know about you," said Alastar, rising from his chair and stretching loudly. "But I'm rather looking forward to leaving this place behind forever. The food, the people, the music—"

"You can't say it's been all bad," said Catriona reproachfully. "I heard you humming that tune the other night."

Alastar shook his head. "And I rather think I shall enjoy laying around a ship for a month or more. What a holiday it will be!"

"Unless you get seasick," Daniel reminded him brightly. "How was the journey from Cork again?"

Alastar paled, and his smile disappeared. "I hadn't thought about that."

"We can always pray we make good time," said Conner, who Finn knew to have been the only other brother who hadn't suffered on their journey from Cork to Liverpool.

Finn couldn't help smiling at the remark, knowing that he had found his sea legs almost immediately. The difficult part of the journey wouldn't be getting sick.

"Can I help you with that?" Norah asked Ma as she moved to begin clearing plates.

"No, no," said Ma. "You've done too much already. You relax."

Finn watched as Norah's face fell, frown lines appearing on either side of her pretty mouth.

"Better let her help, Ma," said Finn. "Norah doesn't like to feel useless. Nor does she like it when people talk about her money or secretive good deeds."

Ma looked to Norah, who had turned to fix Finn with a hard stare. He only grinned in reply, enjoying the ability to get a rise out of her, especially given how their last encounter had left him feeling the fool once again.

When Finn looked back at his mother, she was watching him closely. Her eyes flitted questioningly to Norah, then back to him. Finn grasped for some topic he might turn to engage one of his brothers about, but he couldn't think of anything that would distract his mother from her observations. He was as confused as his mother appeared right now when it came to Norah McGowan—and he had no answer for her unspoken question.

Finn stood abruptly and approached little Oona, who was always happy to play with her uncle, though her idea of play was to speak too loudly and quickly for Finn to comprehend fully.

"Ma says we're going to travel in a big ship to a new place." Thankfully, Finn was just able to decipher her words as she gasped for another breath before speaking again. "And Roisin says if I'm not careful, I'll fall right over into the ocean and be gobbled up by a whale. 'Tis it true? Will a whale eat me up like Jonah?"

"I wouldn't count on it," said Finn with a laugh.

"More likely a shark," said Roisin, coming up behind her sister with a glint in her green eyes.

Oona's head whipped back around, her eyes wide in fear. "Sharks?"

"Stop scaring your sister," Catriona called. But she turned back to her conversation with Bridget the next moment, and the gleam returned to Roisin's eyes.

"What's gotten into you, my rose?" Finn laughed, tickling Roisin's sides. "You are usually so quiet and gentle. Has your uncles' teasing finally rubbed off on you?"

Roisin shook her golden head, a small smile on her face. "Only, I'm excited about our adventure. I don't like this city anymore. Do you think they have farms in America? I miss digging for potatoes with Oona and Cuán."

"I think they have a great many things in America," said Finn soothingly.

"Do they have potatoes?" Oona asked, looking equally excited at the prospect of a new place.

"Aunt Norah says they do," said Roisin proudly.

Finn's eyes shot to where Norah sat. Their eyes met, and she looked away quickly. She'd been watching him—he could tell by the blush creeping up her neck. The fact made Finn grin, though he wasn't entirely sure why.

"*Aunt,* is it?" Finn asked, lowering his voice as he turned back to his nieces.

"I know she isn't really my aunt," said Roisin with a blush of her own. "But couldn't she be my aunt, do you think? Like Uncle Daniel married Aunt Bridget?"

"Conner can marry her," said Oona matter-of-factly. "Or Uncle Michael?"

"Uncle Michael is going to marry Aoife," Roisin reminded her sister with a roll of her eyes.

Finn quickly extricated himself from yet another conversation before the children could make any more suggestions. Unlike Alastar, being seasick was the last of Finnegan Boyd's worries right now. He was more concerned about the damage wagging tongues and the mouths of babes might do when placed in such close quarters.

CHAPTER NINE

20 January 1846, The Bark Rosemary, Dublin, Ireland

The *Rosemary* made port in Dublin, and, for a little while, Finn was able to gaze upon the shores of his home country once more. The green grass on the cliffs was an unexpected but welcome balm to his heart.

Finn's family hurried to say goodbye to Michael, who clung to Ma instead of the other way around, now that it came to it. Finn felt the full weight of his goodbye to his brother. They had been almost inseparable for these past five years since Finn had stepped in to take care of Michael after his wife's untimely death during childbirth. Michael had been despondent for much of that first year, walking through life like a ghost. But he had come out of it stronger than Finn could boast, and Finn admired his brother for that. Moving on had never been one of Finn's strong suits. Too often he let himself wallow in the past. In truth, Finn felt more than admiration for his brother—he envied him. He knew it was wicked of him, and he tried his best to teach his heart otherwise. But change didn't come easily.

"I never imagined my life turning out this way, Finn," Michael had said one morning not long after Finn had moved into Michael's small cottage so that his brother could keep some of his independence but not be so alone.

In truth, it had not been the life Finn would have imagined for himself, either. But even thinking about it was a sin, so he threw himself into caring for his brother. Eventually, Michael's intense grief had begun to lessen. With more time, Finn had begun to relish the comradery between him and his brother.

Now they would be parted—truly parted—for the first time in their lives, and the argument and angry words from the previous week felt petty.

"It goes without saying that I was wrong," said Finn as he embraced his older brother.

"But you'll say it anyway," said Michael with a laugh into his brother's shoulder.

"I was wrong," said Finn. "I was blaming my own troubles on you. You don't dishonor your family by living, Michael. Niamh would have wanted that for you, I'm sure."

"Your own troubles?" Michael pulled back, both hands on Finn's shoulders as he searched his face. "Are you ever going to share your troubles with anyone? Or are you going to keep them locked up in that head of yours?"

Finn shrugged, smiling through tears that threatened to fall. "Tomorrow has trouble enough of its own, and no one needs more from me."

"You're entirely too good, Finn," said Michael, wiping at his eye and letting his brother go.

Finn was relieved to see that his brother didn't press the matter. He wasn't sure how he would react if he had. As it was, they were able to say goodbye as brothers and friends, and both men were glad for it.

Soon after Michael had disembarked, additional passengers were brought on board, and Finn and his family were ushered back down below deck. Finn lingered as long as he could on deck, saying a silent prayer that he would see his brother and his homeland again someday. In his heart, Finn felt a sense of finality about this goodbye. He bade farewell to Ireland's shores, to his home, and to the ancestors whose final resting place was beneath those green hills.

There was a string about his heart that pulled him back to that land, pulled him to *her*. With a deep breath, Finn acknowledged that it had pulled on his heart for far too long, clouding his judgment. He could not quite bring himself to sever it. But he knew that with every mile between his home and his heart, it would stretch and fray until, at last, he would finally be free. He followed his family down into the ship with that small comfort.

The *Rosemary* was not set up as a true passenger ship, as they had discovered when they first began their journey. There were no private cabins, but rather the crew had turned the hull of the ship into a large cabin for all the passengers.

"That's likely why the fare was lower than the other ships we considered, like," Norah had said as she examined the place where they would be expected to spend much of the next six weeks. The bunks were put together quite poorly. After inspecting them carefully, Da had informed the family that only the lightest of them should sleep on the top, lest they unwittingly fall through the thin boards onto the person below.

On the journey from Liverpool to Dublin, the Boyds had been some of the only passengers, aside from a few small English families and one fellow who spoke a language Finn did not understand. Now the Irish passengers poured in, their voices loud as they settled, their faces mirroring the concern Finn was beginning to feel as they all realized together that there was not quite enough room for them all. Beds that had been somewhat cramped before were made claustrophobic by the need to double and sometimes triple-up. Finn was not happy about having to share his sleeping space with Conner, who, if reports were to be believed, kicked violently in his sleep.

But in true Irish fashion, they all endeavored to make the best of a bad situation. Soon enough, people stepped forward to introduce themselves to their fellow passengers, swapping stories and, as some of the passengers from Ulster called it, "o' bit o' craic" or good fun.

Conner especially was enjoying the company of his fellow Irish. Finn knew the lad had struggled the past month or more with the lack of friends, so he was finally in his element. He'd been a popular lad back in Shancloch, after all.

"You're from Cork," a lass who looked to be about Conner's age proclaimed loudly from where a group of youth sat towards the center of the compartment amidst a small collection of tables and benches. "I could tell as soon as you opened your mouth."

"What's wrong with that?" Conner asked, his expression guarded.

"Not a thing," said the girl with a laugh. "I'm Gráinne, by the way."

"Conner," he said with a slow smile.

"Where do you fae?" another lad asked.

"No need to ask where you do," said Gráinne with another laugh. "With that Scotch, I'd say County Antrim, is it?"

"Aye." The lad nodded, his cheeks flushing and accentuating his already red hair.

"And what of you?" Conner pressed. "Since you seem to know so much about all of us already."

"I'm from County Mayo," said Gráinne, pushing her bonnet off of her head to reveal a head of golden hair that might even rival Órla's in length.

"Gráinne from Mayo," said Conner with a laugh of surprise. "Like the pirate queen?"

Gráinne nodded, her smile one of pride.

"My granddad used to tell me stories about her," said Conner as he made his way to join the group. "He said she hid a knife on her person when she went to visit England's queen. But because Gráinne Ní Mháille carried herself with such confidence, Queen Elizabeth allowed her audience anyway."

"Good taste for a tale, your granddad," said Gráinne with a wink. Conner blushed crimson, and Finn had to look away to muffle his snort of laughter.

His eyes found Norah's a few bunks away. She had been watching him again, though she tried to look as if she hadn't. Finn was not the only one whose blush gave him away. Whereas Finn had caught her glaring at him plenty of times in the past, he was almost positive she had been looking at him with a softness in her eyes. He wished she wouldn't, though he wouldn't let himself entertain thoughts as to her motives. It was hard enough to look at her and see someone else's face. But the look she had just given him left him feeling confused. Finn wasn't sure he would know himself if he couldn't keep his heart and head clear. He needed to allow the string to break instead of holding on and allowing himself to get burned by its tugging. But it was becoming increasingly difficult to be sensible.

* * *

Because of the sheer number of passengers—Norah and Bridget were almost certain they had counted over one hundred and fifty, although Daniel insisted his count had been even higher—they had to take turns walking about on deck. Per the captain's order, they were to remain out of the way of the sailors and were only allowed up to thirty minutes at a time. Ofttimes, that was the only time they saw the sun if they weren't the ones in charge of cooking the meal for their families in the little fireboxes on deck. Because of the size of the Boyd family, two of the women usually took on the task of cooking. But, after a week aboard The *Rosemary*, Norah had yet to have been given a turn at it.

"'Tis dangerous business," Bridget had informed Norah after fixing the small meal with their meager rations. "If you knock over the little box, the whole ship could start on fire, and we'd all be as good as dead."

Norah assumed the Boyd womens' insistence that Norah allow them to take care of the cooking was their form of repayment for their passage, but they needn't have bothered. She preferred doing something with her hands. Feeling useless and powerless was its own kind of torture.

Regardless of the limited time, Norah did her best to enjoy her time on deck. She breathed deep the sea mist in the air, reveling in the taste of it on her tongue. It tasted of home, of childhood and days spent at the bay with her parents picnicking and dipping her toes in the sea. She tried to ignore the chill it caused down to her very bones by wrapping her shawl tighter around her head and shoulders.

She was careful not to lock her knees as the ship rolled over a wave on the choppy sea. The wind blew harder than the sailors would have liked, judging by their looks of concentration as they barked orders to one another.

Norah turned to look behind her to the opposite side of the main deck, where she knew Conner and Finnegan Boyd had been walking with Gráinne Dougherty, the lass from County Mayo, and Nolan, the red-headed lad whom Norah hadn't heard say a word since that first day. The girl, Gráinne, was a bit too quick to laugh for Norah's tastes, but Conner enjoyed her company, and heavens knew the lad needed something to bring a smile back to his face.

Norah only caught a glimpse of Conner's brown head of hair before she turned around again to cling to the railing. She hadn't been seasick, exactly, but she had to concentrate on keeping her feet under her. Another spray of mist descended upon Norah, leaving her face wet and cold instead of refreshed, as she would have been had it not been the height of winter. She had almost determined to cut her time on deck short and go huddle under her thin wool blanket. Just then the ship rolled to the side unexpectedly, causing Norah's knees to buckle beneath her as she was pitched forward. Her eyes bulged in fear as she grasped hopelessly at the wet railing. But her hands slipped, and she was still moving forward.

A warm pressure encircled her waist, yanking her backward until she was falling in the opposite direction. The sound of her breath being expelled from her lungs reached her ears at the same moment that a loud groan sounded beneath her. Norah's landing had been much softer than she had expected, and it only took her a moment to realize why.

Finnegan Boyd's arms held her firmly even as he rasped for breath. Norah scurried out of his grasp as they both hurried to their feet, both of their faces burning. He was clutching his middle, the muscles in his face pulled tight in pain. Norah's heart beat too quickly for her mind to catch up, and she stared at him with the wide eyes of one who has narrowly escaped death. *He* was the reason she was able to stand there with her thoughts in complete disarray.

"Thank you," she said with a gasp when she had caught her breath enough to speak.

Finnegan shook his head, breathing fast as he righted himself. "Don't mention it." Then, still gasping slightly for breath, "We're even now."

When Norah continued to stare blankly at him, Finnegan grinned. "The shoes."

The cheek of the man!

"They're hardly the same thing, like, Finnegan," said Norah steadily as Finnegan's grin continued to grow.

"But you aren't denying it anymore," he said. "And I'd say that most assuredly makes us equal."

He turned to walk back to the other side of the deck where Conner, Nolan, and Gráinne stood waiting for him, the thud of his shoes against the wooden deck a mocking reminder of his words. Norah let out a long breath.

"Most everyone calls me Finn," he said, turning back suddenly after a few steps and making Norah's sigh catch in surprise. "You might try it. If we're going to be friends and all."

Norah frowned. "I never said we were, like."

"But I don't save my enemies from going overboard," Finnegan said with that same grin from before. "So I think that describes us by default, like."

He added the last part with a wink, and Norah blushed furiously at his impression of her thick Cork accent. He was gone before she could come up with a properly indignant response. But even after he had returned to the hull of the ship, Norah was left wondering what she would have said to him if given half a chance. He had just saved her life, after all. She couldn't pretend she hated the man after that without looking the villain. *Would it be so bad to be friends with him? With . . .Finn?* She ignored the resounding *yes!* from her head. It was all too easy to do with her heart still pounding in her ears.

CHAPTER TEN

Time passed slowly—far too slowly—Norah felt. Many members of the Boyd clan were brought low with seasickness, forced to stay abed and try to keep down what little food they had been given.

"There's a remedy for this sickness," Gran Boyd insisted. "But there's nothing to be done about it, as we can't go searching for herbs and roots in the middle of the ocean."

Norah looked after her friends the best she could, though she had never treated anyone with seasickness, especially when there was no medicine to be had.

"'Tisn't too bad," said Órla, looking paler than Norah had ever seen her, though Bridget assured Norah that Órla had seen darker days. "I would not say 'twas any worse than some of the early days when I was carrying the twins."

Órla didn't often talk about baby Colum's angel sister, but since leaving Ireland behind, she had become sentimental, often bringing up memories she shared with the Boyds from years long passed.

"Do you remember the time Finnegan pushed Conner into the stream and nearly drowned him?" Órla asked as she shook with laughter.

Gráinne, who sat between Conner and Nolan, the lad from County Antrim, twittered with laughter. "How do you almost drown in a stream?"

"I was only nine or ten," said Conner defensively. "And there had been a rainstorm, so the stream was flowing faster than usual."

"Even so," said Gráinne. "Haven't you learned to swim?"

"Not all of us grew up a stone's throw from the ocean," said Conner grumpily. Gráinne patted his arm in what looked like a patronizing manner to Norah's eyes, but Conner blushed anyway.

"I didn't push him," said Finn with a huff. "He slipped on the mud near the banks."

"Because you shoved me," said Conner. "Though I still don't know why."

Norah looked to Finn to see if he would offer some explanation, but he said nothing, staring only at his feet, lost in thought. Despite all of the things she had told herself about Finnegan Boyd, all the things she'd said to convince herself that he was nothing but trouble, Norah had a hard time imagining him picking on his younger brother for no reason. But it wouldn't have been the first time she had been wrong about a body.

She had noted that Finnegan—*Finn*—liked to tease, as did all of the Boyds, but his words were a bit more calculated and thought out. Whereas Alastar had a tendency to injure unintentionally, Finn was quick to make amends if he ever stepped over the line. Why, just that morning he had teased little Oona about her eyes looking like blueberries and inadvertently made the wee lass cry. For penance, he had spent the rest of the morning by her side, playing games and helping to cheer her up until she was beaming once more.

No, there was more to Conner's story than Finn was letting on, and Norah was irritated that she wanted to know it. She couldn't ask because, despite what Finn may say, they weren't *really* friends. Were they? Or was being friends as easy as saying it was so? Norah wasn't sure, as the Boyd women were the first friends she had in her life since before her parents had died.

Ten years. Could that be right? Before the Boyds, she hadn't had a friend in ten years? She had neighbors and acquaintances and people with whom she'd done regular business, but never proper friends. The revelation came as a surprise to her, but she supposed it explained why she had been so willing to drop almost the entirety of her inheritance on a family that was not her own. They had asked her to come with them to Liverpool and had given her a place in their home, all without a word about the difference in their beliefs. From time to time, Mrs. Boyd had invited Norah to attend Mass with them, but had never said a word when Norah had politely declined. It was as remarkable as it was unnerving.

All the same, she wasn't sure she was ready to be friends with every member of the Boyd clan. But Finn could be entirely too persistent for his own good. He worked hard to include her in conversations, asking her about her life before Cork.

"Were you much of a mischief maker as a child, Norah?" Finn asked after they had all finished laughing at Torin's animated tale about Daniel trying to capture Bridget's attention the year prior. In short, the attempt had been an utter failure, but Bridget and Daniel didn't seem to mind, and they huddled together on their bunk, Bridget looking a little greener than Norah liked to see. She still hadn't found her sea legs, and Daniel refused to leave her side until she did.

"My parents were convinced I could do no wrong," said Norah in answer to Finn's question.

"But were they right?" Finn pressed, his eyes sparkling with amusement.

"I'm afraid not," said Norah dryly.

The Boyds and their friends all laughed as Norah recounted the story of a time when she and one of her neighbors had tried to keep themselves from growing older by mixing a concoction of medicines from her father's medical bag.

"Luckily, one whiff of the mixture was enough to convince us that it would do more harm than good. But my father was very put out at the loss of so many medicines. I don't know why I didn't receive a more severe punishment, but I've always attributed it to being an only child."

"Your father was a doctor?" Finn asked. He was watching her in that careful way again.

"He was," said Norah carefully, her heart rate quickening inexplicably.

"I see," he said, his expression lightening as if this explained everything he had ever wondered about Norah. He likely thought her medical expertise had somehow been learned or inherited from her father. But if he only understood how little he knew, how little that small fact really told him, he wouldn't be smiling at her as he was.

And then he was making his way over to where she sat, his steps measured and slow as the ship rocked beneath them. He kept his eyes fixed on her until he kneeled down beside her, moving to take Cuán from her arms. Finn beamed at his little nephew, bouncing him on his knee as Cuán laughed brightly.

"Bridget mentioned your parents died of cholera," said Finn, keeping his voice low as he leaned closer to her.

"Did she now?" Norah turned to look at Bridget, who smiled feebly, too far away to hear the topic of Norah and Finn's conversation.

"I'm sorry." He sounded so sincere, and his voice was laced with pity.

"'Tisn't your fault," said Norah with a shrug. "Anyway, 'twas a long time ago, like."

"How old were you?" He held her gaze until Norah could bear it no longer, and she found the words she had kept bottled up for so long spilling from her mouth.

"Thirteen. There was an outbreak in Sligo. Once my father saw how bad 'twas getting, my parents sent me to Cork to stay with one of my mother's good friends from childhood. They thought it would be far enough away to keep me safe, like."

"Was it?" Finn asked.

Norah shrugged again. "I didn't die of cholera."

Finn's eyes narrowed between his ginger lashes. "That's not the same thing."

Finnegan Boyd was far too perceptive for his own good. "I've done all right for myself, wouldn't you say, like? I'm alive and have the means to help others. Well, had. I don't know that I'll have much to speak of once all is said and done, like."

Finn handed Cuán back to her without warning, Finn's warm hand covering her own on Cuán's back.

"We'll take care of you, Norah," he said, his voice almost a whisper as his breath tickled the hairs about her face. "You won't be left destitute if that's what bothers you. We take care of our own."

Norah swallowed hard, knowing her voice would be thick should she attempt to speak. Bridget had said something similar, but it was an entirely different sensation to hear Finn declare Norah to be a part of "their own" in that deep voice of his. Even though she knew that she would never really be one of them, she couldn't help being overcome with emotion at the feeling of their acceptance.

Part of her tried to squash down the feelings of belonging, justifying them as empty words meant to pacify their benefactor. Although the Boyds had welcomed her long before they knew she was a woman of means, it was difficult to quiet the voice which told her that she had nothing of her own to offer. Nothing of worth, anyway.

But the Boyds had given her equal shares in all they had, even going so far as to search out a new shawl for her when they arrived in the much colder Liverpool. Norah knew they stood by their word, so if Finn said they would look out for her, it would be so. That was if she could keep the less desirable parts of her history from them. Everyone had their limits, after all. And Norah didn't intend to press her luck.

* * *

Norah all but gasped in the sea air on deck, enjoying the feeling of freshness in her lungs for the first time that day. Unfortunately, the air in the passenger compartment—and she used the term lightly—had gotten increasingly worse as the days passed. The number of people who had fallen seasick as they hit rougher waters, the inability to bathe properly, and the lack of a proper latrine had created quite the noxious odor.

"I haven't seen your face so relaxed in days," said Finn from beside her. He leaned his forearms on the railing, staring out at the vast ocean. A glance between the two confirmed a long-held theory, though not one she would admit to ever having considered. Finnegan Boyd's eyes were the exact same shade as the calm ocean. She didn't let her thoughts linger on comparisons of depth and peace. Years of experience had taught her to school such thoughts, though it had admittedly become more difficult of late.

"What do you mean?" Norah asked. She tried to think if she had been particularly stressed lately. She wondered how he had picked up on it when he turned to her, his nose scrunched up and his lips bunched together in a way that reminded her of a little rabbit sniffing the air.

"That's you," he said, his face relaxing. "Every time someone down there gets sick."

Norah glowered at him as his words registered. His impression had been far from flattering.

"Why don't you go walk with your brother," said Norah, turning away from him with a dismissive huff. "He's more accustomed to your teasing than I am. I think he'd much prefer your company, like."

"I doubt that," said Finnegan with a conspiratorial glance over his shoulder. "He's walking with Gráinne."

"And?"

"I don't think that's all he intends to do with her," said Finn, raising his eyebrows and cocking his head meaningfully.

"I don't follow you," said Norah blankly, still seeing his ridiculous impression of her in her mind. Is that how she looked to him? She knew she shouldn't have felt so disappointed, but she did.

"You know the saying," said Finnegan. "You can't kiss an Irish girl unexpectedly—you can only kiss her sooner than she thought you would."

Norah looked away, blushing at Finn's words. "I thought they were just friends."

Finn was shaking his head. "I haven't seen Conner so smitten since Mary Wilcox."

"Mary Wilcox?" Norah's eyes widened in surprise, and Finn grinned at her, amused by her reaction.

"Didn't you know Conner fancied the lass?"

Norah ran through everything she knew about Mary in her mind. When Norah had first met her, Norah had been suspicious of both her and Daniel, as it was clear there was something between them. It didn't take long for Norah to realize that Daniel's obvious discomfort around the lass stemmed from his desire not to hurt her feelings. Norah wasn't sure she had seen anyone as smitten with someone as

Daniel was with Bridget, so she had been quickly reassured that her friend's heart was safe.

Beyond that brief first encounter, Norah hadn't thought much about the young woman who had befriended the Boyd men. She seemed pleasant enough and generous with her home and food, but time had made Norah suspicious of people who gave too freely. Something was always wanted in return. And it was usually unwillingly given or downright impossible to give.

"Isn't Mary twenty or more?" Norah asked.

"I don't think Conner cared."

"But did Mary?"

Finn chuckled. "Mary was gracious enough never to mention it, I think. She let Conner down easy enough. But his feelings must not have been very strong for him to have moved on so quickly."

"Or perhaps he isn't skilled enough in letting a lass down easy himself," said Norah with a glance across the main deck to where Gráinne and Conner stood with their heads bent closely as they spoke words for no one else's ears. Their usual companion, the redheaded lad, was nowhere to be seen.

"No," said Finn, shaking his now too-long honey hair with a slow smile. "If there's one thing our mother taught us Boyd boys, it's that one should never string a heart along. I suppose she must have drilled it into Bridget as well. I believe that may be why it took so long for her and Daniel to get together."

There was something about his wry smile that made Norah's stomach flutter, and she quickly cleared her throat to distract herself from the sensation. She should be used to it by now—she'd spent enough time in his company the past month or more. She should, but it never seemed to get any easier.

"Bridget's still young yet," said Norah disapprovingly. "A person doesn't have to marry as soon as they are able, you know."

"Aye," Finn agreed. "I think I know that as well as anybody. You must have heard my gran comment on my bachelorhood at least once or twice by now."

A muscle in his cheek twitched, and Finn turned it into a lopsided grin that didn't quite reach his eyes. Norah had heard the elder Mrs. Boyd press Finn on when he would finally settle down, but he had always brushed it off with such ease that Norah hadn't thought much of it before. Looking at him now, at the way he struggled to meet her eyes as if he feared that she too would judge him for something she found lacking in him, made Norah's heart beat uncomfortably. It would have been too easy to press the matter, to put further space between them. It would have been safer than the words she found tumbling from her mouth.

"Then it must be as you said, like," said Norah. She watched the calm ocean as a means of distracting herself, peering down to see if she could see anything beneath the surface. But she never could. "His feelings for Mary must not have been very strong."

Finn's brows pulled together in confusion for a moment until he realized that she was once again talking about Conner. The tenseness about his jaw immediately relaxed, and he let out a breathy laugh which sounded more like a sigh of relief to Norah's ears.

"'Tis all right," said Finn lightly. "The lad is just beginning to learn about not getting everything he wants simply because he's a bit handsome."

"An important lesson to learn, like," said Norah. "I should think."

Finn turned to her, his brows pulled together again, and an amused smile played on his lips.

"Norah."

Norah turned to look at him in surprise; the deep timbre of his voice, of her name on his lips, gave her pause. And she was decidedly unsure what she had said to cause him to look at her so. She reached out to more firmly hold the railing, wet with sea mist, feeling as if her knees might buckle without warning.

"Is it not a lesson you've learned yet?"

Norah blinked several times before his words registered. "I'm afraid I don't have the requirements to have taken that particular lesson."

Finn chuckled, shaking his head with a dubious smile. When she only stared at him in return, Finn's face slowly fell.

"Norah," he repeated her name, his voice full of rebuke. He moved forward, taking hold of one of the strands of hair that had been dancing about her face in the wind. "Surely you must know how pretty you are. I believe you may well be one of the most captivating people I know."

Finn tucked the strand behind her ear and smiled, tapping at the corner of her mouth where a small smile had begun to form without Norah's permission.

"Now I'm convinced," he said, his blue eyes shining.

Norah opened her mouth to speak, but she could form no coherent thoughts. Her heart beat loudly in her chest and drowned out all other sounds, so she couldn't hear the quiet words Finn spoke, let alone think of a reply.

Because she could not hear his words, she was unsure what caused his sudden frown, nor the conflict which filled his eyes. The next moment, he had turned away from her, his back and shoulders rigid as he made his way below deck without a backward glance.

Putting a hand to her burning cheeks, Norah forced the smile from her lips. It wouldn't do. As she had suspected all along, a friendship with Finnegan Boyd was absolutely impossible. Her treacherous heart simply wouldn't allow it.

CHAPTER ELEVEN

F inn was a fool. An utter and unabashed fool. He had to be to attach another string to his heart just when the first had begun to fray. And with Norah McGowan of all people! There was a reason there was usually such contempt between Catholics and Protestants; there was such a differing in their beliefs so as to render them completely incompatible. To put it simply, both believed the other was bound for hell. Had Finn such a weakness for a pretty face that he had lost all sense of reason? The answer was, unfortunately, yes. He had long ago known it to be true, though it had taken only one instance for him to realize the certainty of it. It was one of the many reasons why he avoided spending time with any lass in particular. He attached himself too quickly, with feelings deeper and stronger than could be returned. And it had led to his own detriment.

He had known Norah was pretty since the first moment he had met her on the causeway when she had glared so furiously at him for accidentally knocking her down. Truthfully, he hadn't looked at her beyond a passing admiration and general frustration with her character until the night of Bridget's wedding. That was when Norah had sat by the fire, looking so familiar to him one instant and so ghostly foreign the next. Though . . . he was beginning to doubt that he hadn't truly noticed her before then.

Regardless of when she had captured his interest or when he had first noticed his inclination towards her, Finn had no doubt spent more time in quiet observation of Norah than was probably prudent. No, it had definitely *not* been prudent—he could see that now. Each day had allowed him to see how different she was from that phantom image of the past. And how much he found those differences fascinated and endeared her to him.

Norah was real, tangible, and so incredibly alive. She was quiet, although not shy or afraid to speak her mind as some might assume. She was reluctant to trust others, and Finn guessed there was something to it that he hadn't been able to ascertain yet. *Yet.* Because even now, Finn had every intention of learning more about Norah if he could. If she would let him. It was a fool's errand, but, as he had already concluded, he was just such a fool.

All of these observations had come about on accident. Finn had been trying to find differences between that hauntingly beautiful, yet decidedly ghostly image from his past and Norah's own appearance. But learning more about her had only made him more curious. Once he had allowed himself to look, there had been no denying that she was much more beautiful than he had first thought. Her rare smiles lit up her entire face. Her coppery hair, sometimes more bronze, and in other lights fierier, was so wholly fascinating that Finn almost noticed nothing else. Almost.

"What has you looking so distraught?" Gran asked from the bunk beside Finn's. Gran looked pale, and her hands shook more than ever, but her eyes were bright and full of concern for her grandson.

"Nothing," said Finn quickly. The sharpness of the word left him wincing. He knew his gran well enough to know that there would be no avoiding her questions now. Yet Gran only hummed in response, lying back down and pulling her blanket more closely about her.

"Are you all right, Gran?" Finn asked, moving to feel her forehead. She was a little clammy and cool.

"I'm grand, lad," said Gran quietly. Her speech was slow and her answering smile was weak with sleep. "Leastways, I will be once I've had a bit o' sleep. If only this ship would stay still long enough for me to catch my bearings."

"I think we all feel that way." Finn knew he certainly did. The pitching of the ship left him feeling rattled, and he longed for the peace and quiet of the fields he had once called home.

Just then, Norah returned from the upper deck with the rest of the passengers, all looking less than thrilled to return to the dreary atmosphere. Well, except Conner, who was grinning ear-to-ear. He still held Gráinne's hand in his own, and she looked just as pleased as he was about that fact.

Finn envied how easy things were for his younger brother when they had never been so for Finn. The lad had only had to deal with the rejection of a lass for a few months before he had moved on. What must it be like to not live with hopeless unrequited love for years on end?

Finn looked up at the sound of Bridget moaning. She had been sick several times that morning, and each time Daniel's face had grown paler to match his new wife's. To be honest, Finn suspected his friend and new brother-in-law's pallor had more to do with worry than seasickness.

"Uncle Finn," Roisin said, coming to sit beside him on the wooden floor of the ship. "How much longer until we get to America?"

"Some weeks yet, my rose," said Finn with a wan smile. "We barely left two weeks ago. If we make good time, we may only need to travel another four weeks or so."

Roisin's nose scrunched up, making her look very much like her father, Alastar, when he was being overly dramatic. "That's too long. Do you think you could help the ship go faster if you helped the sailors?"

Finn had to suppress his laughter. "I'm afraid that's not how it works, little one."

"Why not?" Roisin asked, her eyes full of innocent curiosity.

"No amount of men can make the wind or the waves behave as we need them to."

"Oh," Roisin's eyes grew wider. "But Jesus could. He told the seas to be quiet, and they listened. Do you think He could do that for us?"

Finn hesitated, knowing that the intricacies of faith meant nothing to a child of six years. "Yes, probably."

"I will pray, then," said Roisin with determination. "Do you think Aunt Bridget would let me borrow her rosary? Hers is so much prettier than Ma's."

"I don't think it would make much difference either way," said Finn with a smile. "After all, Jesus was born in a lowly stable and all. But I wouldn't worry your aunt about it right now. She's feeling poorly. Why don't you sing us a song? I think that would make us all feel better, don't you?"

"Mhmm!" Roisin nodded enthusiastically. Then her shy smile slipped back into place. "Maybe you could sing, Uncle Finn. There are too many people here."

"We'll sing a tune together, and I bet you my favorite button everyone will join right in."

Roisin eyed him dubiously, her nose scrunched up. "Do you really have a favorite button?"

Finn grinned, nodding. "It's the same color as your eyes. I keep it in my pocket for good luck."

"Can I see?" Roisin asked, a small smile pulling at her lips. She reached for the pocket of his jacket, but Finn was quick to grab her hands.

He held them gently between his own, smiling encouragingly at her. "Only if you'll sing with me."

Roisin nodded, glancing around at the compartment full of people. "You start."

Finn did as he was commanded, looking encouragingly at Roisin as he began a song he knew all the children would be able to join in on—one of the songs that built on itself until it was longer and longer and difficult to remember. The pace also picked up with each verse, which often left the singers breathless and laughing as they struggled to keep pace and remember the words.

Roisin's eyes widened and shifted back and forth, and her lips pressed together in amusement as almost everyone who knew the words joined in. Some people sang different words or pronounced them differently, as was the case in Ireland's various counties. This only added to the fun of the song, as people dissolved into giggles or stopped short in confusion as the others pressed on. In the end, everyone clapped and cheered for another song.

"What should we sing now, my rose?"

"Something sad," said Roisin, laying her head on her uncle's chest. "You know all the best sad songs!"

It was an interesting assessment for her to have made at such a young age, but the lass wasn't exactly wrong. Although a sad song was a staple for any Irish gathering, Finn did know more than his fair share of sad songs whether he had intended to learn them or not.

Settling on a favorite, Finn gave his niece a soft smile before beginning the first meters. It was about a lad whose love had married another and his subsequent broken heart. Not everyone joined in as before, perhaps because they did not know the song or possibly because they preferred to listen.

Finn had received many a compliment about his singing abilities over the years, especially from grandmothers and mothers he knew thought of him for their granddaughters or daughters. He had never given much stock to the praise before. That is, not until he caught Norah looking at him as if she was seeing him for the first time. Finn smiled despite himself and the tale of tragedy about which he sang. He supposed it was entirely possible that she was still surprised at what he had told her before he'd come back down below deck. But, for some reason, he didn't quite think that was all there was to her dazed expression.

More applause followed the end of the song, and the trill of a flute broke through the sound as someone began another tune. It was much livelier than Finn's song by miles, and before long, couples were forming in the small space in the center of their compartment. Tables and benches screeched against the floor as they were moved to make more room.

Roisin begged Finn to dance with her, and he couldn't say no. The lass seemed to know that she had her uncle wrapped tightly around her finger. They danced a reel together, struggling to keep up with the time given Roisin's unpracticed movements. Then Roisin bounded off to claim her da's hand as the notes of the next tune filled the crowded space. More instruments joined the flute as passengers huddled closer to the center of the compartment to hear. If Finn closed his eyes, he could almost imagine he was at a céilí in the Auld's barn back in

Shancloch, with straw beneath his toes and the laughter of family and friends filling up the space.

Opening his eyes once more, Finn found himself searching for a pair of dark eyes amongst the throng.

"Will you dance with me, Norah?" he asked when he had found and approached her. He made sure to keep his tone light, despite the racing of his heart.

Norah hesitated, looking this way and that—for what, Finn did not know. After a moment, she reluctantly accepted his proffered hand and followed him onto the makeshift dance floor.

"I've not danced in many years, mind," said Norah over the sound of the voices and music. "So don't be surprised if I tread on your feet."

"You can tread on my feet all you like," said Finn with a care-free laugh. "They've been idle long enough, they won't know the difference."

She gave him a look that told him she didn't understand his meaning, but she said nothing.

Norah needn't have worried about stepping on Finn's feet, for, when it came to it, she kept better time than he did. Finn wanted to blame his clumsiness on the lack of space for proper reeling, but it had more to do with the lass in his arms. Norah was smiling—truly smiling, as he wasn't sure he had seen her do before. At least, not directed towards him. At that moment, despite the circumstances that brought them to where they were and the impossibility of the future, Finn couldn't remember a time his heart had felt lighter.

He was left breathless when the song ended. He stood with one hand still pressed to Norah's back and the other holding her hand firmly within his own. He knew it was past time to let go and step away, but that new string held him there. Finn wondered that it had already wound so tightly. He didn't want to move, not with Norah still looking up at him with shining eyes and her smile leaving him more breathless than the dance.

"My turn!" Little Oona pulled on Finn's trousers. "I want to dance next."

Oona insisted on not one but *three* dances with her uncle, and by the time the music died down and everyone ran out of energy, Finn felt like he might just fall over and stay that way. Their food rations were less than they had been promised, and they hadn't brought any food with them beyond some preserves and marmalade Mary had given them as a parting gift. The preserves would have been enough to add some flavor to the dry biscuits Ma cooked on the box stoves they used on the deck, but that could only last them so long. Finn was used to hunger, to be sure, but potatoes seemed to have more substance to them than a bit of flour and water. And the rocking of the ship only accentuated the gnawing in his belly.

"You look tired, Uncle Finn," said Roisin as she sat beside him on his cramped bottom bunk.

"I feel tired," said Finn, lying down and wishing there was enough space to stretch out but knowing it would be impossible, given his height.

"I've been thinking," said Roisin, leaning down to whisper in his ear. "You can marry Aunt Norah."

Finn's eyes shot open as he turned to look at Roisin. She was smiling sweetly, utterly unaware of how complicated that situation would be. So he closed his eyes again, hoping the young lass would think he was sleeping and return to her mother. But she snuggled down into the crook of his arm and sighed contentedly. Finn envied the ease with which she fell asleep, snoring softly at his side. He wasn't able to sleep a wink for far too long.

* * *

FINN SNORED. IT WAS ONE OF MANY THINGS NORAH HAD BEEN SURprised to discover since the beginning of their voyage. He snored louder than her father had, though not as loud as Alastar—she had yet to hear anything to rival that ruckus. Norah didn't know why she made a mental note of it nor why she kept comparing him to the other men in her life. Only . . . she did know. But she had no intention of giving the thought power by acknowledging it.

Sleep evaded her, but that was nothing new. She rose from her bunk, trying not to wake Oona or Roisin, who had insisted on being her bunkmates for the night. The girls were as sweet as could be. But they had both inherited their father's snoring. It was a Boyd trait, it seemed. It didn't help any that Norah was such a light sleeper. Back in her boardinghouse in Cork, she would wake multiple times a night to the smallest of sounds—a mouse scratching under the floorboards, the cough of a neighbor through the too-thin walls, or a dog barking. To help settle her thoughts, Norah would often make herself a glass of warm milk or tea. But that wasn't an option here in the middle of the Atlantic Ocean, so she took to walking about the space between bunks and the small area near the ladder leading up to the deck of the ship. She moved slowly, not wanting to increase her heart rate and make it more of a challenge to get back to sleep. And while she walked, she planned.

The *Rosemary* was set to make port in New York. From what she had been able to read in the papers, Norah believed New York to be a thriving city full of employment opportunities. Given her experience in the textile industry, Norah did not doubt that she could get a job in any of the many factories about which she had read.

But she didn't want to be stuck working in a factory if she could help it. She knew all too well the conditions the workers faced, and she doubted America would be much different, given their flourishing cotton industry. No, Norah would need to find more long-term employment if she was going to support herself and begin to build up her savings again. She knew she would never have the kind of security she had known before, but she still had every intention of working hard to be independent.

But what of the Boyds? Would they be forced to labor in the factories, or would they be able to find an opportunity to use their farming skills once more? Given their recent employment, they were more skilled than they would have been before. There was the possibility of some of the womenfolk taking in washing or working as seamstresses. If they were able to find housing close to the port, the men might be able to secure dock work, which would likely pay more than a factory.

"Norah?" a soft voice broke through Norah's thoughts and plans for the future. She turned to the sound of the familiar voice, but she had to wait several moments for her eyes to adjust to the dim light coming in from the stars and moon high above the *Rosemary*.

It was Mrs. Boyd. She watched Norah from a nearby bunk.

"Are you all right, child?" She sounded concerned, and Norah felt the need to assure the older woman that she was just fine—she was merely stretching her legs and that Mrs. Boyd needn't worry about her. But she couldn't bring herself to lie to the woman. Not after the way Mrs. Boyd had accepted Norah, despite all of their differences.

"I'm sure I'll be grand soon enough," said Norah, hoping it was the truth.

Mrs. Boyd rose carefully from her bed and stretched with a small smile. Norah knew that feeling all too well. The bunks were a bit short and narrow, and there was a feeling of relief when standing from them, regardless of the limited space between bunks.

"I don't think your back should ache so after resting," Mrs. Boyd whispered as she joined Norah, looping their arms at the elbows.

They had to walk very close together to fit in-between the bunks and towards the ladder leading above deck. But the closeness helped fight off the chill which, even below deck and away from the wind, had a way of seeping into their very bones.

Norah was thankful she had insisted they all acquire some warmer clothes for their new life in America. As she had researched the country where they would make port, Norah had been careful to consider what they would need to give them their best opportunity for success. She had always been very cautious with how she spent her money, and this instance had been the same. But when Roisin and Oona had begged for dyed shawls and bonnets instead of the plainer, less expensive kind, Norah had been incapable of disappointing them.

"You seem very lost in thought," said Mrs. Boyd after they had completed several laps about the cramped space.

Norah smiled weakly. "I was just thinking of Catriona's girls."

Mrs. Boyd's eyebrows lifted. "Were you now? And what of them?"

"They are sweet lasses," said Norah. "I only hope they can be spared a life of hardships, and that America will be the land of opportunity I've read about."

Mrs. Boyd smiled, causing the corners of her eyes to wrinkle—the same eyes each of her children had inherited. There was a kindness and openness about them which had immediately drawn Norah to them. "We will do our best to give them a life better than the ones we've lived, as every older generation should do."

Norah took to watching their feet as they walked back and forth as quietly as possible along the ship's wooden planks. She took comfort in knowing that she was not alone in her plans for an improved future.

But of course, she wasn't—these children were not her own. They had parents, grandparents, aunts, and uncles who cared for them. This family was not hers. They had each other.

"They do adore you." Mrs. Boyd seemed to read Norah's thoughts and patted her arm comfortingly.

"The girls?" Norah asked, inexplicably startled by the sincerity in Mrs. Boyd's voice.

"Oh, everyone, I suspect," said Mrs. Boyd with a knowing smile.

Norah's face began to burn, and she gently guided them back towards the darker section of the compartment so that Mrs. Boyd might not notice. Norah didn't want Mrs. Boyd to see that the thought of not "everyone" but *someone* in particular being fond of her made her react so swiftly. She wanted to keep the kind woman's favor, and Norah knew that no matter how much she had helped them nor how often Roisin and Oona called her "Aunt Norah," that she could never be one of their clan. Not truly.

"I think I've walked myself ragged," said Mrs. Boyd breathlessly. "You should get back to sleep while you still can, child."

Norah nodded but said nothing as they walked back to their beds. It took her longer than she would have liked to squeeze in between the girls without waking them. They immediately nestled against her, pulling their one thin blanket closer about their shoulders. If there had been more light to see, Norah might have allowed herself to stare at their sweet faces until sleep finally claimed her. But she had noted the lack of one particular snore amongst the cacophony, and its absence left her wide-eyed and wondering if he had trouble sleeping too.

CHAPTER TWELVE

Finn was going mad. It wasn't right for a body to be confined so. He had to constantly remind himself of how he was grateful for his family's decision to find new opportunities in America. The likelihood of him and his brothers eventually being locked up for one reason or another had been too high in England. There was no way his body or soul could have survived such captivity. He definitively knew that now after weeks at sea.

The sharp contrast between his feelings of imprisonment below deck and the utter freedom and fresh air above were the initial justifications for Finn's momentary lapse in judgment. After all, no one could deny that the day was glorious, despite the chill of the February wind. In fact, after the stuffiness of the compartment below, Finn welcomed the crisp bite of the salty air as he climbed above deck. The sun shone brightly above them, adding just enough warmth to make the chill bearable. The sea was calmer than it had been the past few days, and the captain had finally allowed passengers to take a turn about the deck in small groups. Finn had stood back and waited, ensuring that he and Norah would be in the same group, though he wouldn't admit to himself as to why.

He hadn't waited long to approach her at her usual place, ignoring Conner's waggling eyebrows and pointed looks as he, Gráinne, and

Nolan all made their way to the opposite side of the deck. Finn was glad that his brother had found a group of friends his own age, but it hadn't done anything to deter the lad's more annoying qualities. Like not minding his own business.

"There's nothing like a breath full o' sea mist," said Finn as he stood beside Norah at her preferred bit of railing.

She looked up at him slowly, as if she'd been anticipating him joining her there. That thought sent a thrill through him, and he hoped he was correct in his assumption. And then she smiled, and he had to hold firmly to the railing to maintain his own casual expression.

"I've always loved the ocean," said Norah. "Sligo is on the coast, so I've always lived in a port town. I don't know how you lived so far away from Cork all your life, like."

"I never knew what I was missing," said Finn. His eyes hadn't left her face since he'd approached her, so he had the pleasure of watching her smile again as she talked about her former homes and apparent love of the sea. There was no sadness about her face as was usually present when she alluded to her past, so he assumed her love of the landscapes where she had grown up was rooted deeper than any pain.

When she finally looked up at him again, her eyes widened, and her mouth pulled down at the corners. But her face soon relaxed, and she tentatively returned his smile.

"The way Bridget talks about your Shancloch, I wonder if I've been missing something this whole time too, like." She said it so softly that her voice was almost lost in the wind. But her meaning—at least what Finn hoped was her meaning, though he probably shouldn't— resounded in his chest like the beating of a drum. If he'd met Norah McGowan at the céilí or on the streets of Shancloch instead of the dirty causeway of Liverpool, he was almost positive that he would have found himself irrevocably altered on the instant.

"Funny," said Finn, although he wasn't sure where the thought was going when he started speaking. "I'm surprised to hear that Bridget speaks kindly about Shancloch. She was always so eager to get away and do anything other than farming all her life."

"That's the thing," said Norah, her voice almost impossibly quiet now. Finn had to lean down close in order to make sense of her words.

"Sometimes, you don't know what you want until you realize you can't have it after all."

There. He couldn't possibly have been imagining that, could he? But then Norah looked back out at sea, and Finn was left to turn her words over and over again in his head. He resolved at last that they had been talking about Bridget and Shancloch and not—impossible things.

"Unlike my sister," said Finn, embracing whatever madness possessed him to speak on. "I'm not one to give up easily. I made a promise long ago that I'd try my best not to spend my life looking back if there was a way ahead. I haven't done the best job of it in past years, but I am repentant."

"Is there a way ahead, Finn?" Her dark eyes were shining up at him, and he was sorely tempted to lean down just a little closer. As his eyes slid of their own accord down to her lips, Norah blinked and cleared her throat. "That is, do you plan on farming again, if you can, like? Only, Bridget didn't seem too fond of the idea when I first met her."

"Oh," said Finn, following her gaze and stiffly turning his body more fully towards the ocean before them. "I don't know. I suppose I haven't thought about it."

"Haven't thought about it?" asked Norah, her tone teasing. "What have you been spending the last weeks doing? You had better come up with a plan quick, like, if you're going to fare any better in America than you did in Liverpool."

He didn't think she truly wanted to know the answer to her question. If he were to answer honestly, much of his thoughts the past weeks had revolved around puzzling her out. And confusion had followed when Finn discovered that she was not at all what he had expected her to be. Even more of a surprise had been that he had not been even a little disappointed with this discovery.

"I suppose I'll take up whatever factory work is available," he said at last. "Though I suspect I will miss farming. There's something so honest about caring for the land, planting from seedlings, and watching something grow. There's a give and take between you and the land that isn't dependent on anything but the rain God sends you and your own two hands."

The corner of Norah's mouth pulled up at his words. "That's quite poetic—especially considering the latest harvest season."

"You sound surprised," said Finn with a chuckle. "I suppose I am a bit too. As difficult as that life is, I find it rather closely mirrors the lives we've been given. 'The Lord giveth, and He taketh away.' But also, 'Consider the lilies of the field.' The joy isn't only in the bounty of the harvest, but in the honest labor and relying on your own hard work."

Norah stood with her mouth slightly agape until she let out a breathy laugh of surprise. But she didn't say anything, and Finn wondered if he had said too much, let her see too much of himself. But then why were her eyes shining at him with a spark of admiration? Perhaps, he concluded, he was seeing what he wanted to see.

"More than likely," he stumbled on, "there won't be any land to be had for a good, long time once we get to America. So, as I've said—I haven't spent much time thinking about what I will do once we arrive."

"Whyever not?" Norah asked, finding her voice at last. "If you have an inkling of what you might want there."

"Honestly," said Finn, his words coming out of their own accord and far bolder than he felt. "I've been a little distracted."

"Oh?" Her voice was still small, but it was, unless he was mistaken, hopeful. "By what, like?"

He would have answered—he really would have—but that piece of hair kept blowing about her face, caressing her cheek, catching on her lips, and he couldn't help the ridiculous notion that he would like to be that small bit of her coppery hair.

Reaching out a hand, Finn justified that allowing himself this small movement couldn't hurt. As he had done once before, he moved to gently place the lock of hair behind her ear. Only his hand seemed to have a mind of its own, and Finn watched with curiosity as it trailed a line across her jaw to the point of her chin and then back again until it was cupping just behind her ear. And then the rest of him was moving before he could fully register what had happened. His other hand left the railing to rest carefully on her arm as Finn turned to Norah with the intention of pulling her even closer to him.

He didn't think he imagined her lack of hesitation, and he wondered why they had danced around this for the past month. By all appearances, Norah felt the pull just as keenly as Finn did. There was none of the confusion or fear he had seen clouding her eyes during many of their past encounters. Norah was all calm reassurance as she leaned into him ever so slightly, placing a hand on his chest to steady herself as she gazed up at him.

Finn barely had the chance to lift the corners of his mouth into a smile of surprise and joy before his name called across the deck caused Finn to step back, his face a remarkable shade of scarlet as he looked about in search of who had called to him.

There, near the hatch leading to the passenger compartments, stood Conner. He looked stern, and Finn's initial reaction was to bark at the lad to mind his own business, but Finn bit his tongue. After a second look at his youngest brother, Finnegan realized that something was wrong. They were close enough that Finn could see unshed tears in his brother's eyes.

"I'd better go," said Finn, turning back to Norah. Her eyes were wide, and she had placed both of her hands on her cheeks, either to calm the blush there or in horror of what had just occurred between them. Against his better judgment, Finn hoped it was the former. "I'd better see what the lad needs."

He hurried over to Conner's side, trying to soothe his own embarrassment by ignoring the fact that he hadn't been caught with just any lass on the road in Shancloch, but Norah McGowan, their very off-limits family friend. Lapse in judgment, indeed. There was that madness rearing its ugly head once more.

"What is it?" asked Finn, his voice sounding rough to his ears.

"It's Gran," said Conner, his eyes flicking back over to where Norah still stood at the railing.

"I'd appreciate it if you didn't . . ." Finn began but soon trailed off. Didn't what? Tell Ma he'd been fraternizing with a Protestant? That he'd just been caught in an intimate embrace with one? That he was already trying to think of a way to repeat that same scenario if Norah was willing?

"I'll be silent as the grave," said Conner, eliciting a relieved sigh from Finn. "But you'd better hurry. Da is distraught."

* * *

NORAH'S FACE WAS STILL BURNING WHEN SHE EVENTUALLY RETURNED below deck. She didn't know how it had happened, but all of her carefully constructed walls had come toppling down the moment she realized Finnegan Boyd might return her feelings. The feelings she had denied within herself for far longer than she cared to admit. Was she that weak that all it had taken were a few compliments and an ounce of affection to crumble her resolve?

She preferred to blame it on her own weakness—at least that she could control. But she knew it more than likely stemmed from a desire to be wanted and a decided lack of affection from those who should have given it most freely.

Because the truth of the matter was that Norah had known, almost from the instant that they met, that Finn would be trouble for her. With his easy smile and his quiet, gentle ways, he was precisely the sort of man she could see herself falling for. And that just wouldn't do. She had seen too much, had experienced too much to believe that this could end in anything but sorrow.

Norah didn't doubt that some people—rare individuals like Mr. and Mrs. Boyd, Bridget and Daniel, and the other couples in their family—were able to be happy. But then, they were each equals with their partners. They didn't struggle to hide a tattered past from the other. They weren't afraid to show how broken they truly were.

Norah had tried to keep her distance for as long as possible and would never have dreamed in a million years that Finn would see something in her worth admiring. But he had, hadn't he? Why else would he look at her that way as he held her in his arms? Norah's face burned anew at the thought that he hadn't been the only guilty party. And now he would know. There would be no more denying, no more pretending that he irritated her just to keep him at a distance. She was a simpleton for thinking that tactic would work in the first place. Despite his reticence, the man was too determined for either of their good.

Finn had warned her on more than one occasion that he didn't give up when there was still a chance of something working out. His warning had sent a tingle down her spine, but now she felt only curiosity. He had alluded to some event or moment in his life which had fostered this resolve within him, and Norah had the sudden urge to ask him what it was. Despite her better judgment, she wanted to know everything about him. She wanted to fall into easy conversation as they sometimes did, to share her own dreams for the future, and maybe—

All thoughts of what Norah wanted abruptly ended when she saw several members of the Boyd clan gathered around Gran Boyd near her bunk.

"What is it?" Norah asked Bridget quietly as she moved to stand beside her friend.

"It's a fever," said Bridget. Her eyes were glistening, but her jaw was closed tightly. She was trying to remain composed. The sight pulled at Norah's heart, and she found herself pressing forward until she knelt beside the older woman.

Norah looked to the elder Mrs. Boyd for permission before beginning her examinations. "May I?"

Gran Boyd nodded, her mouth pulled into a somber line. Norah pressed a hand to the woman's forehead and visibly started at how hot she was to the touch.

"How long has she been like this?" Norah asked, searching the concerned faces of the Boyds for an answer.

"She wasn't feeling well yesterday," said Finn, kneeling beside Norah. The tips of his ears were still pink, but he spoke calmly—far more than Norah could admit to feeling. "But she felt a little cool then. I didn't notice a fever."

"Mrs. Boyd," Norah called gently, shaking the woman's arm slightly to try and rouse her, as she had closed her eyes once more. "Can you hear me? Can you tell me where it hurts?"

But Gran Boyd only moaned and weakly swatted at Norah's hand. Norah continued her assessment. The woman was clearly in pain, and at one point, her shaking hand flew to her forehead. A headache, perhaps.

Norah sucked in a breath when she unbuttoned the first few buttons of Gran's blouse. A dotted red rash.

"Scarlet fever?" Mrs. Boyd asked, her eyes wide.

Norah shook her head. "I don't know." She didn't want to voice any suspicions. Not yet. "Has the ship's doctor been sent for?"

"I'll go," said Conner. Gráinne followed after him quickly, and Norah frowned at the concerned way Gráinne watched Conner as they made their way up the hatch. It was the same expression she imagined she wore as she looked at Finn, who still knelt beside her, his eyes never leaving his grandmother. Norah felt a sudden kinship to the girl and immediately regretted ever thinking that the lass was too jovial. She looked anything but happy now.

"Has she had anything to eat or drink?" asked Norah, looking to Finn in hopes that he would know or, at the very least, glance her way. It was a selfish thought, but the way he was determinedly *not* looking at her was unnerving.

"I offered her a bit of those flour biscuits Ma made this morning, but she didn't want any." Finn did look up at her then and kept her gaze for several long moments before looking back at his gran.

"Maybe . . ." Norah reached out to gently press her hands on Gran Boyd's stomach. It was swollen. Norah's heart dropped, sinking like a stone in the sea.

"What do you think 'tis?" Finn asked, his voice full of worry.

"I shouldn't say," said Norah, trying to keep the tightness out of her voice. "We should wait for the doctor, like."

A warm hand on her arm prevented Norah from standing as she had been readying herself to do. "What do *you* think, Norah?"

What was he doing, with his family hovering over them and all? What they had shared on deck only minutes before was as close to a scandal as could be had aboard a small ship of over one hundred fifty passengers. Didn't he feel the need for discretion?

As if reading her thoughts, Finn pulled his hand away as though Norah's arm had burned him—or rather, he hadn't realized it was there in the first place, which was far more probable. Norah noted it with a twinge of disappointment she immediately worked to suppress.

She hesitated before lowering her voice and leaning in. There was something about the pleading look, about his gentle encouragement that gave her the confidence to speak the wretched word. "Typhoid."

Finn frowned. Norah could see the stubble on his chin, a shade redder than his honey-colored hair. The faint beginnings of wrinkles bordered either end of his mouth and something told her that he had spent too much time frowning. Somehow it didn't match up with the man she had known the past several months, who was always willing and ready with a friendly smile, despite the difficult circumstances. It was a silly thought, she knew, but Norah resolved to help him avoid deepening his frown lines.

But this . . . this was not something she could control. She hadn't been formally trained, and she had no medicine with which to alleviate pain or fever. No, it was a job best left to the ship's doctor.

"Have you seen typhoid before?"

Norah started at Mrs. Boyd's question. For more than a moment, Norah had forgotten that she and Finnegan were not the only ones worrying over his grandmother. The entire clan pressed close, eyes eager, waiting on her every word. Finn, Norah concluded, must have told them she had some sort of medical training.

"I have," said Norah. "But not for some years. We had best wait to see what the doctor says."

"Is typhoid like typhus?" Torin asked, his normally happy face full of concern.

"They are similar," said Norah. "Both present in some of the same ways, but there are marked differences." Norah avoided explaining what the differences were and which illness scared her more by moving to further examine Gran Boyd.

It was several more minutes before Conner and Gráinne returned. Conner's face was red, and he was scowling at the short, balding man who wheezed as he hurried down the hatch towards them.

"Move aside," the doctor said in a commanding voice, his English accent clipped. "I need to see the patient."

He took his time repeating the steps Norah had already taken, making several short grunting noises when he completed each part of the examination.

"I'm afraid the diagnosis is not good," said the doctor, who had never bothered to introduce himself. "It looks like typhoid fever to me. A little more time will tell for sure. The patient should be handled very carefully; else the entire compartment falls ill with the same."

The doctor was already moving toward the hatch. His lips were pressed tightly, and his nose scrunched against the smell of so many bodies so close together in such a small space.

"Aren't you going to stay and care for her?" Norah asked, standing up and following the man.

He whirled around, shaking his head gravely. "Given the patient's age and general health, I can say that I don't think it would do much good," the doctor said. "You may encourage her to drink as much as possible and try to keep her comfortable if you can. But anyone who does care for her should be prepared to fight the illness themselves. Typhoid is not a kind mistress, I'm afraid."

The doctor was gone the next moment, but the Boyds were looking at one another, each with the same look of determination in their eyes.

"I'll fetch her some water," said Mr. Boyd.

"She's shaking a great deal," said Catriona, turning to Norah. "Should we give her another blanket, or is that not the right thing to do?"

"Should I try and make her something to eat?" Bridget asked, clinging to Daniel, her face still as white as a sheet.

They had so many questions and Norah struggled to answer them. She threw her mind back to the last time she had dealt with typhoid. Could she remember what Dr. O'Shannessy had done to help his patients?

Six Years Earlier

Norah gasped at the sudden knock at the door. No matter how hard she tried, the sound never ceased to rattle her. She worked to quickly slow her breathing and quiet her heart before she made her way to answer. Remaining calm was difficult, given how incessant the knocking was. And how loud. But she welcomed any patient, no matter how boisterous, over the current oppressive quiet of Dr. O'Shannessy's office at present. He had been drinking earlier, and Norah knew it was only a matter of time before she would know whether he had fallen asleep or would emerge, angry and looking for someone to blame for any imagined slight.

The doctor had been holed up for some hours now, and Norah wasn't brave enough to bother him unless it was about one of his patients.

The cool air of early evening rustled Norah's skirts as she opened the door. She squinted ever so slightly in the gathering dark.

"Can I help you?" she asked the woman who stood before her.

Stood, Norah quickly realized, was too generous a word. The woman looked ghastly pale. The hand which held her lantern shook almost violently.

"'Tis my family, like," the woman muttered. "My husband and my babes are ill and I don't know what to do for them."

Norah ushered the woman inside, offering her a glass of water and a chair while Norah tried to muster up the courage to knock on the office door. It was only when the woman began coughing and could not stop that Norah was able to convince herself to raise her own hand and knock.

"What do you want?" came the curt reply from the other side of the door. "I told you to leave me be, woman."

Norah drew in a shaky breath. As calmly as could be, she replied, "You've a patient, doctor."

She jumped back when the office door opened abruptly and Dr. O'Shannessy stepped through, his doctor's bag in hand and his face all business.

"What can I do for you, misses . . .?" the doctor asked as he approached the woman who still struggled to get her coughing under control.

"Kennedy," said the woman between coughs. "And it's my family I'm concerned about. My babes, especially. They have fevers so hot and they won't stop moaning."

"Hm," Dr. O'Shannessy hummed as he opened his bag and began searching around in it. Norah watched his hands carefully for any shaking and noted with relief that he had more control than when he had seen a patient earlier in the day.

After a moment, Dr. O'Shannessy huffed angrily and turned to Norah. "There isn't enough light in here to see my own nose," he said. "Fetch another candle, and be quick about it."

Norah did as she was told, hurrying to the mantle and lighting the candle with hands she tried and failed to keep from shaking. Mrs. Kennedy needed help, she reminded herself, and Norah would be no good to her if she couldn't keep her own emotions under control.

She returned with the candle slowly, careful not to trip over the piles of books that had been thrown from the bookshelves earlier. But her deliberate pace only served to further irritate the doctor.

"I don't have all night," he snapped as Norah held the light a little higher so he could see the contents of his medical bag.

Norah met Mrs. Kennedy's eyes for only a moment, but it was long enough to see the look of curiosity mixed with pity Norah had come to know well. Norah did her best to smile despite this, not wanting to give the young mother further need for concern. She had a job to do, she kept reminding herself. A job to do.

After an examination of the woman's throat and belly, Dr. O'Shannessy stepped back and began rummaging in his bag once more.

"Are your family's symptoms similar to your own?"

Mrs. Kennedy nodded. "As I said, it's my babes I'm most worried about, doctor. If you could just come and examine them—"

"There's no need," said Dr. O'Shannesy. He pulled a number of small, white envelopes from his bag and handed them to the woman. "This is quinine for the fever. Mix the powder with water and drink it. I'll be by in the morning to check on you all, but I expect this should do the trick."

Norah failed to suppress a tsk of displeasure at the doctor's unwillingness to venture out to care for his patients at night, even though she knew any care he gave in his present state would be mediocre at best. Her noticeable displeasure earned her a glare whose meaning was clear. She would regret her moment of insolence later. It took effort at that moment for Norah to put her concern for the Kennedys above her own. She stepped forward to help Mrs. Kennedy stand, bracing the woman as she swayed.

"I think I should help her home," said Norah, trying not to sound too eager that the solution might benefit both herself and Mrs. Kennedy.

Dr. O'Shannesy reluctantly agreed, and he sent Norah and Mrs. Kennedy off into the night, assuring the young mother that all would be well and that he would see her in the morning.

But all had not been well. The quinine had helped both parents make it through the worst, but the children had not been so fortunate. It had left Mr. and Mrs. Kennedy childless, weak, and broken, and both Norah and Dr. O'Shannessy had needed to work hard to keep the Kennedys alive. Norah frowned, noting the hopeful expressions on the Boyds' faces. They believed she could help them—believed she was capable of so much more than she truly was. She hated to disappoint them. Not when there was still a chance.

Norah muttered hurried excuses before she bounded up the hatch after the doctor, calling for him as he hurried across the deck towards what Norah could only assume were the cabins for the higher-ranking crew members.

"Doctor!" she called, still irritated that he hadn't bothered to introduce himself. She finally caught up with him—her legs proved to be just a little longer—and the man turned with an aggravated sigh.

"What can I do for you, miss?"

"Do you have any quinine I can administer to Mrs. Boyd?"

"I have only limited stores of medicine, miss," said the doctor. "I would hate to waste it on a lost cause."

Norah sputtered, unsure how to respond to that.

The doctor's pursed lips relaxed, and he looked at her with an expression that could at least pass for sympathy. "It is the sad reality that the old and infirm have very little chance of surviving such an illness as typhoid. The woman looks to be at least sixty and five years old, perhaps older. I need to save my treatments for patients with better odds."

"You're just abandoning her, like?" Norah asked indignantly. "You are her only chance!"

"It is in God's hands now, I'm afraid." Without another word, the doctor turned heel and hurried the rest of the way to his cabin.

God's hands? That was it then, Norah concluded. Gran Boyd truly had no chance. Norah certainly couldn't be any help to her without medicine. And God had abandoned Norah long, long ago.

CHAPTER THIRTEEN

Finn watched with quiet admiration as Norah worked. Her mouth had held firm in a grim line ever since she had spoken with the ship's doctor, and Finn feared the reason for it. Gran burned hotly, complained of stomach pain, and refused to eat or drink. Da had taken to laying on his bed and weeping like a small child. It felt impossible to watch him grieve his remaining parent and Finn's only living grandparent. The feelings of helplessness only increased when Norah's mouth turned down into a definitive frown.

"Is there anything I can do?" Finn asked, holding onto the thin bedpost to steady himself as the ship pitched back and forth. He prayed they weren't approaching another storm. The first one they had encountered had, according to the sailors, been relatively mild. But it had sent passengers flailing out of their beds and across the compartment in a jumbled heap, which had left more than its share of bruises and injuries.

"There's really nothing to be done, like," said Norah quietly. She looked about her to see if any of Finn's family had heard her, but she needn't have bothered. Once Da had begun crying, even those who had held out hope couldn't deny that the situation looked grave. They had all returned to their bunks, as there was little else to be done.

Norah had insisted she would do what she could to make the older woman comfortable.

"All right," said Finn, bending down to kneel beside Norah. He took the damp cloth she held to Gran Boyd's forehead, allowing his hand to press Norah's for a time before she finally pulled away. "Is there anything I can do for you, then?"

Norah turned to look at him, and her brows pulled together as if she couldn't understand his meaning. His eyes followed the lines of her face, the smattering of freckles across her nose and cheeks, and the sweat which pooled above her lips from the exertion and stress of caring for one so ill. Even under such pressure, and perhaps accentuated because of it, she was beautiful.

Gran moaned and moved about, and Norah moved in closer, whispering encouraging and soothing words.

"It's all right, Gran," said Finn when Norah moved to dip the cloth in the water once more. "Norah here is taking care of you. Her da was a doctor, you know. And she fixed up my foot grand-like when I cut it and all. You'll—you'll be all right."

Gran moved her head towards him, and her eyes opened slightly to peer up at him. But they remained unfocused. Finn could see clear as day that she wasn't truly conscious. Nor was she likely to be before the end.

Norah had confided in Finn the truth of what the doctor—Dr. Smyth, Finn had gleaned from one of the sailors—had said above deck. Dr. Smyth would not give Gran any of his limited stores of quinine because it would be wasting his resources on a lost cause. *A lost cause.* What kind of doctor just gave up on a person without a second thought? Finn wasn't sure, as he'd had precious few experiences with doctors. But from the way the man's indifference had seemed to light a fire beneath Norah, Finn would guess the answer to be "no kind of doctor at all."

"You'd have made a grand doctor, Norah," said Finn, biting his lip to keep it from trembling. "Leastways, you're a better doctor than that poor excuse for a man."

"I don't know half as much as I should like," she said quietly. "If I did, there might be more hope."

"How did you learn so much?" he asked, watching the practiced way she moved as if she had taken care of the ill a thousand times.

"I'm quite observant, you know," said Norah lightly.

Finn could tell by her intonation that there was more to it than that. "Did you ever go on calls with your father?"

"Whenever he would let me," said Norah. "My mother didn't like it, but my father was rather indulgent of me, I'm afraid. I was quite a spoiled child."

"I don't believe it," Finn chuckled. "You're far too selfless for that."

Norah looked up at him sharply, signaling that her willing moment of reminiscing had ended. "Time has a way of changing people."

That was true enough. Time and trials could bring about immeasurable change in a person, either for good or ill, as the wind and the rain could weather down even the strongest of stones. Finn opened his mouth to ask her what hardships had caused her to be so nurturing and giving, but the words died on his lips.

"Excuse me, miss," said a young boy, emerging from the dark end of the compartment where the light from the hatch didn't quite reach. "I heard you know doctorin'. Me ma said she was feeling poorly and now she won't wake up."

"Merciful heavens," Norah breathed, closing her eyes for the length of a breath before turning to Finn. There was an unspoken question in her eyes.

"We'll be fine. I can watch over Gran until you get back." Finn knew his smile was weak, but it was the best he could manage.

Norah hurried away without another word. She did not return for a long time. In her absence, Ma took her turn watching over and caring for Gran. Catriona and even Torin took a turn by her side while Órla took care of little Colum. When Norah finally returned from the other end of the compartment, the tight bun which she usually wore her hair in had come loose, and several strands clung to her sweaty face.

"How bad is it?" Finn asked. Judging by the length of her absence and her disheveled appearance, he guessed he didn't want to know the answer.

"Fifteen sick, at least," said Norah, her voice hoarse. "They all said the doctor denied quinine. Some of the families are too scared to care for the sick. They're afraid of catching the fever themselves."

It was a thought that had not truly crossed Finn's mind before, despite the doctor's warning. Now that it had, his heart lurched. Norah had just spent hours in the belly of the ship, caring for the sick. She was tired and susceptible, and he wanted nothing more than to gather her in his arms. His hands twitched as she sat down beside him and Gran, her frown more pronounced than he had ever seen it. She glanced at Finn out of the corner of her eye, noticing him watching her.

"Go rest," said Finn, his tone somewhere between commanding and pleading, as he was yet unsure which would best convince Norah to do as he suggested. She only scowled at him. He smiled slightly in response, and her lips twitched. Norah McGowan was not half so fierce as she would have him believe, Finn was convinced of it.

"She's still burning up," Norah said gravely. She laid the wet cloth on Gran's head once more and dabbed it about Gran's face and neck. Her lips were pursed together so they almost weren't visible. So it really was that bad.

"I can do that," said Finn. He gently reclaimed the cloth, noting as he did so that Norah's hands were back to the dry and cracked state they had been weeks before. He couldn't stop his thumb from brushing over the back of Norah's hand as she eventually relinquished the cloth to him.

"You're no good to us if you're too weary to lift your head," said Finn, hoping that logic was the way to reach her. After a moment, Norah nodded in agreement.

"All right," she said. "But wake me if you need anything, like."

"Of course," said Finn.

He had absolutely no intention of waking her if he could at all help it. He would keep a silent vigil if he needed to—anything to ensure that she did not succumb to the fever. Finn knew she wasn't his, but if she could only remain healthy and strong and his to regard from a distance, he hoped he could be content.

Even as he thought it, he knew he was only trying to deceive himself. He didn't want unrequited love from a distance—he wanted to admire her from as close as she would let him. Because somehow, in the midst of all the sorrow and hardship, he had begun to fall in love with Norah McGowan. She was the light breaking through the gloom, his hope of brighter days. And he would fight for that light even if his heavy eyes and weary body didn't agree.

* * *

NORAH AWOKE TO THE SOUND OF COUGHING AND HUSHED VOICES. It was still dark, or perhaps the hatch had been closed, as the only light sources were the few lanterns the captain allowed to be lit below deck if the seas were calm enough. He couldn't risk a fire, he insisted, so the passengers were often forced to sit in the dark. During a storm, especially, the deprivation of senses was maddening. When more and more fell sick as the days passed on, all sense of sanity and hope felt like a distant memory.

Someone nearby was snoring, though Norah was still too disoriented to tell if she recognized the sound. Instead, she focused on the voices, trying to decipher their words.

"—no improvement," a deep voice said.

"We should wake Norah," a female voice answered. Norah recognized Bridget's irritated tone. "She might know what to do."

"You didn't see her when she finally agreed to go to bed," the deep voice insisted. She recognized it the next instant as belonging to Finnegan Boyd. "She was exhausted. She has been exhausted for days, what with caring for those who don't have hope. The quickest way to send her to her own watery grave is to leave her with no strength left to fight."

"But the doctor won't do anything," said Bridget helplessly.

"I know," said Finn wearily.

Bridget's voice was muffled when she spoke again, and Norah guessed that Finn had pulled her into an embrace. It seemed the most likely reasoning anyway, and very like Finn to comfort someone when they needed it. Norah had long tried to deny it, but he was just that sort of man.

"Why did we leave England? Why did we leave home?"

"We were trying to protect you. We were trying to survive."

"This doesn't feel like survival, Finnegan," said Bridget. "This feels like slowly losing all we hold dear."

"Yes," Finn whispered. "But not all—not yet. Don't give up hope yet, Birdie. You still have your Daniel, so there's that. Go and comfort him. I'm not sure how he'll fare losing both uncle *and* aunt within so short a time."

The breath Bridget exhaled was shaky. "Don't say that. Don't condemn Aunt Aileen so quickly."

"All right," said Finn. But Norah could hear that he didn't sound convinced.

"Maybe Norah would have an idea—"

"No, Bridget," said Finn with finality.

"Why?" she asked harshly. "Why do you care if I wake her?"

Finn huffed. "Why do you not? I thought she was your friend."

"She is! Which is why I think she would want to help if she could."

Norah let out a short breath in defeat. She had the feeling that they would only stop their bickering if she resolved their argument for them, so she made a point of yawning and stretching as she stood from her bunk, careful not to wake the girls as she shifted. Norah had to feel about her and grasp onto the bunks nearby as she followed the sound of the quarreling.

"Oh, Norah!" Bridget said as she noticed Norah making her way to them in the near-dark. "You're awake." Bridget, who sat beside Finnegan near Gran Boyd's bunk, elbowed her older brother in the ribs, then quickly stood.

"I am," said Norah, eyeing the siblings with apprehension. "How can I help?"

"It's Aunt Aileen," said Bridget, stepping forward to take hold of Norah's arm and lead her in the direction of Aileen's bunk.

Norah offered Finn a weak smile in greeting. He only nodded, his face remaining impassive. Norah's heart ticked faster, and she had to calm her breathing. She wasn't sure how to act around him anymore, not after that revelatory moment on deck. The memory was already blurred with confusion after days of caring for their fellow passengers, but Norah was almost positive that Finn had been about to kiss her. And then they had been plunged into chaos. Norah hadn't had a moment to truly consider what it had meant nor why it had happened.

Well, she could answer the last part, blurred memories or no. For her part, anyway, Norah knew precisely why she had wanted Finnegan

Boyd to kiss her. Though whether she would live to regret this revelation remained to be seen. He had been so attentive and helpful, and just now, he had insisted that Bridget let Norah rest. Why, then, did he not return her smile?

Perhaps, Norah reminded herself, it was because he had nothing to smile about at present. His gran was not faring well, and after a quick evaluation of Aunt Aileen, Norah concluded that things there did not look hopeful either.

"What are we to do?" Bridget asked with tear-filled eyes. "We're still at least two weeks away from America. Dr. Smyth refuses to give quinine to the old or infirm. I fear 'tis a death sentence."

"Keep offering them water, like," said Norah. "And continue with the cool compresses."

"And pray," said Bridget, taking a calming breath.

"Yes," said Norah slowly. "I suppose you can do that too, like."

Norah did not share her doubts that the Almighty heard the prayers of diseased peasants or, more specifically, Norah's prayers. He hadn't answered her prayers to spare her parents from the epidemic or to save her from Mrs. Driscoll's cruelty, or even Dr. O'Shannessey, in the end. She had had to find her own ways to save herself. And when she had resolved to never depend on someone again, she had secretly included God in that pact. She knew she was next door to a heathen for it, but Norah couldn't bring herself to care. Not like she would have if every good thing hadn't been ripped from her.

No, not every good thing, Norah recalled as she glanced to where Finn sat on the edge of his grandmother's bed, her still hand in his, and his head hung low. But none that she could claim.

"Simon?" Gran Boyd's weak voice broke through the stillness, and Norah watched as Finn's head shot up, his eyes searching his grandmother's face. Norah's mind barely registered that his grandmother had called for Finn's father, Simon, before Norah was on her feet, Bridget following close behind.

"No, it's me, Gran," Finn said. "Finnegan. Do you want me to wake Da?"

"I have to tell you, lad," said Gran, her hand shaking slightly in Finn's grasp. "I have to tell you I was wrong."

Her voice was weak and raspy from so many coughing spells and a sustained fever.

"Hush, now, Gran," said Finn. "Save your strength."

Gran smiled weakly. "I haven't had strength for these past ten years, at least. But don't distract me, boy. I have to tell you"—here she broke off coughing until Norah moved closer, offering the woman a sip of water which she only pushed away with a look of determination. When Gran's eyes fixed on Norah, she nodded in acknowledgment.

"She's a good lass," she said, turning back to Finn. "I said she wasn't right for you, but it's plain as day that she makes you happy. And I've not seen you happy since before Niamh. Tell your Da I love him, lad."

Finn sat frozen at her words; his eyes were wide and his mouth agape.

Norah hung her head in disappointment as Gran grew still, her eyes drooping as she lay, struggling for breath. Norah had hoped that, with as lively as the woman had seemed only moments before, she would be on the mend. But Norah knew all-too-well the burst of energy that came to some before the end.

Bridget was sobbing hysterically now, which caught the rest of the Boyds' attention as they awoke from their fitful rest. "She didn't even know who we were," Bridget was saying. "She thought Finn was Da and then Michael. She didn't even know us!"

A moment later, a sailor opened the hatch door, letting in the early morning light. Someone—Norah believed it was one of the Boyd boys—hurried up the ladder to find the priest or minister or whomever it was who had been conducting their Sunday services. Truthfully, Norah had not paid much heed to the gatherings.

The sound of sobs mingled with the stifling air in the passengers' compartment. Norah felt the telltale beat of her pulse in her throat, constricting her breath and filling her with a sense of impending doom. She had to get out, had to get away. So she did the only thing she could do when stuck on a ship with too many bodies—she hurried up to the deck. She was prepared to plead with whichever sailor was closest to let her stay and catch her breath, but as soon as the men on deck took in her appearance and the crazed look in her eyes, they gave her a nod and a wide berth.

It was there that Finnegan found her a quarter of an hour later. Norah still stood at the railing, taking deep, calming breaths. She kept her eyes on a fixed point on the horizon and tried desperately to regain control.

"I'm sorry," she said, not daring to look at him. Her voice felt gravelly and unsteady, and she wanted nothing more than for him to go away and leave her alone with her thoughts and doubts.

Finn's warm hand covered Norah's on the rail, but he said nothing for several minutes. They stood in companionable silence, neither giving nor taking from the other, but merely existing in their grief. Norah had half-expected him to demand answers from her, to chide her for leaving the family amidst their suffering, but he remained silent for a long time. He was not at all the man she had tried to convince herself that he was in an attempt to maintain her distance. He was steady and sure and good.

As if reading each other's thoughts, Finn and Norah turned at the same time. They locked eyes for only a moment before they pulled one another into a firm embrace. Norah turned her head to rest it on Finn's broad chest, and he leaned his chin upon the top of her head. They fit like they had been made to hold each other. Although she had come on deck for air, Norah had only just begun to breathe again. They stood there for what must have been several minutes, finding comfort in each other's arms.

Finn moved to press his head into the corner of Norah's neck, and she could feel his unsteady breath against the skin there. She willed her heart to calm and for her brain to focus on comforting him, but all rational thought flew out the window when she felt Finn press his lips ever so lightly against the place between her neck and shoulder before he quickly stood straight, rubbing a tear from his eye.

"Gran is gone," Finn said at last as he slowly dropped his arms from around Norah and took a step back. "Thank you for helping us make her as comfortable as you did."

Norah bit her lips and inhaled sharply to maintain her composure.

"She liked you, you know," said Finn.

"Me?" Norah asked in confusion. "She barely knew me."

"She knew you well enough," Finn said. His eyes were red and puffy, but he had dried his tears and set his jaw. "You heard her—she said you are a good lass."

Norah scoffed as she wiped away a tear. "Bridget said she wasn't in her right mind. Your gran thought you were your brother."

Finn searched Norah's face, indecision written all over his own. "She didn't think I was my brother. She was talking to me."

CHAPTER FOURTEEN

Norah couldn't understand what Finn was trying to tell her, but it was clear from the pointed look he was giving her that there was some hidden meaning in his words. She turned Gran Boyd's last words to Finn over and over in her mind, but couldn't make sense of them.

"She said something about you being happy—"

Several emotions fought for control over his face—confusion, apprehension, fear. And then he nodded, took a deep breath, and looked at Norah with such resolve that she took an instinctual step back as Finn moved forward and captured one of her hands in his. "Yes. That you make me happy—she was right, in case you were wondering."

Norah did her best to calm her thoughts enough to focus on his words and not the way his eyes were locked on her, causing her stomach to dance about. "Happy like you've not been since Niamh." Norah frowned, trying to recall why the name sounded familiar. "I've heard Bridget say that name before. She was . . ."

"Michael's late wife," Finn said slowly. "Yes."

He didn't immediately explain, and Norah's imagination was left to run wild for much longer than she would have preferred. Her mind twisted about the different possibilities, but none showed Finn in a favorable light, and she was left wishing he would simply explain himself. Not for the first time, she understood why Finn's siblings sometimes complained about Finnegan's proclivity to keep things bottled up inside him.

"Was she—that is, were you—"

"'Twas nothing quite so nefarious as you're imagining," said Finn. He still held Norah's hand in his, and he gently turned her wrist so he could idly examine her palm while he spoke. "I was eighteen when Niamh and I first met. After the harvest, my brothers and I would often travel to neighboring villages to help other farmers or do any odd jobs we could find to help pay our rent. Niamh's father hired Torin and me on. 'Twas the happiest summer of my life. I've always been quieter, so Niamh was like a sudden thunderstorm I could never have seen coming. She was confident and, although I didn't know it at the time, a bit of a flirt. She captured my heart before I knew what hit me."

Norah watched Finn continue to turn her hand over in his own. They were both incapable of looking at the other.

"She enjoyed teasing me about my quiet ways, but she was also very kind. In truth, I don't think she understood the hold she had on me. To her, I was just a summer fling, but I spent the whole of the year dreaming and planning for the following year. Michael came with me that next summer and . . . He can't be blamed for it—he didn't know my plans or feelings about her. I hadn't told anyone, as I preferred to avoid my brothers' teasing. I wanted her answer before I shared my feelings with the world.

"When it came to it, there was no denying that Michael and Niamh were better suited. They grew together quickly, and I was left behind, nursing what should have been a passing wish for a future that could never have been mine. I don't think Niamh ever said anything to Michael, but I always had the feeling he knew. He must have at least suspected."

"You loved her," said Norah, realization dawning just as the jealousy began to creep in. She wasn't sure where it had even come from, but the knowledge that Finnegan had loved someone who, by all appearances, still held a significant piece of his heart pricked her own more than she cared to admit. It wasn't fair of her, she knew, but there it was.

Finn looked up from their hands, face contorted in pain as he struggled to form words. "I tried not to. But I wasn't very good at it."

"Did she know?"

Again, Finn paused before answering. He looked out at sea, his eyes searching the horizon as if he might find the answer there, blue on blue on blue.

"She knew I was hurt when her affections for Michael first became clear," said Finn. "And angry, for far too long after they had married. But I think—I hope I became better at hiding my pain over time. In the end, she didn't tiptoe about me anymore. She treated me like the rest of my brothers. And if anyone suspected my feelings were more than the brotherly sort, they never said a word."

"Which only added to your pain," said Norah knowingly. She knew the pain in his eyes, knew it as well as she knew the pull of the breath in her lungs. To expect love that wasn't returned was unbearable pain. She wore its sister over her own heart, and Norah reached out, placing a hand on Finn's arm in support and empathy. The longing from before was replaced with a desire to take this pain away from him.

Finn looked up at Norah and clenched his jaw. "I think, given time, I could have moved on. But she died barely a year after she and Michael were married. I've spent too many years mourning for what I couldn't have. I stood by my brother's side and watched him bury my first love, but I still wasn't able to let go. I tried to make restitution for my sins by taking care of Michael, by being his friend and a better brother than I had been before. Now that he has moved on, I can't help feeling there might be hope for me too. I'm ready to put the past behind me, Norah. I hope—if—"

Finn went suddenly silent, giving Norah time to let his words sink in. He was ready to move on, ready for a fresh start. Unfortunately, that did nothing to tell Norah whether or not he wanted *her* to be part of that new life.

"Have you ever experienced anything like that?" he asked at last. He was staring at her with intensity once more, silently pleading for something Norah couldn't quite place.

"Like . . ." Norah began, unsure what he wanted from her. "Like falling for my brother's lass?"

Finn snorted, turning immediately somber the next moment. "What I mean is have you . . . have you ever been in love before?"

Norah stilled, sure there was more to his question than he was asking. Did he want to know if she had ever been in love or if she thought herself capable of it? Because the latter would have been a resounding yes. She'd known for far too long that she often cared more deeply than anyone cared to return. It caused her to keep people at a distance. But if she could only live a bit more like Finn, have a bit of his courage and desire to not live with regrets, perhaps things could be different.

"No," said Norah slowly. "I can't say I've ever truly been in love before."

She must have misunderstood his question because his face twitched once more, his mouth falling somewhere between a grimace and a grin. Had her answer upset him somehow?

"But they say America is a grand place for new beginnings, like," said Norah with a levity she did not feel.

Then Finn fully smiled, his eyes lightening as he pulled her hand close to his chest. "Exactly."

The realistic part of Norah couldn't stop herself from adding, "If we live to see it."

Finn's face fell once more, and Norah silently cursed her ability to ruin what could have been a perfectly romantic moment. Only she knew it couldn't be, not really, not with regret and secrets niggling in the back of her mind. Because as much as she wanted him to, Norah couldn't allow Finn to declare anything to her yet. They had already shared more of themselves than was prudent. Regardless of any help rendered to his family, Norah was not under the disillusionment that a relationship between herself and Finn would be a welcome one.

"We must, Norah." Finn pulled one of his hands from hers to cup her face. He was looking at her with such sincerity and desperation that, should he have asked her to run away with him to the moon, Norah might have been sorely tempted to say yes.

They were simultaneously aware of someone stepping up beside them, and their hands snapped to their sides as they took a step back from each other, both of their faces flushing at having been caught in so intimate a moment.

"Oh," said Finn, his face relaxing as he took a step back towards Norah, reclaiming one of her hands. "It's just you."

"Well, that's a fine how-do-you-do," said Conner, his voice holding none of the amusement which would have been present under less strenuous circumstances.

Did Finn not mind Conner seeing them together like this? Norah would have thought he would be ashamed to be found in an embrace with a Protestant lass. But then, the entirety of the Boyd family had never reacted quite as Norah would have expected them to. Were they truly so remarkable a people that the differences between them didn't change the ties that bound them as friends?

"What do you want, Conner?" Finn asked impatiently. He was outright glaring at his little brother, but Conner didn't notice. Or if he did, he simply didn't care.

"I wanted to talk to Norah," said Conner. "If you're quite finished here."

"We're not," said Finn brusquely. "Why don't you go find your own lass? I'm sure she misses you by now."

"Leave Gráinne out of this," Conner warned. He spoke with such ferocity that Finn barked a laugh in surprise.

"All right, lad," said Finn, reluctantly releasing Norah's hand once more. "What do you need?"

Conner nodded to his brother, still scowling. "Daniel would like you to take a look at Bridget," he said to Norah. "He said he's sure it's just an overabundance of caution, but she's taking the news about Gran very hard."

* * *

"When I tell you that you need to rest, lass, you need to listen," said Norah as she finished her examination of Bridget.

"So she doesn't have typhoid?" Daniel asked. He sat beside Bridget on their bunk, smoothing back his wife's hair with what appeared to be a permanently furrowed brow.

Norah hesitated. "She has a fever, but I don't see any other symptoms, like. That's not to say that it couldn't simply be too early to tell. But you've been so sick-like, and you *need* to rest. For both of your sakes."

"My head is pounding," Bridget muttered, placing a hand over her eyes.

Norah bit her lip as Daniel looked at her sharply, waiting to see what that new piece of information could mean.

"I'll see if the doctor has any headache powder," said Norah, pushing herself up from the floor and handing Bridget a small tin cup of water. "Don't drink too quickly, like—you're bound to lose it all again if you do. Little sips at a time."

Bridget started to sob all over again, her tears wetting her pillow and causing Daniel to place an arm around his wife. His face was etched with worry.

"I couldn't even say goodbye to her," Bridget said. "They just dropped her in the ocean like a—some stone or something, not like a person who should be buried in the ground where she could be properly mourned and remembered."

"*Mo chroí*," Daniel murmured, but he said no more. What was there to say? Bridget's sorrow was real and valid, yet becoming hysterical now could only weaken her. It was impossible to ask her to calm herself.

Norah did the only thing she could do—she sought out Doctor Smyth once more, begging him for what must have been the dozenth time in a week for some medicine for her friends.

"I'm afraid I just don't have enough," said the doctor when Norah approached him in his cabin.

"That's not possible," said Norah. "You've barely administered anything, like. There are more people falling ill every day, yet you can't be bothered to treat them!"

The doctor shook his head, the few gray hairs atop it swaying with the movement. "I'm sorry, miss," he said, lowering his voice and looking about to make sure no one was listening. "I think you will find that you are quite lucky to have a ship's doctor on board, as many ships traveling to the Americas just now are not even required that. When I was hired for the job, I was informed that there would only be fifty passengers. My stores are all but depleted already, and I've been ordered to set aside provisions for the crew. As I'm sure you know, I can only help so many. The young and old alike will likely not survive the journey. If you are determined to help, I suggest focusing your attention on those who stand a chance."

Norah slammed a hand down on the desk between them. "You've made a promise, Doctor Smyth, to 'do no harm or injustice.'"

The doctor rose from his chair, his face as hard as a stone. "'To my greatest ability and judgment,' miss," he said. "And I judge that the time spent on those who stand no chance is disadvantageous to those who could still be saved."

Norah scoffed, folding her arms across her chest and shaking her head in disgust. "And yet here you sit—on the opposite end of the ship from your patients, unquestionably *not* treating anyone. You make me sick."

The doctor sputtered indignantly until Norah turned on her heel and pulled the door open, making sure to slam it behind her with as much strength as she could muster. The air shook about her, and she allowed herself a small, satisfied smile before hurrying back across the deck to her waiting friends. The wind whipped at the sails and rigging with an awful moaning. It pulled at Norah's hair and shawl, and she had to fight against the strength of it. Her usually steady stance was put off balance by the rocking of the ship. She looked up at the dark clouds above, silently cursing them—a storm was the last thing Bridget needed.

Norah knew she hadn't exactly been fair to Dr. Smyth by accusing him of not caring for his patients. If there was not enough medicine to be had, there was very little that could be done. She knew her own wounds and past experiences did not mean that all doctors were so neglectful, but fear was a funny thing. It could eat you up inside until you didn't know what was real and what was a memory, reaching out and poisoning all it touched. Calling it by name helped, but no matter how hard she tried, she couldn't seem to move past it.

Daniel looked up at Norah expectantly as she approached, holding a hand out in hopes that she had the headache powder of which she had gone in search. Norah shook her head, trying not to let him see the anger which was still seething inside her.

"We'll just have to pray, then," said Daniel, holding Bridget's hand and bowing his head solemnly.

A short time later, the call to "batten down the hatches" came, and any passengers who had been above deck were ordered below. It was pitch black, as no candles or lanterns could be lit in a storm. They huddled in their bunks as the rocking of the ship intensified.

The crashing of the waves drowned out the voices of the crew above. Would they even know if the entire crew had been swept away? Each time a sailor's muffled shout reached her ears, Norah allowed herself a small sigh of relief. But it was usually short-lived. The next moment they would be clinging to their bunk posts as another wave crashed down, sending anyone who couldn't hold on tightly enough sprawling across the floor.

Those who were ill or already suffering from seasickness had the worst of it. Norah sat with Aunt Aileen, making sure the older woman didn't roll off her bunk and into the growing pile of passengers.

"Thank you, child," Aunt Aileen managed to breathe out when there was a moment of calm just before another wave pitched them to the opposite side. Norah had to hold on tightly to avoid crushing her.

Hours passed with no reprieve.

So this is it, Norah thought in disbelief after what felt like an eternity. They were to be left to their own devices without a soul in either heaven or earth to care if they lived or died. They were to suffocate in the darkness, consumed by the raging seas.

Just when Norah felt the despair building inside her, when she was ready to cry out like so many of the other passengers who sobbed and called for someone to help them, a voice rose above the sounds of the storm, strong and clear and familiar.

She already knew Finn sang well—she'd heard him sing many times with his family and on that day only weeks before, but which now felt like months ago. She thought about that day when they had danced together more often than she probably should. There was something different about hearing his voice now, in the dark and despair, the stink and the suffocation.

Be Thou my Vision, O Lord of my heart;
Naught be all else to me, save that Thou art.
Thou my best Thought, by day or by night,
Waking or sleeping, Thy presence my light.

Like a light in the dark, the words he sang gave Norah hope in a way she had not thought possible. Though the circumstances did not change—the sea still raged about them, and they still struggled against being flung from their beds—the light remained. It was only a spark, but in the pitch black of hopelessness, it felt like the sun.

Be Thou my battle Shield, Sword for the fight;
Be Thou my Dignity, Thou my Delight;
Thou my soul's Shelter, Thou my high Tow'r:
Raise Thou me heav'nward, O Pow'r of my pow'r.

As other voices joined in, Norah felt compelled to do the same. She had not sung a hymn in at least five years, but there was no denying the power of so many voices raised in lyrical prayer. She used to love to sing. It had been her favorite part of attending Sunday services with her parents. She wondered that she had forgotten that fact and that the sorrow and years of loneliness had wiped the simple joy from her memory. The song was both a comfort and a pleading and, though a voice in the back of her mind told her there was no one to hear her anyway, Norah did not cease.

High King of Heaven, my victory won,
May I reach Heaven's joys, O bright Heav'n's Sun!
Heart of my own heart, whatever befall,
Still be my Vision, O Ruler of all.

Silence followed the end of the song, and it was only then that Norah realized they were not being thrown about quite as much as before, though the boat still lurched from side to side. Time passed slowly, but Norah was left with a sense of calm. This storm, at least, would not snuff them out entirely.

The hatches were opened at last. Norah sucked in a deep breath of air, her head spinning with it as she looked about her in the dim light to assess the other passengers. Many would need medical help—there were more than before who appeared unable to move—brought lower by either seasickness or the spreading of the fever. Doctor Smyth, she knew, would be no help, so it was left to her and anyone willing to render aid.

She took another deep breath, trying not to think about the smells and sounds that still accosted her, and readied herself.

"What will you need?" Finn stood before her, his jaw set with determination. He glanced from her to the moaning passengers, clearly troubled by what he saw and heard.

"Strips of cloth, if they can be had," Norah said, taking another deep breath as she stood to join him. "I will need water—as much as can be spared. And . . ."

"What is it?" asked Finn. He waited patiently for her response, the steady and familiar rise and fall of his chest grounding her to the present.

"Doctor Smyth has denied my request for medicine at every turn," Norah said. "There's nothing else to be done. Except . . ."

"Name it, Norah," said Finn. He placed a hand on her arm, rubbing it gently with his thumb before lowering his hand once more. His eyes flickered to his family nearby, but they were too preoccupied to have noticed.

"You might sing again," said Norah, smiling weakly. "That seemed to lift everyone's spirits, if only for a time."

"Did it lift your spirits?" he asked curiously, searching her face.

Norah hummed a laugh. "More than you might think."

Finn smiled softly at that. "All right," he agreed. "But let me help you assess things first."

Norah nodded her thanks, picked up her skirts, and went to work.

CHAPTER FIFTEEN

24 February 1846, the Bark Rosemary, the Atlantic Ocean

"Ten more sick this morning," said Norah.

Finn stood beside her as she examined Bridget for the third time that morning, the worry in Norah's eyes growing more defined each time.

"How many dead?" Finn asked quietly, not wanting to frighten his sister. He needn't have bothered. Bridget was burning with fever, as were the majority of the Boyds at this point, and was not coherent enough to hear him. That a few had been spared the worst of it was a miracle Finn could only attribute to God.

"Three," Norah rasped, her voice strained from answering so many questions from worried family members as she did her best to make as many as comfortable as she could.

"The Bourke baby?" Finn asked. He knew Norah's answer without her needing to speak. He recognized the sorrow and defeat in her eyes which grew with every day in the belly of this stinking ship. "He's at peace now," said Finn flatly. It was a fruitless attempt to offer comfort, he knew, but he struggled to watch Norah suffer so.

She looked at him sharply, but her expression was guarded. "Will you say that if your sister dies next?"

Daniel, who lay next to his wife, his own brow glistening with sweat, groaned. "Don't say that," he begged. "She can't—" But Daniel's words were cut short by a coughing fit.

Finn frowned. He had listened to enough of Daniel's coughing to last him a lifetime. Finn worried that his friend's lungs were not recovered enough from the last fever Daniel had suffered. Finn knew this was a different illness than had plagued Daniel before. And then, they'd had Mary to help and the medicine necessary to allow Daniel to recover quickly. The medicine that was sorely missed now, as Daniel struggled to suppress the violent coughing.

"Rest, Danny," Finn commanded. "Norah's orders."

"Oh, I'm grand," said Daniel, moving closer to Bridget to wipe a strand of sticky hair from her face.

"Don't worry," said Órla from the bunk beside them. She was one of the few who hadn't taken ill. Finn hesitated but reluctantly added *"yet"* within his mind.

"I'll keep an eye on them both," Órla continued. "You should both rest—you've been taking care of everyone all morning."

"Step away for a moment," said Finn to Norah. "Get a breath of fresh air."

Norah paused before she finally nodded her agreement. He could see how torn she was about the decision, but a body could only spread themselves so thin before they didn't have anything left to give.

"But I won't go far," Norah promised Órla before she slowly ascended the ladder.

"Keep an eye on her," Órla ordered Finn as they both watched Norah. She moved too slowly; each step was measured as if it took more effort than she could give.

Finn nodded grimly and hurried after her. He knew he shouldn't be, but he was relieved to have an excuse to be alone with the lass without having to think up one for himself. For days he had been by her side, offering aid and helping to care for those who couldn't care for themselves. Although he had already had a good idea before the ordeal, Finn was even more convinced of the fact that Norah McGowan was without a doubt the strongest, bravest, and the most brilliant woman he had ever had the pleasure of knowing.

When taking care of a patient, she moved with a confidence and self-assurance he was rarely able to see in her outside of those moments. She was decisive and unafraid of speaking her mind. He had seen only a glimpse of this part of her character as she took him on, calling him out on his words and deeds, whether he was deserving of it or not. In this capacity, at least, Finn could not deny that it only made him admire her more. And, though admiration was a fine thing, he knew his feelings ran much deeper. Much deeper, indeed.

Finn found Norah standing just outside the hatch, leaning on the wall near the cabins towards the ship's stern. Her eyes were closed, her face utterly relaxed as if she were so fatigued that she had not the strength for any emotion. Regardless of the fact that they had been stuck below deck in horrible conditions, surrounded by the dead and the dying, Finn felt a tugging at his heart which pulled him forward—toward her. He craved her company, her words of reason, her elusive smile. Now more than ever, he needed the hope she gave him just by being near.

Finn leaned next to her, his back to the cabin wall, one hand running over the wood paneling and the other capturing her hand in his own as it rested by her side. Norah's eyes remained closed, and she said nothing, but she heaved a great sigh, exhaling slowly through her nose. Finn continued to watch her until she finally turned to look at him. She looked so tired, so forlorn, that he couldn't help reaching out to pull her into his embrace. Norah leaned heavily against him, and her own arms about him felt weak.

"I can't do this," she murmured into his chest, her breath warming him to his very core.

"You can," Finn promised. "I know you can. Though I've suspected for some time, over the past four weeks we've been at sea I've come to believe that you are quite the bravest, strongest person I've ever met."

"And here I thought I was just one of the prettiest, like," said Norah. Her face was still buried in his chest, but Finn could hear her smile.

He couldn't remember the last time he'd seen her smile, and he savored the idea that he had caused it. Finn chuckled, tightening his arms about her ever so slightly. "I'm afraid I've quite changed my mind on that point."

"Oh?" There was no mistaking the disappointment in her tone.

Finn felt his grin might tear his face in two. "I'm positive you're the most beautiful lass who ever lived."

Norah pulled back to study his face, her expression dubious. "Ever, is it now?"

Finn nodded silently, relishing the way Norah was looking at him and the blush creeping up her neck.

"Have you seen the state of my hair, like?" Norah reached her hand in an ineffectual attempt to smooth down her flyaway locks.

"Have you seen the state of mine?" Finn countered with a laugh, mirroring her actions.

Norah only scoffed, her mouth twitching with amusement as she stared at him. After a moment, her gaze lowered to his lips. He needed no further incentive.

In the back of his mind, Finn felt the levelheaded part of him shouting a warning to be sensible. But he had spent too many years wishing for something he could never have. Norah was here with him now, and, judging by the way she placed her arms around his neck to pull him closer, she felt the same way about Finn as he did about her. He hoped. And it had been so long since he had really, truly hoped.

As their lips met once, twice—he lost count of how many times— he heard that voice again, a little louder than before. *How will this end?* it wondered, tugging at the back of his mind.

Quiet, he countered angrily. He let his hand trail up Norah's back and get lost in the coppery curls at her neck. One of Norah's hands tentatively caressed the stubble along his jaw, and she pulled away for the briefest of moments to lay a feathery kiss there as well before Finn moved to reclaim her mouth with his own.

He wasn't sure how long they stayed like that. Long enough to silence the voice that Finn used to call "reason." Long enough to continue tying the knot around their hearts that Finn was sure could never be undone.

When a jeering whistle sounded across the deck, courtesy of a group of sailors, Finn finally allowed reason to return. What was he doing, standing above deck, thoroughly kissing a lass his parents were bound to disapprove of, all while his family lay below deck sick or—heaven forbid it—dying? What right had he to be so wholly content, so entirely happy holding this woman in his arms? He made himself sick. Finn immediately relaxed the arms he still held about her, though he could not convince himself to release Norah completely. No, he didn't feel quite enough guilt for that.

Norah seemed to be experiencing a similar internal struggle. There was a puckering between her brows, and her eyes kept darting from side to side. "I need to tell you something."

There was no accounting for the way those words caused Finn to tense. He couldn't stop himself from pulling her back to him, allowing her closeness to dull reason once more.

"I'm listening," he said as calmly as he could manage.

"'Tis about my past, like," Norah began slowly. "But where to begin?"

"I've heard the beginning is generally best when telling a story," Finn teased. He wanted to see her smile again, wanted to wipe away the look of worry she wore on her face like a badge of a war he knew nothing about. Maybe then he could calm his fear of whatever she was about to tell him.

Norah tapped his arm, glaring at him. "I'm serious, Finnegan."

Finn quickly sobered, nodding gravely at her, though his lips still twitched. Norah appeared unfazed by his amusement and looked away from him as she began.

"You know I was raised in Sligo," she said, her voice quivering. She cleared her throat, her eyes locked on his shoulder as she continued. "That my father was a doctor. You know my parents died of the cholera epidemic when I was only thirteen."

Finn nodded, wary of what she could say that would account for the way she was beginning to tremble in his arms. He was tempted to tell her all of the other things about her he already knew—either that she had told him or that he had gleaned from Bridget as indifferently as he could manage—but he abstained.

"You know that, shortly before their death, my parents sent me to live with a friend of my mother's."

Again, Finn nodded, waiting to hear something he did not already know.

Tears were already glistening in Norah's eyes as she continued. Finn brushed them away with the pads of his thumbs as he listened.

"Mrs. Driscoll was kind enough when she thought I would only be staying with her and her family for a time, but it soon became obvious that she had been unprepared to be my permanent guardian. To put it mildly, she was . . .unkind. I suffered unnecessary hunger and cruelty at her hands."

"But you didn't have anywhere else you could go?" Finn asked, his throat constricting at Norah's distress. She wiped at her eyes and took a calming breath before she continued.

"I was only thirteen. I was on the opposite end of the country with no living family and no guarantee that any of my old friends were alive. I wanted to write letters, like, but Mrs. Driscoll said she couldn't afford the expense. She had ten children of her own, after all. They were another reason I found it difficult to leave. The little ones depended on me and I . . ."

"You have a tender heart, Norah," said Finn. "You have a difficult time watching anyone suffer."

Norah looked up at him in disbelief, and Finn chuckled. "Why does it surprise you that I've noticed? I can promise you that everyone aboard this ship knows of your kind heart. 'Tisn't hard to see, though I admit there was a time I wondered."

"That's only because you have the uncanny ability to infuriate me, Finnegan Boyd," said Norah, her lips pursed in mock displeasure.

Finn smiled at that. "Do I? I rather thought that was your way of keeping me at arm's length, given that I am so handsome and charming."

She was giving him that disbelieving look again as though he had found her out. Her mouth was agape, her eyes wide. Finn couldn't resist the urge to press a quick kiss to the corner of her pink lips before straightening, suddenly serious once more.

"I'm sorry," he said. "You were telling me a story."

Norah's mouth snapped shut, and she nodded brusquely. "Where was I?"

"The children."

"Yes," said Norah. "I didn't want to abandon the children, like, so I stayed. For four years, I endured Mrs. Driscoll's treatment of me. She didn't seem to notice any good I did, seeing me only as an expense. She tried to force me to attend Mass with her family, but it was the one thing I could stand my ground on without harsh consequences."

"Did she . . .beat you?" Finn asked.

Norah shook her head. "No, but she had other means of getting her way, like. She knew I had a soft spot for the children and would isolate me, locking me in my room if I displeased her. Which was often."

"Oh, Norah," Finn breathed. What else could he say? Nothing would change the past or undo the hurt of feeling so unwanted and unloved. How she had endured such cruelty and for so long was a further testament to the strength Finn had come to see in her.

"Don't," Norah commanded, pulling away from him. Finn's arms hung loosely at his sides, and he felt the cold of the ocean blowing over him, chilling all the places which had once shared Norah's warmth. "I'm not telling you this to gain your sympathy, like. But if you're going to keep kissing me and looking at me like that, then you need to know the whole story."

Was he going to keep kissing her? He certainly hoped so—he had no immediate plans to stop, anyway, as long as she would allow it. Finn had already admitted himself in love with her but had not thought much beyond that fact. She was, after all, still a Protestant, and he was still a Catholic. But surely there had to be some solutions there. A marriage between the two was not altogether unheard of, though it was undoubtedly frowned upon. But they were headed to America, and perhaps things were different there. Given its founding in religious freedom, Finn hoped that there would be acceptance and understanding. Because he *did* want to marry her. Finn smiled as realization dawned over him, bright as a new day. If they survived the journey, Finn didn't want to stay another day apart from Norah.

"I'll listen to whatever you want to tell me," Finn promised with what he hoped was a reassuring smile.

"There was a man—a neighbor of the Driscoll's," Norah continued, her words halting. "A doctor—Niall O'Shannessey. He was several years older than my seventeen years. He was twenty-five when we met, like. By all accounts, he was a kind and educated man. He was a member of my own congregation, though he was only known to me because of his profession. I found him to be rather quiet when we first met, but I thought nothing of it. He took an interest in me, though I still don't know why, like. And, because he was a man of means, when he asked Mrs. Driscoll for my hand, she readily agreed."

Finn stiffened. He had to work very hard to focus on Norah's words and their meaning. Another man had wished to marry her—had been given *permission* to marry her. It shouldn't have come as a surprise to him as Norah was stunning, but it made him inexplicably cold all the same.

"In the end, I was part of a business arrangement. Dr. O'Shannessey actually *paid* Mrs. Driscoll for my hand. Mrs. Driscoll's money troubles were solved. Niall had himself a wife to take care of and serve him. Everyone got something out of the arrangement . . .except for me. Niall—Dr. O'Shannessy was . . . not what a husband ought to be."

Norah paused, wiping her face with a shaking hand as if it might wipe away the memories Finn could see flooding her eyes.

"It didn't take me long to realize that he had no intentions of loving me as a husband should. He drank a great deal, more so in the second year of our marriage. I was only eighteen then, but more often than not, I was the one seeing after his patients because he was too incapacitated to treat them properly. I was careful to observe him when he was sober because I knew I would need the knowledge on how to care for them when he was not capable. And when he was out drinking, I was studying his books."

Finn had to place an arm on the cabin wall beside him to steady himself before he could find his voice. "That's how you know so much about doctoring—not from your father. But from your husband," he said. The frown on his face was painfully deep, and he could hear how hollow his voice sounded. But there was nothing to be done.

Norah nodded in understanding. She pulled her shawl closer about her as she continued. "In addition to being negligent, like, he was also an incredibly mean drunk. I had gone from one kind of abuse to another. When I told him I might be expecting—" She stopped abruptly, perhaps noting Finn's rigid stance.

"What, Norah?" Finn's jaw was clenched so tight he had a difficult time forming the words. But he needed to hear; he *needed* to know the whole of it.

"He was angry." Norah's voice was soft and hesitant. "I knew I couldn't suffer any more at his hand, not after that last time. I left. If I hadn't, I was afraid of what he might do. But I couldn't go back to the Driscoll's, so I found a job and worked hard to support myself."

"And the baby?" Finn asked, his voice strained.

Norah looked up at him sharply for a moment, her eyes guarded as they followed the lines of his face. "There was no baby. I was mistaken. But I thanked whatever higher power might be listening that it hadn't been true. I don't know if I could have handled having any lasting connection to that man. After I realized my marriage was over, I resolved to never depend on anyone again—"

"W-what?" Finn shook his head, his thoughts shuffling around as he tried to make sense of them all. He had tried to listen, tried to remain patient, and tried not to react to any of the shocking details of her story, but this . . .this realization settling into his mind was too much. He looked about him, desperate to find something, some answer that would make this all easier somehow. But there was nothing.

"Norah," a soft voice called, and Órla emerged from below deck, her head swiveling about in search of them. Finn could see her taking in his rigid stance and what must have been the tortured expression on his face. She looked back and forth between him and Norah until she focused on Norah's tears. After a moment, Órla looked at them both with understanding.

"I know we're all tired," she said, approaching them slowly, little Colum attached to her hip by the shawl wrapped about her waist. "I hope the fresh air has done you some good. But . . .Catriona is asking for you."

"Is Alastar worse?" Finn asked. His brother had had a raging fever for days, but it had broken the night before, and Norah had declared him out of danger. Finn had been grateful to have at least one member of his family through the worst of it. They had a long way to go before he would breathe a sigh of relief, but, when all was said and done, they had already fared better than many of their fellow passengers.

"No," said Órla carefully. "'Tis Roisin."

Finn's heart stopped for a painful second while he tried to catch his breath. They had been so careful to keep the children separated from the sickest of the family, but in such close quarters, it had been quite impossible. "Is it bad?" Finn asked when he had gathered enough air in his lungs once more.

"She couldn't stop coughing," said Órla.

Finn raced below, struggling for a moment to remember which bunk the children had been huddling up in the last time he had seen them. It didn't take him long to find the source of the coughing.

"Oh, my rose," said Finn, sitting beside the girl and slowly stroking her back. Roisin's face was red, her eyes bulging from the force of the wracking coughs.

When Norah had offered her some water, and she was finally able to calm down enough to breathe, Roisin's eyes filled with tears.

"Am I to die now like Great-Gran?" asked Roisin in a raspy whisper.

"Never," Finn vowed. "If the angel of death comes, I'll fight him off myself—tooth and nail."

Roisin smiled weakly. "You're so brave." She coughed again, weaker this time. "I just wanted to go to America."

"You will, my rose," said Finn. "I promise."

Roisin only closed her eyes, moaning. She was too tired to do anything else.

"Uncle Finn," Oona's quivering voice broke through Finn's panic. She stood at his shoulder, her eyes full of fear. "Is Roisin going to die?"

"No, little lamb." Finn smiled at her weakly. "But you must let Roisin stay with your ma and da now. You keep close with Aunt Órla and the babes so you can be healthy and strong for me."

Oona smiled at him, although it did not quite meet her wide eyes like he was used to seeing. Finnegan tried to return her smile but was not successful. The Boyds were a strong bunch made of proud Irish stock, to be sure. But he wasn't able to conjure up the same optimism of only an hour before. Instead, Finn was kicking himself that he'd been so rash, jumping into things without thinking them through. He had allowed himself to be tangled so thoroughly that he wasn't sure how to proceed.

Another coughing fit from Roisin helped Finn to clear his head immediately. His pathway was sure, though he could only see a step or two ahead of him. He would throw himself into taking care of his family, as he had done for Michael all those years ago. In doing so,

Finn would do his best to distract himself from the fact that he had once again given his heart to a woman who wasn't free.

There was no denying he had thoroughly mucked things up. Innocent interest had evolved into harmless flirting. But there was no taking back that kiss nor his confession.

Blast.

Unfortunately, Finn's newfound resolve to distract himself didn't stop him from thinking of all the moments he and Norah had shared together. And even now, even as he tried not to observe her ministration to his sick family members, she was still so incredibly beautiful. *She's not yours,* that little voice reminded him. It needn't have bothered. The words were written upon his heart.

CHAPTER SIXTEEN

25 February 1846, the Bark Rosemary, the Atlantic Ocean

"Save your strength," Norah commanded, though she didn't know how much longer she could take her own advice.

Bridget nodded weakly. She was able to sit up on her own now. Her fever had broken sometime during the night. Daniel, who had already fared better than the sickest members of the Boyd family, had returned to his sickbed as his fever raged once more.

Norah wasn't sure how many times she had hollowly promised people that they couldn't all possibly die from the fever. Although the elderly and youngest of them undoubtedly fared the worst, there seemed to be no rhyme or reason to who was well and who was sick.

Conner, for example, had been a great help in caring for his family, as he might have been the healthiest of the lot, but Alastar still struggled as one of the hardest hit among them. Norah worried for him, given how seasick he had been in the first place.

Norah was only thankful that Finn remained as yet unscathed. *If only*, she thought with disappointment, *he would speak to me.*

She knew they hadn't had time to speak in private since the day before when Norah had finally resolved to tell him the whole of her story. Now she could see what a horrible mistake her confession had been. Finn had been so detached, so distant ever since. She tried to attribute his sudden aloofness to the fact that Roisin was gravely ill, as Norah knew that Finn shared a special bond with his eldest niece. However, she could not shake the feeling that there was something more to it.

The day marked Ash Wednesday, but there were none of the usual feelings of anticipation and devotion that came with the holy day. The priest was far too busy administering last rights to hold a meeting, so the Boyd family made due, as was their way.

"I don't know about you," mumbled a miserable-looking Alastar. "But I'll be abstaining from all this rich food they've been feeding us."

Norah knew Alastar was referring to Lent, the period of time between Ash Wednesday and Easter. This was a time when many Christians, including both Catholics and Protestants, actively fasted or worked to give up something about their actions or characters that might be considered a sin or an indulgence.

"Don't be blasphemous, Alastar," Catriona warned, looking about her as if lightning might strike at any moment.

Alastar, too weak for his usual booming laugh, only smiled wanly from his bunk.

They all took turns sharing how they would be observing the forty days, forty-six if you included Sundays. Most of the Boyd brothers kept what they would be abstaining from light, as Alastar had done. They were all anxious to make their loved ones smile, in spite of their desperate circumstances.

When Mrs. Boyd softly asked Finn, who had been very quiet during the whole exchange, what indulgences he would be avoiding, there was no mistaking the pointed look he gave Norah. But he quickly turned to his mother, at whose bedside he sat, reapplying the cool cloth to her forehead.

"I shall try to be more grateful, Ma," he began softly, "for the things I do have, instead of dwelling on the things I cannot."

Mrs. Boyd patted Finn's hand lovingly. "There's my smart boy," she said with a weak smile.

What could he have possibly *meant by that?* Norah wondered. Why had he looked at her with that mixture of pity and disappointment? Was she, then, the thing he could not have?

So they had come to it at last. Norah had wondered when Finn's conscience would finally prick him—when he would finally declare himself ashamed of his dalliance with her. From everything Norah had seen, he was faithful and dedicated, and she could only assume that extended to his relationship with the Almighty. As far as she knew, Finn had kept their brief rendezvous above deck a secret from all except Conner, though she couldn't account for the exemption. And Gran. Somehow his grandmother had known . . .but she had not, apparently, entirely disapproved of Norah.

No. Something else must have changed between them. Norah feared her honesty was the culprit. It was the first time she had felt safe enough to relate her history to anyone, and she had thoroughly spoiled things by doing so. She wished for nothing more than to find a private moment with Finn so that she might complete her story and clear up any misunderstandings between them.

But Finn was set on spending as little time alone with her as possible. When Norah made her regular rounds to check on the other passengers—a task which Finn had been sure to do with her almost since the beginning—Conner was suddenly present as well.

The lad did not appear comfortable with the arrangement, and more often than not, he could be seen eyeing his brother warily as both brothers were given instructions to change out a cloth or help a fellow passenger take a drink. There was, quite suddenly, none of the ease between Finn and Norah that there had been for the weeks they had been aboard the *Rosemary*.

Norah mentally kicked herself. She had been very careful over the years not to grow close to anyone, to avoid attachments or friendships. The fact that she hadn't had a friend in over ten years had been purposeful. How could she have forgotten that? She knew the answer, of course. She had learned very early on in their acquaintance that she was hopelessly attracted to Finnegan Boyd. The initial fear of him and his similarities to Niall—similarities that had only been made stronger when Finn and his brothers had become involved in a bar fight—had faded as she had watched his interactions with those closest to him. He was gentle, thoughtful, and, for all that she could see, sincere.

Learning about his lost love and his loyalty to her had only solidi-fied Norah's good opinion of him. She had thought that even his hon-esty with her had proven his worthiness. Now she feared she had been mistaken, and her face burned at the thought that he knew so much of her history. If she had been wrong about him not judging her, not blaming her for her past, what else had she been wrong about?

Norah tried not to think about which part of her history was so repulsive to Finn. For the time being, she needed to put all thoughts on the matter aside and take care of her patients, as she had secretly begun to think of them.

"How's your mother today, Gráinne?" Norah asked as she approached the fair-haired lass. Gráinne, who was sitting beside both of her parents, turned at Norah's greeting. Norah's quick intake of breath immediately caught Conner's attention, and he hurried to his sweetheart's bedside, placing a hand tenderly to Gráinne's forehead.

"You're burning up," said Conner, fear lacing each word.

"Tell me something I don't know," said Gráinne with a humorless snort.

"How long have you been like this?" Norah asked as she moved closer to her. She carefully examined Gráinne's throat, wincing when the lass flinched in pain.

"Maybe since last night sometime," said Gráinne, holding a hand to her head. "I figured there was nothing to be done about it anyway, so why bother you?"

"Because I could have helped take care of you," said Conner, clearly exasperated at the lass's stubbornness. "You shouldn't have to care for your ma and da when you're ill as well."

Gráinne attempted what Norah guessed was meant to be a sweet smile, but it looked more like a grimace as the lass slowly lowered her-self until she was lying beside her parents and two younger sisters. The Dougherty's were not the illest of the passengers by any means, but Norah did worry about Gráinne's sisters, who were only twelve and eight respectively. The young were so susceptible.

"I'm staying here," Conner informed Norah and Finn as they fin-ished checking on the Dougherty's and prepared to move on. Norah didn't miss the pointed look between the brothers. Finn grunted softly, and Conner all but ignored him, moving to help Gráinne put one of the too-hard pillows under her head.

"You can stay too if you like," said Norah as she stood up, dusting off her skirts while carefully avoiding Finn's gaze.

"No," said Finn. The word came out roughly, and Finn cleared his throat. Norah looked up at him quickly, searching his countenance for any sign of illness. He looked back at her steadily. "I'm well, Norah."

She breathed an audible sigh of relief, not only at learning that he was still healthy but also at hearing him speak to her directly for the first time in what felt like too long. She had given him instructions on how to help, and he had readily complied but had remained mostly silent.

"I'll come with you," he continued, no longer looking at her but instead directing his gaze at the many bunks full of the sick and dying. "Someone has to do something."

They worked together almost without a word, as Finn appeared to be most comfortable when Norah allowed silence to pass between them. By the end of their rounds about the ship, Norah was so utterly drained that one more look of regret from Finn might break her. So she didn't look at him, she didn't say a word to him. Instead, she slowly returned to her bunk, to Órla and the healthy babes, and closed her eyes. She did her best to ignore the rocking of the boat and the pounding in her head, knowing that neither was likely to stop anytime soon.

* * *

AFTER GOING TO BED WITH A HEADACHE, NORAH FEARED SHE WOULD awake with a fever. But the reality was far worse.

"It's Finn," was all Conner said, his eyes crinkling painfully as he shook Norah awake with the dawn.

"I'm fine," Finn insisted, waving a hand to shoo Norah away when she came to kneel beside him. After the initial hurt at having been dismissed so easily, Norah grit her teeth and continued her evaluation. She justified his behavior by blaming it on the fever, though she knew it was far too early for him to be experiencing any sort of delirium. Instead, Norah was afraid it meant that Finn indeed had hardened his heart against her. She only wished she knew why and how she might reverse the process. She couldn't quite bring herself to believe that he could consider her spoiled, given all that she had endured. But the thought lingered there in her mind all the same. She had never wanted her words to him above deck to be unsaid so desperately as she did when Finn turned over in his bunk, his back to her as he coughed helplessly into his pillow.

"I'll check on you later, like," said Norah softly when he had finished his coughing fit.

"Conner can keep an eye on me," said Finn weakly. "You needn't bother yourself."

"You could never be a bother," Norah admitted, her voice a whisper. She didn't want his family nearby to hear his rejection of her, though they still knew nothing of what had passed between them.

"Don't mind Finn," Conner said as Norah finally stood and made to go check on Roisin nearby. "He's an idiot."

"He's not," said Norah regretfully. "But thank you."

"No, he is," Conner insisted. He followed her to Roisin's side and watched her quietly as Norah checked the girl's temperature, throat, and abdomen. Norah knew her face must look grave. Little Roisin was not faring well at all.

Norah glanced back over to where Finn lay, her thoughts wandering to moments she had seen Finn share with his niece.

"He's not an idiot," Norah breathed, not wanting to disturb the fitful rest of the sick Boyd clan. "He must have his reasons, like, I'm sure."

"Finn's biggest problem is that he keeps everything bottled up inside," said Conner with a roll of his eyes. "It's like he thinks he is protecting us from whatever melancholy thoughts have taken up residence in his head. But it really only serves to worry Ma."

Norah looked to where Conner's eyes had been drawn. Mrs. Boyd still lay beside her husband, both of them sleeping fitfully.

"She doesn't need any more worries than she already has," Conner whispered. "Maybe you could knock some sense into Finn for her sake."

"I'm not sure how effective that would be," said Norah a little bitterly.

"Then you might try that other method you two have been employing," said Conner with a smirk. Norah's mouth hung agape at Conner's reference to her and Finn's time above deck. Conner only continued to smile knowingly at her. His brow suddenly furrowed as he wiped his hands on his trousers as he stood. "I'm going to check on the Doughertys. Let me know if you need me."

"But what about Finnegan, like?"

Conner turned back to her and wriggled his eyebrows. "I believe you're the one with the medicine, Norah."

Norah sighed long when Conner had gone, disappearing around the corner of bunks. There were too many of the sick for her to treat everyone as she would have wished. But, with the exception of Roisin, the other Boyd children remained in as good of health as could be expected aboard a ship with no proper sanitation and not enough rations to go around. They were thin, far too thin for Norah's liking, and she spent much of the day imagining what she could do to fatten them up again with her remaining money once they finally arrived in New York. She had already resolved that she would do everything in her power to help the family who had taken her in as one of their own, even if Finn had concluded that she was undeserving of such a place. The Boyds needed the money far more than she did. Far more than they needed her.

"Norah," a soft voice called from behind. Norah turned to find Bridget standing close by; her face was ghostly pale. There was the Boyd determination in her eyes, and Norah braced herself for whatever the lass might have to say. "I want to help."

"You're not fully recovered yourself," said Norah kindly, knowing she had to tread carefully whenever Bridget got an idea in her head.

"I can't sit here any longer," said Bridget. "I can help."

"I don't think that's a good—"

"Norah," Bridget began firmly. "If I sit in that bunk thinking about all of my losses any longer, I will go stark raving mad. Give me something to do."

"Only if you promise not to overexert yourself," said Norah reluctantly. As much as Norah disliked it, Bridget was right. Norah needed more help, especially with Finn now sick and Conner preoccupied with his mother's and Gráinne's illnesses.

"You have my word," said Bridget with as bright a smile as Norah had seen from her in weeks, at least.

"Will you sit with Roisin?" Norah asked. "I need to . . .check how Finn is faring."

"Finn is sick?" Bridget asked, paling even more, though Norah hadn't thought it possible.

"He'll be all right," said Norah, attempting a brave front. "He's strong, like your Daniel. How is your Mr. O'Callaghan, by the way, like?"

Bridget was too distracted at first to answer her. She felt Roisin's forehead and cheeks, shaking her head at the heat radiating off of her. "He's doing better," said Bridget. "Leastways, his fever has broken again."

"That is something," said Norah encouragingly as she moved back to Finn's bunk. She sat down beside him as cautiously and quietly as she could, not wanting to startle him or give him reason to send her away again. But Finn didn't stir. Perhaps he didn't have the strength to do so. For reasons that Norah could not explain, his illness was the one that made the least sense. He was as strong a man as any of his brothers—healthy and fit—yet it quickly became apparent that his illness would rival Alastar's in ferocity. Finn burned too hot too quickly and moaned from the pain in his head and belly. The cough intensified not long after, and he soon struggled to breathe. The symptoms were not the same as described in the books she had studied, as was the case with many of the sick. Norah knew she was no doctor, but she feared a secondary infection.

What had been an overwhelming number of passengers to care for before quickly became a mad attempt just to keep the Boyd family alive. Those who were well enough could often be heard praying over those who were not, begging God for a reprieve from their tribulations. There was little improvement among the family. In the case of Roisin, Alastar, Finn, and Mrs. Boyd, their conditions continued to deteriorate.

* * *

Norah tried to take heart and detach herself from the situation, but seeing Finn reach delirium only days into his illness was almost more than she could bear. At one point, he even called out for Niamh. Bridget, who had been attempting to cool his brow, was so surprised that she sat frozen by his side for a good minute before Norah could hurry over and relieve her. Norah hastily muttered something she hoped would quiet Bridget's mind about the outburst, knowing Finn would wish to keep that part of his past private. Bridget only nodded, her weak smile indicating that she was not entirely convinced.

"You'll have everyone knowing all those thoughts you keep locked as tight as a barge, like, if you don't stop that now," Norah whispered soothingly as she felt Finn's wrist for his pulse. It beat too quickly beneath her fingers.

Finn's hand twitched beneath her touch. Norah looked to find him looking at her through hooded lids.

"Norah," he breathed, the ghost of a smile playing on his pale lips. Norah shushed him quickly, her eyes flicking to the nearby bunks and their occupants. Bridget had moved on to care for Alastar and was out of earshot once more.

"Are you come to take care of me, lass?" he asked, his voice hoarse.

With no little effort, Norah helped him sit up enough to drink a small amount of water, most of which he coughed out. She watched helplessly as it dribbled down his chin, collecting in his whiskers as his face contorted in pain. Then she carefully patted his face dry. It felt bittersweet to be able to be so close to him, to care for him in this way. Yet she could not shake the feeling that he was too far away from her now, in more ways than one.

She mentally counted the days until the captain believed they would arrive in New York. The multiple storms they had encountered had blown them off course. Norah would have supposed that was the nature of sailing in winter, but the captain had apparently not planned accordingly. They were running low on their already sparse rations. Water would be next, and then they wouldn't last long, no matter how few of them were still alive in the end.

"Can I tell you a secret?" Finn asked when Norah had laid him back down.

"Don't you think there've been enough confessions between us?" Norah whispered, hoping that he would simply slip back into unconsciousness once more. She winced at how bitter her words both sounded and tasted coming out, but Finn seemed not to notice.

He beckoned her closer, and Norah was obliged to lean in quite close until he was satisfied. Finn grinned at her, though it was lopsided, and there was something about it that didn't look quite right to Norah's eyes.

"Your eyes are the color of dried turf," he said, his eyes drooping so low that Norah thought they might close altogether.

"You're delusional, Finnegan Boyd," Norah scoffed with a tinge of regret. She tried to pull away, but Finn's surprisingly firm hand on her arm kept her there.

"I'm in love," said Finn conspiratorially. "But I've heard they're the same."

Norah stilled, stunned into silence for a good minute while Finn continued to grin at her stupidly. Perhaps, she reasoned, he was in the midst of a delirious episode and thought he was confessing his feelings to Niamh.

"You rest now," Norah ordered in what she hoped was a firm enough tone that Finn would feel inclined to listen.

"Did you hear me, Norah?" Finn asked a little louder, putting his sweaty palm on her hand. "*Tá mé i ngrá leat.*"

Norah did her best to ignore her racing pulse and resisted the urge to place a hand over his mouth in a desperate attempt to silence him. "Will you be quiet now, like? Your family is trying to rest."

Finn closed his eyes and took a deep, rattling breath. After a moment, he nodded.

"I'm so tired," he muttered.

"I'll come to check on you later," she said as she made to stand.

"Later," Finn muttered, his face contorted for a moment in pain and his eyes closed against it. Then, "I love you."

His words hung before her long after Norah had scurried off to check on some of the other passengers.

I love you. I'm in love *with you.*

The reasonable part of her told Norah not to take the ravings of a man stooped in delirium seriously. But when was the last time someone had told her they loved her? Mrs. Driscoll had never said it, to be sure. Niall never had, neither in word nor in deed. Perhaps some of the Driscoll children might have muttered it to her as she cared for them a time or two. But when had someone told her they loved her and really, truly meant it?

The answer was jarring. Her mother and father had both reminded her that they loved her before they sent her off to Cork to stay with Mrs. Driscoll. It was too long—far too long for a body to go without hearing that they were not only wanted but truly cherished. All of the fear from her confession to Finn began to fade away with the knowledge that, no matter what still stood between them, he loved her. Loved *her*. Did she dare to believe it?

"Norah," Mrs. Boyd's voice called Norah from her thoughts and back to grim reality. Norah hurried to the woman's side.

"What can I do for you, Mrs. Boyd?" Norah asked quietly, not wanting to disturb Mr. Boyd, who slept fitfully beside her.

"Oh, child," Ma Boyd smiled weakly. "You've done so much already. You've taken such good care of us from the very start to this wretched end."

Norah was unable to prevent a small gasp from escaping her lips. "Don't say that, like."

"I'm not blind," said Mrs. Boyd. Although she spoke softly and with no little effort, her words and eyes were clear. "I can see where this is headed. As I've said, you've taken care of us. But I worry for you."

"I'm grand, Mrs. Boyd," said Norah, her smile tight.

"You're two peas, and no mistake," the older woman said with a small laugh, reaching up to brush a strand of her fair hair away from her sticky face. "At first, I couldn't decide if that would play out in your favor, but I feel it will all work itself out in the end, God willing."

Norah couldn't make sense of the woman's words. She didn't want Mrs. Boyd to exert too much energy by pressing her to explain, so Norah remained silent. It was what was best for the patient when the delirium set in, after all.

Mrs. Boyd reached out to place an unsteady hand upon Norah's. "You need to let others care for you, Norah," she said. "You can't give and give without needing a bit o' love to fill you up again. I had hoped you would—"

"A man just came asking for help," said Órla, her quick footsteps coming up behind them. She sighed quickly, looking about her as she spoke. "He seemed distressed—said 'tis his child. Bridget and I will do our best to help while you're away."

Norah looked back at Mrs. Boyd, who nodded slightly. "Just think on what I've said," she said, closing her weary eyes.

Norah nodded before hurrying away. She tried not to let Mrs. Boyd's words affect her, but she couldn't ignore that even in her weakened state the woman had the uncanny ability to get to the root of things. Norah wanted to be loved. She craved affection, yet for years she had denied that part of herself and pushed people away for fear of being hurt or rejected. And yet, here she was, unsure of where she stood with the man who had feverishly proclaimed his love for her. Yes, she needed love—craved it—there was no more denying that. But would it break her in the end?

Norah stayed away for longer than she had planned. She had to rein in her emotions before she rejoined the Boyds, so she checked in on the Doughertys and Conner, who refused to leave Gráinne's side when his family didn't absolutely need him.

Gráinne's father's condition had worsened, and it was clear that the normally strong-spirited lass took comfort in Conner's presence. So many others required Norah's help, if only for her to offer a word of hope, however fragile. In the end, Conner and Norah returned together and were greeted by a weepy Órla.

"It's Ma Boyd," she said, her voice catching. "It happened so quickly. I wanted to come find you, but I didn't want to leave her, and Bridget wouldn't. Ma seems so scared . . ."

Norah hurried to Mrs. Boyd's side. Mr. Boyd lay on his side next to her, his eyes large and fearful as he watched helplessly.

"She's had a great many issues with her lungs these past years," said Mr. Boyd. His voice was raw with emotion. "Do you think that's weakened them?"

Of course it has, Norah thought as she watched Mrs. Boyd struggle for breath, the skin at the base of her neck contracting. But Norah couldn't say that. She couldn't say that she didn't know what to do for the woman, not without some medicine or a clean place to lay her down. And even then . . .

Mrs. Boyd was breathing too quickly, which was not abnormal for typhoid fever, but there was something different about the way she struggled for breath. Norah's chest constricted painfully, cutting off her own ability to breathe properly. She wanted to run. She wanted to escape to the deck and breathe deep the sea air until she could calm her racing heart and mind. But the Boyds needed her—Mrs. Boyd needed her—and she could not—*would* not—abandon them because of her own fears.

"Daniel, Conner," Norah called to the only men who had enough strength to help her. "Will you help me to put a few more pillows under her? Perhaps we can open up her lungs a bit by elevating her."

It took Daniel and Conner longer than Norah would have liked to reposition Mrs. Boyd. Daniel was still weak, his muscles straining from the ordinarily simple task. When at last Mrs. Boyd was sitting up, propped up by the pillows of several family members, Norah leaned down to listen to the woman's heart and lungs. There was so much wheezing and rattling that Norah had to fight against the frown pulling at her lips. She didn't want to scare the Boyds, but she had no answers for them when they demanded to know if Mrs. Boyd would be all right. Judging by the defeat in their expressions when Norah could not answer, they, too, feared the worst.

Not long after, the delirium set in, and Mrs. Boyd cried out several times for people Norah was unfamiliar with. Bridget shakily informed Norah, both of their eyes and noses red from crying, that Mrs. Boyd was calling for Bridget's sisters, Deidre, who had been a few years younger than Conner, and Fiona, Finn's twin sister, who had died in infancy.

"Is there anything we can do for her?" Mr. Boyd asked Norah before turning back to his wife. "How can we help you, Miriam?"

But, of course, Mrs. Boyd didn't answer. She had neither strength nor presence of mind to speak. Before long, she descended into the "typhoid state" Norah had always wished she could unsee. Mrs. Boyd's eyes drooped heavily as she continued her mutterings, her hands twitching at her sides. Norah tried to convince the Boyds to return to their own bunks and not to watch as the life slowly drained from their dear mother, but they all refused to leave her.

Conner went to fetch the priest for last rites, as it was obvious to everyone that there was little hope. They had seen enough of their family and fellow passengers by now to know what the end looked like, and Norah hated that fact more than words could say.

She couldn't stop shaking her head as the priest muttered the words which had become too familiar to her. She knew them almost by heart. She shouldn't have to. The illness shouldn't have spread so quickly, taking so many and within such a short time before they were supposed to reach America and their new lives.

What life would look like and how many of them would survive the remainder of the journey, Norah did not know. What she did know was that the God the Boyds kept praying to didn't seem to hear them, as their loving mother—and one of the kindest women Norah had ever had the pleasure of knowing—slowly slipped away.

CHAPTER SEVENTEEN

Finn's condition did not improve, and in his semi-lucid moments, Norah didn't have the heart to tell him about the passing of his mother. From time to time, he would open his eyes, meeting Norah's for a brief moment before smiling through his pain, the whisper of her name on his lips. Norah tried not to let those moments fill her up with hope, reminding herself that the feverish mind was not to be trusted, but she couldn't seem to douse the spark once it had been lit.

He still burned too hot, still coughed too violently. Each expression of pain mirrored in Norah's face as she watched him. If she gave him impartial attention to her other patients, his family never said. But she felt the pull to stay by him, to watch over him whenever she could.

The only thing that was able to pull Norah from Finn's side was when sweet Roisin took a turn for the worse. Norah had needed to leave Conner and Órla to watch over Finn, knowing that there was no guarantee he would be alive when she was able to return to him. Nothing was certain anymore, and Norah felt the frailty of life more keenly than she ever had before. Life was as easily lost as a wave moving across the surface of the water. It was a natural, unstoppable fact, but it didn't make the loss feel any less real and senseless.

"You must fight, dear one," Norah whispered to Roisin as she listened to the girl's breathing. It was shallow and labored, but her heart, Norah discovered, still beat strongly. Norah only hoped that it would be enough—though it hadn't been for Mrs. Boyd or Gran or Mr. Dougherty or any number of the other passengers Norah had tried her best to care for—in the end.

"Your ma and da need you," Norah continued softly, caressing the child's face. "And your sister and brother, too. Where would we all be without your soft smiles, child?"

Roisin did not respond but instead continued her labored breathing. Overcome with a feeling of complete helplessness, Norah did the only other thing she could think to do—the only thing she hadn't yet done to care for the lass.

She prayed.

She wasn't sure she had prayed in earnest for the last several years at least. She had stopped attending services on a regular basis shortly after marrying Niall when it became too difficult to hide her bruises or explain for the dozenth time that she had simply been clumsy while the matrons gave her looks of either censure or pity. When she had begun working at the dyebaths, Norah had not sought out a new congregation. She had still been too angry to rely on anyone or anything but her own wits. She would not, she had resolved, be beholden to anyone. Not anymore.

But if there was any time to hope that there might be a higher power—to hope that perhaps all the years of silence had merely been some sort of test and not apathy towards her—it was now.

"Please, Lord," Norah pleaded, her whispers drowned out by the moan of the ship on the waves. "Don't abandon us here."

Sometime later, Dr. Smyth came to do his one round of the day. It was not often that Norah saw the doctor checking on the few patients he deemed worth his time, so she was a bit taken aback to see him move to Alastar's side. Dr. Smyth listened to the eldest Boyd son's heart and lungs while quietly asking Alastar about his symptoms.

"It's the fever I'm most concerned about," Dr. Smyth said quietly, speaking more to Alastar's wife, Catriona, than to Alastar himself. Even from two bunks away, Norah could see the sheen of sweat on Alastar's pale face.

"I'm going to administer three grains of quinine," the doctor said, pulling out a small envelope.

Norah recognized it as those used to hold quinine powder which could be mixed with water and drunk by the patient. The use of tonic water instead of powdered quinine was becoming more commonly used now, but transporting bottles of the liquid was impractical during such a long journey. With so many passengers, it was much wiser to carry as much of the powder as could be had. And even that was not enough for the number of passengers who needed it when Doctor Smyth was willing to give it at all.

"That should help to alleviate the fever and, with it, I hope, the delirium."

"Thank you, doctor," Catriona said, the frown lines which had seemed permanent about her face lessening in relief. "Should we give the same amount to my daughter?"

Dr. Smyth's eyes followed Catriona's gaze to where Norah sat with Roisin. Norah did her best to remain unaffected by the way the doctor's eyes flitted over her and barely settled on Roisin, but she feared she didn't do a very good job of it. He didn't step closer to examine the child. He shook his head once without looking at Catriona as he answered.

"I'm afraid I only have enough for the one."

Norah wanted to ask about medicine for Finn or Mr. Boyd, but relief flooded the doctor's face as a voice from somewhere farther down the line of bunks called for the doctor. He hurried towards the sound, mumbling his excuses and leaving the small envelope in a startled Catriona's hand.

After she had recovered enough from her shock, Catriona shakily asked Norah to help her prepare the quinine for Alastar. She moved to sit by Roisin's side. Both father and daughter's conditions only worsened as time passed. Norah's hands shook as she carefully mixed the powder into a tin cup of water. Every drop was precious.

"Alastar," Norah said. "I need you to try and drink all of this."

"Is it medicine?" Alastar asked drowsily, his speech slow and breathless.

"'Tis," said Norah with a forced smile. "To help with your fever."

Alastar closed his eyes tightly for a moment before he opened them again, determination written all over his face. "Give it to Roisin."

Norah paused, unsure what to do. The man was delirious, after all. He wasn't in his right mind—he didn't know what he was saying. If the doctor thought Alastar stood a chance at beating typhoid, drinking the quinine water would be his best chance. And yet, delicate Roisin suffered as well. She had little chance of surviving such a formidable disease, as small and young as she was. At last, Norah understood the dilemma Doctor Smyth faced and, perhaps, why he had no desire to labor over patients he knew stood no chance of defeating the disease. It was hard—too hard a decision to make.

"I know what I'm asking of you, Norah." Alastar's voice was weak, but his eyes burned with resolve. "My babe needs that more than I do. Give it to her. I won't drink a drop of it."

Across their respective patients, Norah caught Catriona's eye. It was an impossible thing to ask of her—to choose between being a wife and being a mother. But from what Norah knew of Catriona, she might have been the only one strong enough to make such a decision. Perhaps it was because she was several years older than her sisters-in-law, but Norah had long-admired how unruffled and calm Catriona was wont to be. Silently, Catriona nodded, standing to switch places with Norah once more.

"He wouldn't ever forgive me otherwise," said Catriona quietly as she moved to sit beside her husband. She took his hand in her own, bowed her head in silent prayer, and said no more on the matter.

It was difficult to convince the *wean* to drink when she complained of stomach pain, but Norah was patient and took her time to ensure that Roisin drank every bit of the bitter liquid. Then, with nothing else to do, she, too, resumed her prayers.

Norah wasn't sure how long she begged and pleaded and made all sorts of promises to the Almighty. She prayed for Alastar, for Roisin, and for Finn, all of whom currently fought for their lives as the latest and likely not the last of the Boyds to brush up against death's door. She hadn't even realized she had fallen asleep until she awoke to the feel of a hand on her face, slowly and carefully moving the hair from her face to the place behind her ear. For a moment, Norah had a memory of a time above deck where her face had burned in confusion. But this hand was too delicate and small to belong to Finnegan Boyd.

"You slept for a long time," said Roisin quietly when Norah finally found the strength to open her eyes. "I wasn't sure if you were dead."

Ignoring the pain in her shoulders and neck from sleeping in so awkward a position all night, Norah let out a cry of joy. It took all of her self-control not to take the lass in her arms and pepper her with kisses.

"How are you feeling, like?" Norah asked softly, sitting up straight and moving to feel Roisin's pulse.

"Like I almost died," said Roisin in a whisper. "Did I?"

"Very nearly, love," said Norah. "But I think you'll be all right now. Let me just tell your ma—she'll want to know you're well."

Norah moved to do just that, standing up from her place beside Roisin. She glanced in the direction of the bunk Finn had been lying in the night before, only to find it empty. Norah's mind went blank as her head swiveled this way and that in search of him—of anyone who could tell her what had happened while she slept. But the Boyds' bunks were empty, all except for Roisin's.

"Norah," acknowledged Bridget as she climbed down the ladder a moment later. There were dark circles beneath her reddened eyes, and her hair looked dull.

"Where is everyone?" Norah asked, the worst possible scenarios running through her mind. "Alastar? Finn? They aren't well enough to be up and about."

Bridget's face was set in a pained rictus as if she might never smile again.

"Alastar didn't make it through the night," said Bridget feebly. "Everyone is above deck saying goodbye to Ma and Alastar and the others who didn't make it. Torin said he saw a shark in the water."

Norah's heart dropped, and guilt flooded over her like a tidal wave. Alastar hadn't made it. The quinine had helped break Roisin's fever, but Alastar had suffered for too long without relief. If only there had been enough for both of them—Norah stopped the thought there, knowing that spiraling down into what-ifs would only leave her too weak to face what was to come.

The next moment, Norah was holding Bridget up as she sagged in Norah's arms, her grief too heavy for her to carry alone.

"Even . . ." Norah hesitated, not wanting to sound as desperate as she felt to hear Bridget's answer. "Even Finnegan? Only he wasn't doing well last night, like."

Bridget allowed Norah to lead her to her bunk. She sunk into it without a word and let Norah tuck her in before she finally answered.

"Finn looked to be over the worst of it sometime last night. He asked after you—he wanted to know if you were well. Then he heard about Ma and Alastar, and he's barely said a word since."

"Oh, Bridget," said Norah, feeling her face crumble. "Your ma was such a fine woman. And your brother gave up his own medicine for Roisin. I don't know what I could have done differently like, but I wish—I wish—"

"No one blames you," Bridget said. She looked too tired to carry on their conversation, and Norah gladly quieted so that her friend could find some form of peace in sleep.

Norah knew all too well the pain of losing a parent. She desperately wished she could have saved the Boyds from that pain. Norah had never had a brother to lose, but she imagined that the sorrow would be similar. It tugged at her heart until she found herself climbing the ladder to the deck with only one goal in mind—to offer comfort to her friends.

Her eyes sought out Finn of their own accord. Norah immediately felt her eyes softening as tears sprung at the corners. She did not often allow herself to cry, but she couldn't bear to see him in so much pain. Conner and Torin held their brother up as the Boyds huddled together, their soft cries making their way to Norah on the wind.

Catriona held Oona and Cuán close as both children cried to the sea for their da to come back to them. Norah joined them without a word as the cold bit through her skin, freezing the tears which had begun to track down her face. The air was colder than it had been up to this point, and Norah idly wondered if they were traveling farther north or if they were about to encounter yet another storm.

Órla pulled Norah into a hug, her small frame shaking in Norah's arms. Above Órla's head, Norah caught Finn's eye, and she immediately felt the painful tugging again. His gaze was much the same as it had been before he had fallen ill—emotionless and empty.

But what did it mean? Shouldn't he feel *something,* or was it merely a way of keeping his heart from breaking completely? Norah had to resist the urge to go to him and hold him like she wanted to. There was still so much unsettled between them. But oh, how she wished to be his comfort as he had been hers many times before. Even with the seemingly smallest of gestures, Finn had a way of making Norah feel safe and cared for as she had not felt in far too long. She wanted to offer him the same, but, based on the way he was looking at her, she wasn't sure that her comfort would be appreciated. She wasn't sure of anything anymore.

He said he loves you, she reminded herself. But could love cut through grief? Norah wasn't sure; it wasn't something she had any experience with. So she remained silent and still, only offering comfort to those who sought it out. She embraced both Catriona and Conner. Torin dipped his head in acknowledgment. Mr. Boyd was too overcome by grief to do much of anything. And Finn still would not look at her.

* * *

If Finnegan Boyd had more strength, he would have set aside his principles and self-preservation and knocked the captain of the *Rosemary* square in the gob. He'd been back on his feet for almost a week now, meaning the *Rosemary* should have made port in New York more than two weeks prior. The food stores were almost depleted, and there was very little water left. When Finn and a few others had mustered up the strength and courage to confront the captain about it, they had not been prepared for his answer.

"We aren't going to New York," the captain had informed them, looking at the group as if they had lost their minds. "We were never headed for New York."

After the initial confusion and anger, someone had the sense to ask the captain to explain himself.

"The Americans have far too many costly regulations. We're headed to Canada. You can travel to New York from there if you like."

"With what supplies?" one of the other passengers asked. "We have no money to buy food or shelter."

"Aye," another man agreed, his face contorted in anger. "By all accounts, Canada is much harsher terrain than any of us are used to. We were depending on getting jobs right away—"

"I'm sure there are jobs in Quebec City," said the captain with a dismissive wave of his hand. "And anyway, this is not up for debate." He swiveled about with an arm extended towards the port side of the ship. Finn had to squint, but he could just make out the outline of what must have been land jutting out from the haze of the ocean. "That's New Brunswick, gentlemen. We're drawing near to the Province of Canada. So you'd best ready yourselves and your families."

Ready them how? Finn wondered. Whether they were to make port in New York or Quebec City would make little difference in that regard. Without the generations of matrons to help guide and direct them—save Aunt Aileen, who barely clung to life as it was—Finn felt much like a boat adrift in a storm. And the thought of not having Alastar to make them all laugh left Finn reeling. It was as if the waves of grief might swallow him up at any moment.

"Can we—can we talk?" Norah approached Finn as he returned to the passenger's compartment. It was the first time she had attempted to talk to him alone since before Finn's illness. She had been watching him, he knew. But he couldn't bring himself to care.

She was clasping her hands in front of her, her knuckles white with the tension of it. Instead of feeling concern, as Finn might have done before, he felt oddly detached—he was watching a stranger instead of the woman he had admitted himself in love with. It was an odd, almost surreal experience, completely devoid of the emotion he was used to feeling when he looked at Norah. Finn was empty—numb.

He silently followed her to the opposite end of the compartment and waited with folded arms for her to speak.

"We haven't had an opportunity to speak, like," said Norah. She wasn't looking at him, but rather everywhere about them, especially where the members of his family sat or lay resting in their bunks. She was nervous, Finn noted with an air of detachment.

"No," said Finn simply. "We haven't."

"Only, I got the impression that you misunderstood me," said Norah. "Or that I somehow upset you with my tale."

Finn looked towards the wooden boards above their heads in an attempt to muster patience he did not feel. "I can't talk about this, Norah."

Norah went suddenly still, and Finn knew she was watching him carefully.

"You're upset," she said, her voice smaller and more timid than he had ever heard it before. Instead of the usual tugging on his heart this should have caused, and like it might have done *before*, Finn felt anger bubbling inside him. It was the only thing that explained what he said next.

"Why do you care?" he asked, his voice hollow.

Norah blinked and Finn could see that she held her breath.

"I . . ." she began, but no more words came.

Anger rose inexplicably within Finn's chest. In the back of his mind, a small voice whispered a warning that he should calm down and wait to have this conversation until he didn't feel so much sorrow. He should wait until he wasn't so angry at the captain for lying to them again and again, but he snapped back at it. *Nothing will ever be the same again. There's no point in waiting.*

"I just wanted to know if I could help somehow," Norah said quietly as she searched Finn's face. He didn't try to hide his anger, as he might have done in the past. There was something freeing about letting it go.

"Help, is it?" Finn asked, his words clipped and sharp. "Like how you helped Ma? Or Alastar? Catriona told me the doctor gave him medicine. But you didn't give it to him, did you? I think you've helped quite enough, Norah. Go find someone who *wants* your help."

"Finnegan Boyd!" Bridget called from nearby. From the look of censure of her face, Finn gathered that she had been watching their exchange. She stood there with her hands on her hips and an expression of such fierceness that it almost gave Finn pause. In that instant, she looked so exactly like Ma that it physically hurt. But feeling the pain of loss wasn't half so freeing as letting the anger take him.

"Mind your own business, Bridget," Finn snapped at her before turning on his heel and escaping back up the hatch. It wasn't his turn to be above deck, but he didn't care. All sense of reason was gone, replaced with the raw emotions Finn had worked so hard to school over the years. His life was crumbling about him, and he couldn't seem to make himself care if he went down with it.

CHAPTER EIGHTEEN

25 March 1846, Quebec City, Province of Canada

"I've never been so glad to have snow beneath my feet," said Conner with a contented sigh.

"That's only because you have a sturdy pair of shoes," said Finn with a mirthless laugh.

Conner nudged Finn's shoulder playfully. "You say that as if you don't own the best shoes in the family."

Finn didn't smile at his brother's teasing, remembering all-too-well from where said shoes had come.

They slowly made their way down the stone streets of the fortified city. They had spent the last several weeks of their ship's mandatory quarantine at Grosse Isle, an island in the middle of the St. Lawrence River, some thirty miles from Quebec City. During which, Finn had plenty of time to think about what had passed between Norah and himself and the words he had spoken in resentment and sorrow. His anger had eventually subsided once more to reveal the grief he was feeling. He still had enough sense to know that Ma's and Alastar's deaths weren't Norah's fault, but he couldn't bring himself to broach the subject with Norah. She was avoiding him. And rightly so—he had lashed out in anger and laid blame on her which belonged to no one, except perhaps the captain of the *Rosemary* for taking on too many passengers and not attempting to maintain sanitary conditions.

And then there was the matter of Norah's past and the impossibility of a future together. She was, after all, bound to another man—in the eyes of God, if no one else. It was, he concluded, for the best that whatever he and Norah had been to each other come to an end. He had no desire to make the same mistake he had before. No, it was better to make a clean break than to allow himself to hold onto something which could never have been his. He only hoped he could sever the string between them more quickly than he had been able to do with Niamh.

However sensible this course of action might have been, it was by no means easy. Finn had to fight the urge to speak with Norah as they waited their turn for the passengers on their ship to be cleared to disembark, and then as they were assigned a shed wherewith to wait out their quarantine on the island. It became only minutely easier to resist speaking to her as Norah had thrown herself into caring for everyone around her, as was her way, and had hardly so much as glanced at Finn. But that did not mean he didn't still long for the way things had been when he had been unaware of her past. Ignorance, as they said, truly was bliss.

Now that they had been released from quarantine, the family had to scramble to survive in an environment that was, even in the middle of March, entirely too cold for a group of people used to an admittedly wet and windy but temperate climate. When they had arrived in Quebec City, Norah had taken the womenfolk and children in search of a few items of warmer clothing. The men had been tasked with trying to find temporary lodging until they could decide what was to be done.

Finn and Conner had come up empty-handed and were already past due when they were to meet everyone else at the Cathedral of Notre-Dame de Québec. The building put Saint Peter's in Liverpool and even Saint Peter and Paul's in Cork to shame.

"There you are," a voice called as they approached. For a moment, Finn thought it was Órla, but the girl was a bit too tall for his sister-in-law. Finn only had to glance at Conner to confirm his suspicions. The lad wore a satisfied smile on his handsome face as he called back.

"If I'd known you were waiting for me, I would have ditched ol' Finnegan here and hurried on my way," said Conner as he caught his lass in an embrace.

"I heard Norah tell you where to meet her, and I thought I would come to see if you had better luck than we did," said Gráinne with a grin as Conner leaned down to kiss her cheek.

"I'm afraid we didn't," said Finn, turning away from the young couple with a sudden interest in the architecture around them.

"What?" Gráinne asked. "Nothing?"

Finn looked back at her concerned tone. She wore the same look of worry he had seen on her face many times since her father had died. The Dougherty's were in worse straits than the Boyds, to be sure. With two younger sisters and her mother to care for, Gráinne doubtless felt the strain of finding shelter and work for her family in a strange new land.

"Maybe we just didn't choose the best neighborhoods," said Conner hopefully, but Finn could see the uncertainty in his eyes.

"It will be growing dark soon," said Gráinne. She looked about the square, her eyes flitting this way and that in search of someplace that would offer shelter from the biting wind.

"Don't worry," said Conner. "Why don't you go find your mother and sisters and bring them back here. I'm sure that we can figure something out if we all put our heads together. And if we're very lucky, my da will have already found us a place to stay. I'm sure he wouldn't mind you staying with us. Right, Finn?"

Finn only hummed dubiously, doubting that there would be enough room for the Doughertys as well. There were four of them, after all, and—Finn's thoughts halted as he remembered that that made only one more than the original number the Boyds had left Liverpool with.

"We'll figure something out," Finn agreed. What other choice did they have? They couldn't just let Gráinne and her family freeze to death. It wouldn't be right.

"But where is everyone else?" Conner asked, turning himself and Gráinne by extension, as he still held her hand, about as they searched the square.

"They should have been here by now," said Finn.

They didn't have to wait much longer until the womenfolk—Órla, Catriona, Bridget, Aunt Aileen, and Norah—and the children returned, huddled together for warmth.

"Aunt Norah bought us some blankets!" said Oona brightly, indicating the woolen blanket wrapped around her and Roisin's shoulders.

Finn made the mistake of looking up and meeting Norah's gaze. He'd done his best to avoid it the past weeks, but it was still a struggle. Regardless of the silent understanding that whatever they had been was necessarily over, his eyes still sought her out whenever she was near, and he was only ever able to stop them just before they reached her face. But not this time.

Her gaze felt like fire on his freezing skin, her dark eyes boring into his own with an intensity he couldn't account for. Was she trying to tell him something? If so, he had no clue what it could be. He looked away, feeling more lost than he had before.

"These should help a bit," said Catriona, pulling her own blanket closer about her. "They are a nice addition to the new shawls we bought before crossing over. But I had no idea of this place being so very cold. Poor Cuán was near to freezing."

"We have fixed that, *mo leanbh*," said Aunt Aileen, patting Catriona's arm comfortingly. "Don't you think on it. Your babes will be taken care of."

"We can thank Norah for Cuán's toes remaining intact," said Bridget with a pointed look toward Finn. She indicated the thick wool socks that now covered the toddler's feet peeking out from the blanket which covered him in his mother's arms.

It had been like that between Finn and Bridget since the conversation Bridget was never meant to have heard. She had been increasingly suspicious of Finnegan ever since, always shooting him meaningful looks whenever anyone said a kind word about Norah. If only Bridget knew how little she needed to defend Norah from him.

Finn had wanted to apologize a million times over for what he had said to Norah that day. His high opinion of her had only grown stronger as he'd watched her care for his still recovering family members. But that only made it more complicated.

That Norah had not fallen ill herself was a miracle. Finn was not sure his self-control could have handled watching her lay there helpless and in pain. He would not have been able to hide his feelings for her from his family, which would only have ended in shame and embarrassment for all involved. His family would never have known the whole of it. That Norah was not free and that he had once again fallen for a lass that could never be his were tales which were not entirely his to tell. The very thought of doing so felt like a betrayal of more than one heart.

"Where will we go now?" Conner asked. He held Gráinne's hands within his own, trying to rub some warmth back into them. She had already returned with her mother and sisters, but there was still no sign of Da and the others. It was almost dark before Da, Torin, and Daniel met up with them, a full two hours later than they had planned.

"Do you want the good news or the bad news?" Daniel asked, wheezing as he stumbled to the base of a nearby statue where he hurried to sit and catch his breath. Bridget and Aunt Aileen rushed to sit beside him, fussing over him like a couple of mother hens.

"The bad news," said Finn and Norah together. Norah gave no indication that she had even heard him, and Finn quickly closed his mouth, not wanting to be caught staring stupidly at her for something so trivial.

"My toes are freezing," Torin moaned dramatically, speaking for Daniel as he struggled to catch his breath. "But we found a place we can stay for the night. 'Tisn't permanent, mind, as we don't have enough money for more than the one night, but it should get us by until we can make a plan for tomorrow."

"Anything to get us out of this cold," said Conner. "It's almost planting season, but there's snow on the ground. This makes no sense!"

"I imagine planting season is quite different here," said Daniel wearily.

Finn held his arms more tightly about himself in a futile attempt to ward off the cold. "I imagine everything is quite different here."

"Not everything," said Órla, indicating the cathedral behind them with a look of reverence. "God is here, even in this frozen, foreign land. That's something, I think."

Finn watched in anguish as Catriona hummed thoughtfully, holding Cuán a little closer. She brushed away several tears before agreeing, "Yes. That's something."

* * *

"I vote we stay here," said Torin. "I don't like the idea of taking my wife and son on a journey over a land we know nothing about."

The Boyds, the Doughertys, and Norah were all crowded together in the small room they were renting from a local widow. There was a small fireplace, one bed, and a collection of mismatched chairs. But it was warm, and that was a vast improvement on the chilly evening air. "This is for one night only," the widow had insisted. But she had also given them the name of a local priest who might be able to help them find more permanent lodging, should they need it.

Órla was already shaking her head. "We said we were going to New York. That's where the work is, after all. With as many of our people as are likely to follow us here, it will be Cork and Liverpool all over again. And I don't know French! I've only just started to improve my English."

"Listen to your wife, Torin," said Catriona in such a perfect impression of Mrs. Boyd that it gave everyone pause.

"What do we know about New York?" Mr. Boyd asked quietly. He sat bent over with his arms on his knees, staring at his boots. He was trying, Norah knew, but his was a pain his children could not fully comprehend. Save perhaps Michael, but he was not here to either comfort his father nor mourn his grandmother, mother, and brother.

"It's a large city," said Daniel. "There are a great many factories."

From beside him, Bridget scrunched up her nose. "Linen?"

"Cotton, most likely."

"But is it the only city like that?" asked Mr. Boyd. He shook his hands in front of him as he spoke. "What are the advantages of such a journey?"

"If I may?" Norah asked. Everyone's eyes turned to her, and she took a deep breath before she spoke again. It was becoming easier to act as though Finnegan's gaze didn't leave her a little shaky and unsure of herself. She hoped it didn't show that she was not always entirely successful at being unaffected.

"I did a great deal of reading before our journey to help us prepare," said Norah. "None of us could have predicted that we would end up in a different port than the one we paid to be delivered to, but there's nothing to be done about it now. The way I see it, we can try and stay here and find work. It may well be that there is plenty to be had. The temperatures are considerably colder than we had prepared for, but that isn't to say that we can't rally what money we have left to fix that."

"What money *you* have left," Finn reminded her. Their eyes met for an instant and then, like his father, he kept his gaze locked on his shoes.

It helped Norah feel a little braver not to have him staring at her with those regretful eyes. Brave enough to speak her mind.

"I'll not withhold help, as you well know, Finnegan." Her voice was sharper than she had intended it to be, and, for the length of a breath, his eyes flicked up to hers again. He nodded once, his lips pressed together, but said no more. That was how it had been between them. Barely a word was spoken for weeks and, when it was, someone was always left hurting. There was none of the openness they had felt with one another on the *Rosemary*. They hadn't had a true conversation since Norah had recounted her history to Finnegan, although she had tried the once, only to be left sorry for even attempting it. She again lamented having been so foolish to think that he wouldn't judge her for it. Especially when he could barely look her in the eye. She disgusted him; it was clear as day. She supposed it was yet another dismissal to add to her collection. Norah McGowan: unworthy of love.

Torin let out a long, low whistle, his eyebrows raised as his eyes flickered between Finn and Norah. Órla quickly swatted his arm and shot him a warning look.

"The fact of the matter," Norah forced herself to continue. "Is that I don't know the employment situation in the area. I do know there are some reputable mills in or around Boston specifically. That is closer than New York, at any rate."

"I have a cousin in Boston," said Mrs. Dougherty. "If we could send a letter, you might be able to ask questions to find out more about the situation. But either way, I don't think we'll be coming with you."

Conner stilled, his wide eyes reminding Norah of the fear in the eyes of the rabbits her grandad had used to catch in his snares every summer. Conner looked helplessly about the room, waiting for some-one to say something.

"Y-you can't stay," he finally said, his desperate tone filling the crowded room. "You'll freeze here! And there's more work in America, surely."

"I'm weary, lad," said Mrs. Dougherty kindly. "I'm not sure my bones could handle such a long journey after all we've lost. We are barely recovered, and I won't risk losing my girls. They are all I have left."

"But Ma—" Gráinne began but stopped abruptly after seeing her mother's despondent expression. The lass's head hung down in defeat. She slowly pulled her hand out of Conner's and used it to cover her face as her shoulders shook with silent tears.

Everyone looked to Mr. Boyd to see what he would say on the matter, but he remained lost in his own thoughts. Then he finally looked up at them all. "If we can find a way to do it, we might as well head to this Boston. It's better than the children freezing to death in what should be spring. Heaven knows we've said goodbye to enough of our loved ones. I understand your staying, Mrs. Dougherty, and I don't fault you for it. We all must do what is best for what is left of our families, now."

And that, it seemed, was that. There was no more conversation about what would be the best course of action or which location would benefit the most members of their group, and though it looked like Conner wanted to say a great deal on the matter, there was noth-ing he could do. He was only sixteen years old and without a penny to his name. He couldn't exactly marry his sweetheart and bring her with them; her mother and sisters needed her. So he remained still and silent, defeated once more by circumstances beyond his control.

Mr. Boyd had finally given his opinion on something after weeks of near silence, and his family was ready to follow him, wherever he may lead. Norah was not a proponent of important life decisions being made in the wake of grief, but it could not be avoided in this case.

They would go to Boston, and Norah would find work in one of the mills she had read about. She would help the Boyds however she could—but at a distance.

She hadn't wanted to be right, but there it was. She had known being stuck in such close quarters with Finnegan would be dangerous business, but back then, she had been sure only her heart had been engaged. Now they were both broken, with grief and angry words, and the salt of the sea still between them.

Norah would never forget their time on the *Rosemary*. Some of it she wished she could; other moments would be treasured memories until the end of her days. The way he had looked at her that first day he had captured that lock of her hair between his finger and thumb, the way he had kissed her when he had thought there was a way forward, a way to move past his grief . . .

But she needed to move on because being so close to him but not being able to enjoy the pleasure of his friendship, his company, and his love was more than even her strength of spirit could endure.

CHAPTER NINETEEN

30 March 1846, Outside Manchester, New Hampshire

They were less than two days from Boston when Aunt Aileen, already weak from her illness and advanced years, began to slow, complaining of pain in her stomach and increased fatigue. A short time later, Torin, Conner, and Oona came down with the same symptoms. A worried glance between himself and Norah told Finn his initial thoughts were correct. The fever had returned.

They sought out lodging within the city of Manchester, but with little money, few were willing to listen to their pleas for aid. No one wanted sickness in their homes or rented rooms, so the Boyds were forced to camp outside the city, using their blankets as makeshift tents to shelter from the cold. Norah was quick to separate the sick from the still recovering members of the family and insisted that she be the one to nurse them back to health.

Finn paced outside the patched-up canvas tent he had been able to barter for with Mary Wilcox's preserves. He prayed it wouldn't rain—or worse, snow—for he didn't trust the structural integrity of the shelter. It was tattered and torn in more than one place, there was an odd smell about it, and the older man with whom Finn had traded had been far too happy with the exchange for Finn's comfort.

Finn wanted to help in whatever way he could. After all, his brothers were ill, and he wasn't sure he could survive losing all of them in such quick succession. But Norah had been adamant that the healthy remain as far away from the sick as possible. Bridget, Catriona, and Órla had tried to persuade her otherwise, insisting that they help take care of their loved ones, but Norah would not be moved.

"If you all take ill, there will be no one to take care of the *wean*," Norah had said.

As much as Finn's sister and sisters-in-law had disliked it, they were able to see the logic in it. So they waited, camped haphazardly on the side of the road, doing whatever odd jobs in town they could find to earn enough money to keep themselves alive until such a time as they could resume their journey.

Finn had never considered himself a particularly impatient person, but after months at sea and weeks of waiting to leave their quarantine shed, he wasn't sure how much longer he could handle living life without any idea of what might come next and when. His patience wore out entirely when, during his nightly vigil of the sick tent, he heard a cough that made his heart stop cold in his chest.

"Norah?" he whispered into the dark. He needed to hear her voice to confirm to him that she was safe, that he had imagined it. The only response was a series of coughs, each one more powerful than the last until Finn could hear the wheezing for breath through the canvas, even from several feet away.

With a shake of his head, he gave up trying to keep his distance and from fighting the urge to offer aid. If she couldn't even breathe to answer him, Norah certainly couldn't take care of his family.

"What do you need?" Finn asked, moving to close the flap of the tent behind him and hurrying across the small space towards Norah. She was bent over, holding her chest as her eyes watered and her face grew redder.

She quickly swatted him away and, as soon as she could catch her breath, gasped out, "You shouldn't be here!"

"You need help," said Finn as evenly as he could manage. It was no easy feat to be so close to her, and her looking so helpless only complicated matters.

"But if you get sick again—" Norah began, her eyes wide with fear. Fear for him.

Finn was quick to cut her off. He'd already heard her give the same speech to his sisters-in-law and Bridget more than once.

"I'm no one's husband," he said, abruptly putting an end to her argument. The awkwardness of the statement hung in the air. It was almost as if Norah could hear his thoughts wishing that weren't the case, especially when she couldn't say that she was equally unbound. He hurried on, "And I'm no one's father. No one depends on me. So that argument won't work here."

It was both a blessing and a curse that Norah was too weak to argue. Her once neat hair was matted in some places and clung to the sweat on her face in others. Her patients slept fitfully on either side of the tent, and Norah's eyes darted back and forth, ensuring that everything was as it should be before she allowed herself to fall to her knees near Oona's makeshift bed. Finn could see that it took effort for Norah to lift her hand to check the wet cloth resting on Oona's forehead, though she tried to hide the shaking in her hand.

"How is she?" Finn asked.

"She's faring better than Roisin did," said Norah weakly.

"And the others?"

Norah took a moment to answer. "I'm worried about Aunt Aileen. But Conner and Torin are fighting hard."

Finn nodded. "Rest, Norah. I know what to do from here. I learned from the best, after all."

Norah opened her mouth to protest, but she began coughing once more. She slumped down beside Oona, unable to hold herself up any longer.

The ordinarily strong, confident Norah had never looked so diminished in Finn's eyes, not even when he had learned of her past. No, that wasn't right. Even then, he had seen her as a survivor, resilient, as someone stronger than he could ever hope to be. She was capable of rising from the pain of her past like a phoenix from the ashes. Then, she had been a beautiful bird he could admire from afar but never, never touch. But now, she looked as though one stiff breeze might blow her away.

Norah made small noises to protest as Finn dipped a strip of cloth in the nearby bowl of cool water and gingerly applied it to her forehead.

"Let someone take care of you for once," said Finn, acutely aware of the multiple meanings of his words.

Where was her husband? He should be here caring for her, the scoundrel. How anyone could treat such a woman so deplorably was a mystery Finn would never understand. But to abandon her, to allow her to travel to a distant country without, Finn assumed, so much as a word, was incomprehensible. She deserved better than that. She deserved so much more.

Norah had been right in her assessment of her patients' health. Torin, Conner, and Oona were all able to sit up within a few days and take the small amount of broth the womenfolk had tried very hard to make palatable with the limited ingredients they could purchase. Norah and Aunt Aileen were not fairing as well. The older woman was still so weak from the long journey that, despite his best efforts doing everything Norah had taught him, Finn was beginning to wonder if all his administrations were in vain.

"What needs to be done?" Da asked as he and Finn both stood outside the tent while Finn took a moment to breathe in the cool morning air and consider the best course of action.

"I need quinine," said Finn at last. "If I can bring their fevers down, perhaps they will have a bit more strength to fight off the infection."

Da nodded silently, staring off into the distance as he was wont to do more often of late. "I'll see what we can do. Bridget was talking about selling her necklace again."

Finn bit the inside of his lip, unsure whether to be relieved or saddened by that revelation. *Both*, he concluded at last. He knew how much that necklace meant to his sister—it was a token of Daniel's love, the only thing he had of his mother's. But Bridget also knew how much Aunt Aileen meant to Daniel. She was the only remaining family he had, excepting his estranged father back in Ireland, and the closest thing to a mother he had had since his own had died when he was just a boy.

Losing a mother was a pain that was already too fresh for Finn. He wanted to spare Daniel the renewed pain if he could. And, if Finn was honest, he wanted to spare himself having to watch Norah in pain. He wasn't sure what he would do if she—

Finn shook his head to clear his thoughts, steeling himself against the fear of the unknown. He wouldn't be able to help anyone if he let his worries consume him.

"Whatever can be done," said Finn at last, turning back toward the tent stiffly.

"Are you taking care of yourself, son?" Da asked just as Finn moved to pull back the flap of the tent.

"I am," said Finn without hesitation. At some point in his life, caring for others had become a way of caring for himself. Making sure that they were safe and whole, that they were at least contented, had become a method of survival. Because even if Finn were miserable, to know that everyone else had what they needed lessened his sorrow by degrees.

"Don't worry about me, Da," said Finn with a smile that felt plastered into place with the practice of years. "Torin and Conner should be back on their feet before too long—Oona too, the little fighter that she is. I'll do my best to pull the others through just the same."

Finn bade his father goodbye and secured the tent behind him. He took in a shaky breath of the muggy air inside the tent, made warmer than the outside by the fevers of those around him. Conner mumbled something in his sleep, and Finn hurriedly exchanged the cloth on his youngest brother's head for a fresh one before moving back to check on Aunt Aileen. She was still too hot, and Finn feared the worst should his father and the others not be able to acquire medicine. He then moved on to Norah.

"Is it very bad?" Norah asked, stirring when Finn knelt down beside her.

"No," Finn murmured, praying that his words were true. "Not very bad. I've sent Da in search of some quinine if it can be had."

"The others?" Norah was careful to keep her eyes fixed on the tent above her, never meeting Finn's gaze. Even feverish, she showed more self-control than he felt around her when he was in full control of his faculties. He wanted to reach out and clasp her hand in his own, to reassure her that he was caring for her, that he wouldn't leave her side. Never mind that all of this was true; he wasn't free to say it, nor was she free to hear it. Once again, Finn cursed her estranged husband, wherever he may be.

"Aunt Aileen is very weak," Finn said. "She complains of her stomach and head whenever she is awake enough to speak."

"And yet Conner is the one who can't stop his moaning," said Norah. She smiled wanly, her eyes flickering to Finn's face before she closed them once more. "Might be able to get some rest if he'd quiet down, like."

Just as she finished speaking, Conner let out a moan so pathetic and long, Finn was sure it rivaled one of the Auld's milking cows.

"It gives him something to do," said Finn, trying and failing to hold back a smile when Norah's eyes opened wide at the sound. They both let out a burst of laughter, which quickly turned to coughing and gasping for breath for Norah.

The ache in Finn's heart at watching Norah suffer was an acute reminder that these moments between them must cease. If only he could make himself stop loving her. He had known better. His voice of reason, which he had been so careful to heed in the past, had tried to warn him. With her so close, helpless and needing someone to care for her, he couldn't quite regret not listening to that voice. After all, wasn't loving and losing someone better than never knowing the joy and pain of love? Was ignorance truly bliss, as the poets suggested and as he had thought not long ago, or was it just . . .regret?

"My head," Norah whispered, raising a shaky hand to her fore-head and the cloth that lay there. "It's pounding."

"I know," said Finn, covering her hand for the duration of a breath. He savored the feeling of her warmth beneath his hand for the briefest of moments before he forced himself to pull away. The gesture reminded him that she was still alive, but just out of reach. It was one thing to take care of her when she was unconscious or delirious or when she was just another patient, but quite another entirely when she was fully aware of him. The very air was charged between them every time she met his gaze, and Finn had to shake his head against the tugging he felt to be near her. "I'll talk to Da about medicine for your head too."

He stood quickly, taking the few short steps to the flap of the tent and hurrying out once more. He fought the desire to go back to her, to apologize, to grovel and beg her forgiveness for the harsh words he had once spoken in anger. But it felt like it had been too long. He'd lost his chance, and it was likely for the best. Words did not have the power to change the past.

A million thoughts competed in his mind, rushing and whirling about until he was dizzy. But only one reached the forefront. He needed to ease Norah's suffering. Everything else would have to wait.

* * *

THE QUININE, SO PRECIOUSLY ACQUIRED WITH BRIDGET'S NECKLACE and the pennies from odd jobs about Manchester, worked. At least, for some. In three days' time, Torin, Conner, and Oona were back on their feet; weak, but stronger than they had been. Norah, too, was gathering her strength bit by bit after her fever broke. Despite the medicine, Aunt Aileen was still too weak. In the end, Norah had sat by the woman's side, instructing Finn to fetch Daniel so he might say goodbye.

One look at Norah's face when he returned told Finn that she took this and all the losses before it personally. Did she truly blame herself for not being able to save them? With newfound conviction, Finn resolved to finally say, at the next opportune moment, all the words he had kept locked inside. It wasn't her fault. It could never be her fault—none of it.

Aileen Sullivan was the first of their party to receive a proper burial. The local priest had not arrived at the outskirts of town quickly enough to give her the last rites. However, he had assisted Daniel in arranging for her to be buried in the cemetery of the local Catholic church. It was a small comfort, considering the magnitude of the loss, but it was more than could have been done for Gran or Ma or Alastar.

It was with a heavy heart that Finn and those who had had enough strength to make the journey into town returned to their little camp. Da instructed Finn to gather everyone for a meeting so they could discuss what they would do next. Relieved at being given an opportunity to seek out Norah, who had remained resting in the quarantine tent, Finn struggled to keep the smile from his face. He knew it wouldn't mean mending everything between them—as nothing truly could— but perhaps they might both find a bit of peace by speaking the words they had avoided up to this point. They both needed that closure, Finn was sure. Perhaps they might, at least, be friends. As they should always have been, despite how adamant Norah had been about keeping Finn at a distance.

But there was no Norah resting on the makeshift sickbed. Only a folded piece of paper lay in the center of the bed. Finn's heart pounded as he reached out to pick it up with shaky hands. Even before he opened it, he was sure he could guess at the contents. He was not prepared for the small bundle of paper money which fell from it, however, and almost cursed in surprise.

After that, he didn't need to read the words. He brought the note straight to Bridget, informing her of the empty tent and Norah's absence. He turned away from his family, watching the line of trees which lined their camp with bleary eyes as Bridget haltingly read Norah's words aloud.

I hope this bit of money helps more than I have done to help your family heal and move on from the hardship and loss of the past year. I need to find my own way for a time, and I hope you'll forgive me leaving like this, but I don't think I could bring myself to say goodbye. Thank you for being like family to me. You are all dearer to me than words can say.

Always,

Norah

Silence followed the closing of the letter, and Finn could feel the eyes of his family on his back, but he couldn't bring himself to face them, nor to let them see him dry his eyes. So he stood still, his hands on his hips, holding his breath in hopes that depriving himself of oxygen might help him gain some semblance of control.

As usual, Norah was stronger than Finn. She could do what he had ultimately found impossible. She could walk away. He tried to find comfort in reminding himself that, as she had once said about Conner, perhaps her feelings weren't so very strong if she could walk away so easily. But it hadn't been easy, had it? She had to sneak out, weak and still recovering so that she didn't have to endure saying goodbye. Finn had half a mind to follow her—she couldn't have gotten far in her condition—to bring her back and assure her that her place was with them. He could put his feelings aside. He *could*. He'd done it before, though it had felt unbearable.

But she had asked for time. And he had, as yet, been unable to deny her anything. She deserved that much. After all he had done to hurt her, the least he could do was respect her wishes. Even if that, too, felt like it would destroy him.

CHAPTER TWENTY

6 June 1846, Lowell Mills, Lowell, Massachusetts

Even in sleep, Norah could not escape the sound of the wracking coughs which had haunted her for months. They had set her on edge aboard the *Rosemary* when every cough had threatened to be their last. Again they had plagued her on the journey to Massachusetts when a new wave of fever had overcome them and left even some of the healthiest and strongest of them fighting anew. And here, where the bits of stuff in the air were a common occurrence, the coughing never seemed to cease. It invaded her dreams and memories of the months past, months she wished she could forget but knew she never would.

> *"Can't you do something?" the voices pleaded. They sounded so helpless, so desperate that Norah longed to reach out and comfort them, to snap into action and do whatever was necessary to calm them.*
>
> *"She's so cold!" one voice rose above the general moanings.*
>
> *Again, Norah longed to offer aid, but she couldn't move. And even if she could have, she didn't have Doctor O'Shannessy's physician's bag. She'd sold it long ago, wanting to rid herself of*

every part of him. She could never have foreseen the need, but it didn't stop her from berating herself even now.

"Someone do something!"

"Time to get up!" the matron called, rapping on the door with her cane and sending Norah's heart racing in her chest just as the four o'clock bell chimed outside the window. She knocked her head on her bedside table as she moved to sit up in bed. She held it as it smarted, and she cursed low and strained her eyes in the dark, looking for any traces of blood on her hand. She had been lucky—this time.

"Hurry up," the matron called before moving onto the next door of the boarding house for the "mill girls," as all of the lasses who worked at Lowell Mills were known.

"Esther," Norah called into the dark, reaching about for a match with which to light her candle. "You'd best get up, like."

Esther, Norah's bedmate, sighed long before she sat up in bed. "I feel as if I've only just closed my eyes."

Norah snorted in agreement as their other roommates, Abigail and Helen, hurried to dress. Although Norah was used to working long hours, as she had done since her days at the dyebath in Cork, it never got any easier to work twelve-hour days. She knew it shouldn't have surprised her, but Lowell Mills was not the respectable employer they had advertised themselves to be. The advertisement Norah had read boasted of safe work conditions and an environment where the girls employed at the mill were encouraged to improve themselves. Where this was true to some degree, there was rarely time for improvement, as the work hours were so long. And there had been an influx of male workers, predominantly Irish, which changed the dynamic even more. Norah couldn't have said for certain what things were like before she'd arrived, but from what Esther had told her, the changes were not always positive ones.

As with employment in England, the Americans offered less money to the Irish workers. Esther, who was only seventeen, made a significant amount more than Norah every week, despite Norah's years of experience in the textile industry. Still, it was steady work and paid more than her job as a scullery maid in Liverpool had.

Norah hurried and dressed for the day, pulling her hair back into a tight bun and putting on her apron with practiced precision.

"Oh no!" Esther cried from across their small room. She turned to show Norah her apron, where a rip several inches long outlined one of the pockets. "I forgot all about this last night. I was going to fix it when we got back, but I fell asleep right after dinner, remember?"

Helen and Abigail tutted, muttering how unfortunate Esther was but hurried out of the room without an offer to help.

"Give it here," said Norah, hurrying to take out her small sewing kit. "I'll have it done before we need to walk over to the mill, like."

"But we'll be late," said Esther in surprise.

"You can go down without your apron if you like," said Norah, already working to thread her needle. "I'll be down in ten minutes either way. Better hurry! I'll catch you up."

Luckily Norah had learned a few tricks from her time with Órla Boyd, who was, without a doubt, the finest seamstress Norah had ever known. Before long, Norah was on her way downstairs with Esther's mended apron. She had to run to catch up with Esther, but she was used to running about by now; they were kept on such a tight schedule. Tardiness was not tolerated, and Norah could not afford to be tossed out. She didn't have savings anymore, so keeping in line was more important than ever before.

Finishing more quickly than she had anticipated, Norah did her best to ready her mind for the day ahead of her as she caught up with Esther. They and a few of the other girls walked across the way and between tall buildings of imposing red brick towards their assigned building.

"Hurry up, girls," one of their fellow weavers urged them as Norah and Esther entered the large weave room. There were only a few looms yet without a girl in front of them, so Norah and Esther did not have the chance to work beside each other. It was a shame because Norah preferred Esther to either the talkative or begrudging neighbors she sometimes got. Regardless of the fact that she made a lower wage than many of the other girls, some still held Norah's presence among them against her. Esther was quiet while she worked and allowed Norah to work in silence, which was all that she wanted.

Whoever had last worked the loom Norah chose for the day had not replaced the thread within the wooden shuttle. So Norah quickly went to work, not wanting to be seen as slow. She had worked hard to keep her head down at the dyebaths in Cork and had been able to do so for five whole years before she had been unjustly let go. She didn't blame Bridget or the Boyds for the hand they had in her losing her position there—dropping that linen could have happened to anyone. It had been a bit of bad luck, exacerbated by the fact that the overseer had been in a poor mood that day. But Norah sometimes wondered what would have become of her if she had not stepped in to help the struggling farmer's daughter from Shancloch. Would Norah have stayed in Cork? Would she be working in the dyebaths even now, day in and day out? If so, little had changed except for her lack of financial security and the place within the world which she now called home.

A memory of smiling blue eyes reminded her that some things had changed irrevocably, though for better or worse, she couldn't always determine.

Norah sucked the end of the thread through the shuttle with her breath. It was the quickest way to re-thread it, and she needed every advantage she could get. She replaced the shuttle and moved to pull the lever that would start the weaving motions. The loud clacking of the looms filled the air, creating such a ruckus that Norah felt the sound of it vibrating in her chest. It would be like this for an hour or more before the bell rang, signaling they could stop for breakfast.

Norah had been working the looms for over a month, and by now, everything had become instinct. She ran her hands over the weave of the fabric as the threads wove together and made their way through the machine. Her fingers knew the feel of imperfections at this point, and she was able to correct them and move on quickly. Capable of working without thinking about it, Norah often had to make a conscious effort not to get too caught up in her thoughts. The sound of the machines was helpful in this. Whereas many of the girls stuffed bits of cotton in their ears to block out the sound, Norah welcomed it. When the noise surrounded her, it made it difficult to focus on much of anything else. She craved the numbing effect. After the past several months, she needed not to think or feel. Because she had never been good enough at simply forgetting.

Another benefit of living on such a tight schedule was the lack of time to socialize. Norah spoke with the other girls during meals, but she rarely spoke about herself or her history. She had made that mistake too many times, first with Bridget and finally with the lass's brother. It wouldn't happen again. The only thing the other girls knew was that Norah's parents had died many years ago and that she had used to work in a textile factory in Ireland. Everything else was unnecessary.

The meal bell rang at the appointed time, and the overseer motioned for girls to turn off their machines and hurry for their half-hour break for breakfast. Norah let the machine run for another moment or two to allow her time to check for what she suspected might be a tangled thread, but she didn't have to be told twice to take her meal. Although the meals were nothing special—usually consisting of a simple pie—it was more steady nourishment than many of the girls had been used to before their life at the mills. The smell of bread wafted in the air, and the grumbling of her stomach told Norah she couldn't afford to miss a meal, especially when they had to work such long days. She would need her strength and wits about her to avoid injury and mistakes.

"Some of the other girls are talking about attending a lecture this evening," said Esther as she and Norah hurried back to the boarding house. "Do you think you will come?"

Based on the tentative way she asked, Norah could tell Esther already knew the answer.

"I've some of my own mending to do, like," said Norah slowly. "I think I'll just stay in and read, maybe write some letters."

"That's what you did last Saturday," Esther said. "Abby says some of the men were talking about going to the lecture as well." Esther was eyeing Norah carefully, looking for any sort of reaction.

"That's nice," said Norah noncommittally. "I'm sure you'll have a grand time."

"Don't you want a chance to talk with some of the men, Norah?" Esther asked. "That Irish fellow who comes in to fix the looms always has a smile for you."

Norah smiled weakly. "I've no interests in Irish lads, Esther," she said with as much levity as she could manage.

"There will be plenty of American men as well, I'm sure."

"I've no interests in romance at present," Norah amended. "But I hope you and the rest of the lasses have a lovely time, like."

"Oh, I'm sure we will," said Esther, who then proceeded to tell Norah all about the last lecture she had attended and the ideas that were discussed. Norah found the concept of educating and improving oneself fascinating and hoped that, with time, she would feel ready to venture out to some of the lectures and expand her mind. But she wasn't ready; she had already pushed herself far beyond what was comfortable and familiar. Time, she hoped, was all that was needed to heal and get beyond all the things that kept her spirits low.

The workday passed slowly. By the end of it, Norah's brain rattled within her head from the noise of the machines and the racing thoughts not even her pounding head could seem to drown out. She headed straight for bed, lying down without so much as a thought for how wrinkled her dress would be in the morning.

The room was pitch black when Norah awoke with a start to the feel of someone's hand on her arm.

"It's only me," Esther whispered.

"Gracious, Esther," said Norah as she placed a hand over her heart. "Don't wake a body like that. Light a candle first, like."

"I didn't want to draw the matron's attention," said Esther. "There are a couple of Irish fellows who have been looking for you. I told them to wait out of sight, and I would see if you wanted to talk to them."

"Whatever would I want to talk to them for?" Norah asked, sitting up slowly to test the pounding in her head. It had subsided significantly, as she thought it would. She usually only needed a bit of rest in such cases. "And who would be asking for me, like?"

"One of them said he was your brother," said Esther. "Though I don't know why you wouldn't have mentioned you had such a handsome brother. He has the bluest eyes"—Esther sighed dramatically, making her look every bit her seventeen years—"And he sounds quite a bit like you, I think. Lilting, I think I heard Helen call it. At any rate, he sounds nothing like the friend he has with him. I think the other boy might be Scottish."

Blue eyes? Lilting speech? Norah's stomach twisted at the possibility, but she quickly corrected her heart. It couldn't be. The Boyds were miles and miles away in Boston. And she wasn't sure she knew any Scottish lads.

"Where can I find this brother of mine?" Norah asked, not bothering to correct Esther as to her family tree. Knowing the matron's tendency to chase away any and all menfolk, having a temporary brother was the only chance she would have of speaking to these Irishmen, should she want to take it. She couldn't deny that her curiosity was piqued.

Some of the girls were still trickling in from the lecture they had attended, so Norah didn't have to worry about sneaking out past curfew just yet. Esther went with her "just in case," but Norah suspected the lass simply wanted another look at the men she thought so handsome. Esther led Norah around the back of the boarding house and between two other buildings within the mill compound to where she said she had talked to the two men.

"There they are!" Esther whispered excitedly as she pointed to two figures standing below a lamppost, their backs to Norah.

Norah's shoulders sagged, though she knew she should have felt relief instead of disappointment. Not only their hair but their forms were all wrong. The one lad had hair as red as fire and the other dark, but both were too short to be Finnegan, no matter their coloring.

When they turned about, Norah couldn't help but smile as she raced across the yard to meet them.

"Norah!" Conner Boyd called as she wrapped her arms around him in a tight embrace. She smiled at his companion over his shoulder, whom she recognized to be Nolan, the lad they had met and Conner befriended on the *Rosemary*.

"I'm guessing he is your brother after all," said Esther with a shy smile.

"Close enough," Conner muttered into Norah's shoulder.

Norah pulled back, placing both arms on Conner's shoulders and examining him closely. "What are you doing here, Conner?" she asked, suddenly concerned. "Is everyone all right, like?"

Conner's smile slowly fell at Norah's look of concern. "Everyone is grand, I suppose."

There was something about the way Conner frowned that was familiar. The muscle in his jaw was so defined, she could tell he was clenching his teeth together fiercely. She had seen that look on his face before. And then it hit her—the day he had come looking for Alastar. The day he had confessed to injuring a man beyond repair.

Everything was decidedly *not* grand.

CHAPTER TWENTY-ONE

6 June 1846, Boston, Massachusetts

Finn ran a hand through his hair, not caring that it stood up in odd places nor that it had been too long since he had trimmed it or even shaved. He was too tired to care as he made his way back to the room his family rented on the far end of the city. And anyway, it was not like his family cared much about how he looked. They all tended to look a little ragged of late, especially Da, who had let his beard grow longer than ever before.

"Is Conner with you?" Catriona asked as soon as Finn opened the door to their cramped housing made smaller by the damp clothes hanging on lines strung up and down the length of the room. She handed Finn a crying Cuán as she hurried back over to the stove to stir whatever she had cooking in a large pot.

"I've not seen him all day," Finn called over the sound of Cuán's shrieks. Finn swayed back and forth, speaking quietly to the toddler in hopes of quieting him. "But that's not unusual. I did think it a bit odd that he wasn't about when it was time to walk home, but he sometimes walks home with Nolan."

"He was supposed to run an errand for me," said Bridget, who stood in the corner of the room over a large washbasin. "I need more soap to finish up this order of clothes for tomorrow."

"He probably just forgot," said Finn. "If you give me the money for it, I'll go get some soap myself."

Bridget looked up at him and frowned, the tiny hairs about her face curling from the steam. "I already gave the money to Conner, and I don't have any to spare."

Finn clicked his tongue. "Lucky that I got my wages today, then," Finn said as he put down a now calm Cuán. He dug into his pocket to pull out his week's pay. He deposited most of it into the jar they kept above the mantel, leaving only a few smaller coins he hoped would be enough to cover the price of soap.

"Thank you, Finn," Bridget sighed. "Will the other men be along soon, do you think?"

"I couldn't say," said Finn. "You know dock work doesn't keep the same hours as the factory."

Bridget nodded, her lips pursed in displeasure.

"And don't you worry, Birdie," said Finn with a smile. "I'm sure your Danny will be along soon enough."

"If you don't stop your teasing, I'll make *you* do the laundry while *I* fetch the soap," said Bridget, her eyes narrowed at him.

Finn hurried out the door, only pausing for a moment to look back at her and wink. Bridget harrumphed, but Finn could see she fought against a smile. As much as his sister tried to deny it, Finn knew she enjoyed the banter more than she let on.

It was dusk when Finn had begun his walk home, but now it was full-dark. His way was lit only by the sparse gas lamps along the more prominent streets. He hoped the usual grocer where the Boyds did their business would still be open, but he knew it was a gamble. The Boyds had settled in one of the more Irish neighborhoods of Boston. East Boston was complete with Catholic churches and businesses bearing Irish surnames. It was a stark contrast to Liverpool's Irish neighborhoods, where the Irish feared being their true selves, that was for certain, though the level of poverty was not much different.

It had not yet proved to be the second chance Finn's family had been hoping for, but then, nothing had gone quite how they had expected since they walked down the grassy path leading away from Shancloch.

"Oh, Mr. Burrows!" Finn called as the shopkeeper stepped out of his shop, moving to close the door behind him.

"I'm closed, lad," said the older gentleman. He pointed to the sign above the shop's door with a severe expression on his thin face.

"I only need some soap, sir," said Finn.

"Like I said—"

"I can give you two pennies more than the price," said Finn, hoping he actually held enough in his hand to pay the difference.

Mr. Burrows hesitated for a moment before nodding and slipping back inside his shop. He was out again a moment later, unceremoniously dropping the brick of soap into Finn's hands as he held his other hand out, awaiting payment. Finn slowly counted out the price that Mr. Burrows named, sighing with relief when he realized he had just enough.

"Come before I close next time," said Mr. Burrows with a tip of his hat. "*Slán*, Boyd."

"*Slán!*" Finn called to Mr. Burrows's retreating form.

Finn's task completed, he turned back the way he had come, enjoying the cool breeze blowing in from the ocean after a stifling day of grueling work within the factory. Sometimes Finn wondered if he and Conner had chosen the right jobs by working in the factory, but he quickly corrected himself. There hadn't been enough dock work to go around, even if he had wanted it, but there were factories aplenty that were always needing more hands.

For the first time since leaving home, everyone had some type of job to do. Bridget was taking in washing and watching the children. She could have easily found work in the sugar factory where Finn and Conner worked, but Daniel worried about her. She had recently announced to the family that she was with child, and Finn wasn't sure he had ever seen someone so protective as Daniel at the news.

"She's already lost so much," Daniel had said to Finn. "I just want her to be careful. I'm not sure how much more loss she can endure right now."

Órla and Catriona had found work at one of the better dressmakers that were willing to employ the Irish. Daniel was the only one who hadn't found a job doing menial labor—the lad had been fortunate enough to find work as a grocer's assistant on the other end of the city. As long as he kept his mouth shut around customers and didn't let on that he was Irish, Finn hoped that it would help his friend make his way up instead of being trodden down like so many of their fellow Irishmen.

"Is Conner still not here?" Finn asked when he had returned home. The rest of the family was back at that point, and they were all gathering about in preparation for dinner.

"Perhaps he's over at Nolan's apartment," said Órla. "He's been spending a lot of time with that lad of late."

"He's not a bad lad," said Daniel. "I could think of a lot worse people for Conner to be spending his time with."

"I only wish he'd spend more time here," said Bridget, taking a seat beside her husband at the dinner table. She sent a worried look to Da, who sat silently looking at the table before him, lost in thought.

"I'll go fetch him," Finn said, already out the door again. Nolan's family, the Cochrans, lived on the third floor of the same building where the Boyds rented, whereas the Boyds were on the second.

Finn took the stairs two at a time, wanting to hurry so he could ease some of the worries he knew certain members of his family, himself included, felt when they were not all together. Although, without Michael, Ma, Gran, Alastar, and Aunt Aileen, that sense of someone missing threatened never to go away. And Norah, Finn reminded himself a little bitterly. She had become a part of them too, but her leaving had been her own choice. That felt different somehow—like more of a betrayal than simply dying. He knew it shouldn't—Finn knew why she had gone, and he was trying to respect her decision. But it didn't make her absence any easier to bear.

"Hello, Finnegan," Mrs. Cochran greeted him merrily as she opened the door. She held a red-haired toddler on one hip while another little girl clung to her other side, staring up at Finn shyly. "You're a little earlier than I was expecting."

"You were expecting me?" Finn asked in confusion. "Is Conner here, then?"

"No," said Mrs. Cochran. "But he's left a note for you." She resituated the child in her arms so she could search her apron pocket. She handed the folded paper over with a smile and waited while Finn opened and read it.

Dear Family,

I'm sorry for the worry this will cause you. I don't know why, but I can't seem to be happy in Boston. Not after all that has happened. I know my mood is only making it more difficult for you all to move on, so Nolan and I are headed north for a time. We'll find work, so don't worry about us. I'll write soon.

Love,
Conner

"Do you know what this says, Mrs. Cochran?" Finn asked. How could she? She was smiling so pleasantly at him that there was no way she could know that one of her sons had all but run away. Mrs. Cochran shook her head, and Finn found himself shaking his own in anger at having to be the one to break the woman's heart.

To his surprise, Mrs. Cochran took the news remarkably well. She had several sons and daughters of working age. The loss of Nolan's wage would not be so very great that they would be left out in the streets. It was a small comfort, Finn agreed, but only a very small one.

"No Conner?" Bridget asked when Finn returned to their room, Conner's note crumpled in his hand. He was too angry to explain and simply shoved the note into Daniel's hand, knowing that, as the best reader of any of them, he would be able to read it aloud without pause.

Daniel looked up as he finished, his eyes going straight to his wife, who had already gone pale.

"Gone?" Torin said. "But why? Why didn't he say anything to anyone? We might have helped him."

"Helped him how?" Da asked, and everyone turned to listen. "He's lost his ma, half his family, and said goodbye to his lass. I can tell you from experience that there isn't much help that can be given save for from God."

"So we should just let him go?" Catriona asked, her brows furrowing with worry. "He's just a boy!"

"He's seventeen," Da said. "He's a man now. We can't make him stay if he doesn't want to."

"Sure we can," said Torin. "Do I need to go find him and drag him back here for you?"

"You'll do no such thing," said Da so firmly that Torin bristled slightly.

Since Alastar's death, Finn had noted how Torin had tried his best to fill the role their eldest brother had once held within their family. Alastar had always known just the right thing to say to make them all laugh and put them at ease, but he had also been the most passionate among them by miles. They were big shoes to fill—shoes Finn should have tried to fill himself, as the next oldest brother in Michael's absence. It was too far a stretch for him, as reserved as he was. But there was something he knew he could do.

"I can go," said Finn. He'd been watching the faces of his siblings, the desperation to not lose yet another part of them. "I'll see if he's all right and in need of anything. I won't force him home, but I'll let him know he's a fool if I think it'll help any."

The tension in Bridget's and Catriona's faces loosened, and they even shared a look and a nod. Finn resolved it was a solid plan. If there were anything he could do to relieve his family's sorrow, to help ease the tension about Catriona's eyes, he would do it. After all, they had come to America to prevent the family from being torn apart. And here they were, irreparably separated from some by force and others by their own choices.

It wasn't too difficult to guess where Conner was headed. There was more employment in Boston proper than in many of the surrounding cities north of them. There could really only be two reasons Conner would head that way—Gráinne, of course, being the first. Finn couldn't decide if he was excited or terrified at the prospect of the second.

* * *

7 June 1846, Lowell, Massachusetts

"THIS ISN'T A PROTESTANT CHURCH, NORAH," CONNER WHISPERED as he walked alongside Norah and up the row of benches and marble columns towards the front pews of St. Patrick's.

"Isn't it?" asked Norah with an air of indifference. "See, I just followed the other Irish, and I hadn't really noticed."

"Hadn't noticed you were attending a Catholic church?" Conner's tone was somewhere between teasing and confused.

"Well, the matron of my boardinghouse doesn't care overly much where us girls attend our services," said Norah with that same light tone. Based on his dubious smirk, she wasn't sure how convinced Conner was of her excuse. "She merely 'strongly encourages' us to go. And this is the closest church to the mills. We only had to cross two bridges to get here."

At least, that was what Norah had told herself when she learned she was all but required to go to church every Sunday, a practice she had long ago ceased entirely. But if she were honest, she had also been curious what all the "hullaballoo," as those in Liverpool might call it, was really about. Perhaps it was because she had gone so long without attending her own services, or because she missed the company of the Boyds so much that it hurt, but stepping inside the chapel made Norah feel more at home than she had in longer than she could remember. Never mind that it was a Catholic church and her dear mother was likely to be turning in her grave. There was something decidedly peaceful that washed over her in this place. There was no way she was going to divulge this detail to Conner, of course. She wasn't quite ready to fully admit it to herself, a little afraid of what it might mean.

Norah had assumed Conner would wait until Norah finished with services, but the lad had been eager to tag along. They'd not had a chance to talk the night before, as Norah had needed to hurry back to her boardinghouse for curfew, but Conner had assured her they would get a chance in the morning. There was something bothering him, some worry in his eyes that left Norah with a feeling of disquiet.

When services were over, all Norah wanted was to hear Conner's story and whether all the Boyd family members were safe. They headed back in the general direction of Norah's boardinghouse but with no sense of haste. Conner preferred to have their conversation without prying ears like Esther, though Nolan was welcomed as a silent witness to whatever he had to say. He was a quiet one, but Conner liked his company, and that was enough for Norah.

They stopped in the shade of one of the many brick buildings. Norah leaned against the cool wall, welcoming the reprieve from the heat. She was still unused to the extreme temperatures of this new country. It was different than the sea air or almost continuous drizzle and almost constant breeze of *Éire*. And she had the feeling she would never quite be used to the way she felt like she was being drenched by the air around her when there was no rain to be seen.

"All right, Conner," said Norah when they had rested for a moment. "Time to talk, like. Why are you here?"

"What? Can't I just come for a visit?" Conner asked, putting on a look of offense.

Norah stared at him blankly, waiting for him to drop his joking façade. It didn't suit him, she felt. It was too much like Alastar and not enough like the serious side of Conner she had seen before. It worried her more than she would care to admit.

Conner leaned forward at his place on the wall to look at Nolan. Some silent conversation took place between them and Nolan rolled his shoulders as he straightened. "I'll go see if I can find us a bite to eat," the lad said with a faint smile and nod.

When Nolan was gone, Conner led Norah to the side of the building they had rested against, away from the main walkway between mill buildings and boardinghouses.

"Are you ready to tell me what you're doing here?" Norah asked, crossing her arms in front of her. She prepared herself for whatever Conner was about to tell her, trying not to let her imagination wander.

"I don't know," Conner said after a long moment. "I suppose I needed a change of scene."

Norah waited for him to continue, knowing that the lad might need some time to sort through his thoughts. She was right as, several minutes later, Conner finally looked up at her. Tears pricked the sides of his eyes, but his jaw was set as if he were determined not to let them fall.

"Everything's gone wrong," said Conner. "I tried just to keep going like Da does, but I don't know how. Not with the likes of Bridget and Órla looking at me all pityingly. I feel like I've lost everything that was good and . . ."

"And what?" Norah asked softly when Conner didn't speak again.

"Like no one understands. Even though I know they do, to some extent—Da especially."

"Is this about Gráinne?" Norah asked as delicately as she could manage.

Conner nodded, then quickly shook his head. "As I said, it's about everything. I suppose . . . I suppose I'm mourning the life I know I should have had. I thought maybe you'd have some advice for me."

Norah started, her eyebrows raised in surprise. Had Finnegan already divulged her history to the Boyds? Did they know the depth of her disappointments and the drastic way her life had differed from the one she had expected to lead when she was just a girl?

"You gave me such good advice before," Conner amended, noting her surprise with a touch of confusion.

Norah relaxed, trying not to let her relief be too obvious. "You want advice on how to get over the disappointments of life?"

Conner nodded. He was eager to hear what she had to say, his eyes full of hope Norah knew she was incapable of sustaining. Because, if she were honest, she hadn't gotten over her disappointments. Not really. But what could she say that would offer comfort?

"I don't know that our disappointments have been quite the same, like," said Norah slowly. "I lost my parents at a young age. You're a few years older than I was like—and you still have your Da and some of your brothers and sisters."

Conner only watched her steadily, his eyes shining with unshed tears as he waited for her to continue. He was either unable or unwilling to speak, and his jaw was trembling fiercely as he fought against his emotions.

"And I had never known love, Conner. Not like I think you and Gráinne were beginning to share, like. I . . ." Norah paused, wondering if telling more of her history would be worth it if she were able to help him. Her desire to offer comfort warred against her need to protect herself. But this would likely be the last time she saw Conner, as she had already all but severed her ties with the Boyds. There was very little chance of her acquiring more regrets than she already carried with her every day. She hoped.

"I was married once," Norah said at last. Conner's eyes flew to hers in confusion, so Norah hurried to explain. "He . . .wasn't a good man, to keep it brief, like. I wasn't loved as you have been. The only comfort I have is that he's buried in the earth where he can't ever hurt me again. And the only man I have ever truly loved . . .didn't like that I had a past. So let's just say our disappointments aren't the same, like. But I'm sorry—you want advice on how to move on."

Norah sighed, wondering if she had just made a monumental mistake. Conner could benefit nothing from knowing about her. In all likelihood, it would change his opinion of her forever, as it clearly had done Finnegan's. Not for the first time, Norah wondered if there was something about her, some fundamental flaw that rendered her incapable or, worse, unworthy of being loved once a person saw it.

"You just *do*," Norah pressed on, resisting the urge to hold her breath, to stop the words, to run away before Conner could see her fatal shortcoming. "You take it one moment at a time. You try not to think too much about the future because that will send you to a dark place you might not be able to climb out of—not without a great deal of help you are not guaranteed to find. 'Tisn't easy, but time and focusing on my most immediate needs are what brought me through it."

To her surprise, Conner was slowly shaking his head with chagrin.

"What?" Norah asked, her voice quivering slightly in anticipation of his rejection.

"You're such a decent person," said Conner, his lips pulled into a frown.

Norah searched his face, trying to decipher his meaning.

"I'm sorry my brother is a complete fool."

Norah made a strangled noise, somewhere between a snort and a groan, at the mention of . . .*him*. Would it ever stop pricking her heart? Would the pain of his rejection never cease?

"I'm just so tired," said Conner, wiping at his nose and eyes. Norah pretended not to notice, and that put him at ease enough to open up once more. "I'm tired of the nightmares. I can still hear Ma coughing—all of them. Coughing and choking and dying every time I close my eyes. We were so close! Why did—how could they just die when we were so close? And then the Dougherty's staying in Canada when they could have come with us. We could have helped each other. We *needed* each other."

Norah closed her eyes against his words but quickly opened them against the images of so many fighting and gasping just as they all had in the end. The memories of Norah trying her best to save them despite her own fears and, in the end, raging fever proved too much. Conner was right; it didn't make sense.

Norah had begun to wonder if, after everything she had been through and survived, watching so many people she had grown to care about die had broken her. Perhaps beyond repair.

And here Conner was now, broken in much the same way and begging her to help him again. She was just as helpless as she had been in the spring. The change of season and passage of months had done nothing to heal her. So why did she hold out any hope that she could help anyone else when she couldn't even help herself?

"I'm sorry," Norah breathed, unsure what else she could say. She took a step towards Conner, and he willingly let her wrap him up in her arms. Though it was really more like her being wrapped up, as he was quite a few inches taller than her by now—he must have grown in the last few months they had been apart.

"It just seems like every time I readjust to things, something else happens to throw everything on its head," Conner mumbled into her shoulder.

"I'm probably not helping, like," said Norah with a mirthless laugh, thinking of the weight she had added to Conner's shoulders in telling him even a sliver of her history.

"No," said Conner, pulling back a bit to look at her. "You are like the calm in the storm. You always know what to do when everything is going wrong."

"But I'm not always able to fix it," said Norah, deflating as Conner took a step back.

"But you try," said Conner. "Look at you—barely recovered from our journey first from Ireland, then to England, on to Canada, and then through America in temperatures I've never felt before. You have steady work, a new home, and friends!"

Norah didn't bother correcting him regarding her friends. He had already solidified in his mind the kind of life she was living now, and it apparently gave him hope. She couldn't take that away.

"I guess I just needed to see that 'twas possible to move on. After everything," Conner finished with a shrug.

"You don't resent me for leaving you?" she asked. "Bridget's letter said you were angry with me.

"Resent you?" Conner laughed. "Why do you think I'm here in the first place? You gave me the idea. I think I just needed a bit of space, a bit of time to see what I'm made of. And to heal, if I can."

"To be honest, I thought you might be on your way back to Canada."

Conner nodded thoughtfully at that as if it were a real possibility. "Maybe if we can earn enough money. Nolan and I were looking for work," he said. "We figure we might head over to the coal mines. I hear the wage is decent."

Norah paled. "Oh, Conner."

"I know, I know," said Conner with a wave of his hand. "It's dangerous work. But no more dangerous than all those machines Finn and I have been about fixing in the factory in Boston."

Norah tried not to react at the sound of Finnegan's name. She bit her lip to keep from asking after him. She could barely remember seeing him during the time she was sick, though hazy memories told her he had been near more often than not.

"Sorry," said Conner. "I shouldn't keep mentioning him. I know you didn't part on happy terms."

"I don't know what you're talking about," said Norah as lightly as she could, looking about to check the position of the sun and glance around the corner of the building.

"I'm not blind, you know," Conner snorted. "You forget that I saw the two of you on deck more than once. You didn't try very hard to hide things. I think even Alastar suspected there might have been something going on between the two of you and you know how unobservant he is. Was."

The last word was added hastily and with a bittersweet smile.

"What?" Norah sputtered. "I find it hard to believe that your brothers would never have said a word if that were true."

"Only because Ma threatened them within an inch of their lives," he said with a laugh. "The minute she suspected Finn might be a bit soft on you—which was very early on, you should know—Ma took all my brothers aside and told them to leave you alone. You weren't to be teased or treated poorly. Not when Finn might finally 'have a chance at love again.' Though whatever that meant, she never said."

Norah allowed herself to sag against the wall of the building by which they stood, her gaze searching unseeingly as she struggled to find truth in Conner's words. "But—but they never said, like. Not even after . . ."

"You think my brothers would go against my ma just because she wasn't there to follow through on her threat anymore?" Conner shook his head with a sad smile.

"Conner, I'm—I'm Protestant."

"Are you?" he asked meaningfully, holding her gaze for several long moments. He ignored the way Norah turned bright red, and he eventually pressed on. "So was Ma before she met Da, though she never talked about it. Her grandparents were English, after all. Da met her when he went to look for work up north. My granddad had a farm up near Tipperary."

"Met her when he worked for her da?" Norah asked absently, her mind still racing. "Like Niamh?"

The confused way Conner looked at her gave Norah the distinct impression that he at least didn't know the whole of Finn's story. None of his siblings did, by the sound of it. But, from what Conner said, both the elder and younger Mrs. Boyds might have. The women had been far more observant and understanding than Norah had ever given them credit for. A pang of disappointment shot through Norah's heart at the realization that she would never be able to express to them what their acceptance had meant to her.

"So I guess the question is, does it change anything?" Conner asked, looking at her expectantly. "Knowing that no one was ever going to stand in your way?"

No one, that was, except for the one person that mattered. Finn had never seemed overly concerned about her religion—he had never even brought it up. No, he had distanced himself from her immediately after she had told him about herself. If he couldn't handle her past, he couldn't have ever truly loved her, could he?

"No," said Norah after a moment's thought, answering both Conner's question and her own internal musings. "Things are the way they should be. Except . . .I can't let you go to those mines, Conner. Your mother would never forgive me, knowing I had the chance to say something. Stay here. There are plenty of men working at the mills now. There are lots of Irish lads like yourself who are boarding in town and making a better wage than some of the factories in Boston. Besides, I'm sure I can put in a good word for my *brother.*"

She winked, and he laughed heartily, moving to put an arm around her shoulders as they slowly made their way back to the main walkway. Nolan was walking back towards them, a hand pie in each hand and a hopeful expression.

"Maybe we can stay for a while," said Conner, a bit of optimism trickling into his voice. "Until we find something better."

"Something your ma would approve of," agreed Norah. After everything Mrs. Boyd had done for Norah, all the kindnesses, the least Norah could do was try to be the voice of reason for the wayward Boyd son.

"I think I can do that," said Conner, taking in a deep breath. His eyes were a little brighter than before. It was all Norah could ask for.

CHAPTER TWENTY-TWO

The handkerchief Finn was using to wipe his brow was entirely drenched by now. He could feel his hair sticking to his forehead and was sure that the moisture worked to darken his hair to a truer red. The oppressive heat and humidity would take some getting used to. Or perhaps there was a place within this new country that wasn't as hot. But then he remembered the frigid cold of only a few months before with a shiver and tried to feel more grateful.

Bridget and Norah had been corresponding since the Boyds had settled into Boston. It was the only reason Finn knew where Norah was living. And yet, he hadn't heard a word from her himself, either through Bridget or in a letter addressed to him. He hadn't expected to, really. There had been a finality to the way Norah had disappeared from their lives. She had left them the rest of her money. And that was that. *How easy had it been for her to just walk away?* he sometimes wondered a little bitterly, though he knew it wasn't fair. She had the strength to do what he did not.

And yet now he was expected—nay, had *volunteered* to come to talk to her and to ask for assistance in his search for Conner. He'd long ago admitted to fits of madness when it came to Norah McGowan, but this was an entirely different type of insanity.

To distract himself from what he was about to do, Finn focused on taking in the city about him. He marveled at the genius of how the city of Lowell was set up as he walked through the heart of it and along its many canals. The river that the town had been built around had been channeled into a canal that ran the length of the mills and powered the factories themselves. Although Finn wouldn't have considered himself brilliant by any means, simply witnessing such a modern marvel inspired him. What new contraptions could be thought up to make life easier or to improve efficiency and safety?

As he made his way between the tall, red-brick buildings, Finn slowed his pace. Without thinking about it, he wiped his face on his shirtsleeve, trying to make himself more presentable. He held the direction of the last letter Norah had sent to Bridget a few weeks prior and looked around for anyone who might help him find the boarding-house in question. Several people were walking about the area, most of them lasses in what looked like their Sunday best. Finn thought it a little late in the afternoon to be attending church, but with as many people as it took to work in all of the buildings, he thought perhaps they might have to take turns attending services.

"Excuse me, miss," Finn said as he approached a young woman and her two companions. "I was hoping you might help me find this boardinghouse."

The young woman, who couldn't have been more than fifteen or sixteen years old, squinted at the paper in Finn's hand.

"Oh, but you've passed it," said the girl, spinning around and pointing to a building several hundred feet back. "That's the one you want."

"Thank you," said Finn as he pointed his feet in the right direction. He had to force himself to breathe normally, but he could do nothing about the pounding of his heart. At least, he thought with a little relief, his ears were already red from the day of walking under the summer sun. They couldn't give him away in their current state.

Finn knocked on the door, looking up at the size of the building as he did so. It looked sturdy enough—better than his family's tiny apartment in Boston, at any rate. It was a comfort to know that Norah was able to call such a place home.

"May I help you?" an older woman with spectacles and a sour expression asked as she looked Finn up and down disapprovingly.

"I'm looking for Miss Norah McGowan," said Finn, not sure if he should act contrite or stand taller under the woman's scrutiny.

The woman's eyebrows rose in surprise at his request. "Visiting hours are almost over," she said. She leaned in closer, squinting at him as if only just noticing something. "Are you her brother, too? You look a bit like the other boy."

"The other boy?" Finn wondered aloud. He had never been told he looked like anyone before. He had a different coloring than all of his siblings, though they did share the same color eyes, and someone had once said their mouths were similar. "I don't suppose you've seen Conner then?" Finn asked, knowing it would be too great a thing to ask for him to be able to stop looking for his brother and rest like his body wanted to.

"I think that's his name, yes," said the woman. Her pursed lips relaxed somewhat before she opened the door a little wider. "You might as well come in, then. As I said, visiting hours are almost over, but you can find Norah in the sitting room there." She indicated a room off the hallway, moving to close the door behind Finn as he shuffled in the direction she had shown him.

Finn paused just outside the open doorway. Norah, Conner, and Nolan sat on chairs around a little fireplace—although there was no fire in the hearth—laughing at something Conner had said.

As soon as he had determined that his brother was safe and in one piece, Finn's eyes turned to examine Norah. Her cheeks were fuller and had more color than the last time he had seen her. Her hair was pulled into a fashionable knot at the base of her neck and tied back with a ribbon, but a few wispy curls still framed her face. Although her hair was still that beautiful coppery shade that was unlike any he had ever seen before, he had never seen it look so bright, nor her wear it in quite that way before. Finn found it and her to be as devastatingly beautiful as ever. He closed his eyes in an attempt to steel his heart and features and prayed it had worked as he took a step inside the room, his cap in hand.

Finn felt almost guilty, barging into their perfectly happy circle. He had thought about turning around and walking all the way back to Boston, but then he'd remembered the full reason for his journey.

"Have you come to bring me home?" Conner asked as he looked up at Finn. It appeared the lad wasn't surprised to see Finn there.

"No," said Finn slowly, commanding his eyes to remain trained on his brother.

Conner turned to Norah, and Finn's gaze followed without his permission. She was looking at him as if she had seen a ghost. He knew he looked a disheveled mess, but this was not quite the reaction he had been hoping for, though he couldn't have said what reaction would have pleased him.

"Then why are you here?" asked Conner.

"I've been tasked with a message," said Finn, forcing his eyes back on Conner.

"All right," said Conner, folding his arms and sitting back in his chair. "Go ahead."

Finn nodded. "You're a man now, little brother. You're old enough to make your own decisions. I only beg you to consider your family and the heartache they're already going through."

"What about *my* heartache?" asked Conner, standing abruptly and taking a step towards Finn. Finn stood his ground.

A door down the hall opened and closed, and the sound of laughter followed. A moment later, several young ladies passed by the sitting room door, their faces full of curiosity.

"Perhaps we could talk somewhere more private?" Finn suggested.

"Fine," said Conner, though he looked far from pleased. He took another step towards Finn, then turned back to Norah and Nolan. "Well, you're not going to let him drag me back to Boston, are you? You'd better come along."

"But—" Norah began, her eyes flitting back and forth, likely in search of some excuse not to be alone with Finn. He knew the tactic well; he'd used it enough himself for the same reason in the weeks before they had parted. "Visiting hours will be over soon, and I'm expected to be in before dark."

"We won't keep you long," Conner promised, offering her his arm with a dramatic bow. Norah's lips twitched, and Finn frowned as she accepted his younger brother's arm.

They made their way beyond the buildings quietly, Norah still holding onto Conner's arm, Finn and Nolan following behind silently until they reached the canal. Conner stopped there, allowing Norah's arm to fall, and turned back to his brother expectantly.

"What would you like me to say, Finnegan?" Conner asked. "That I'll come home with you now that you've found me? That everything will be as it always was? Because I won't, and it can't."

"I know," said Finn.

Conner had no response to that, and Finn had the suspicion that his younger brother had been expecting to have to fight to maintain his freedom.

"As I said, you have to make your own choices now, Conner," said Finn. "The family and I just wanted to make sure you knew you will always be welcomed home. Bridget is worried about you—we all are. But I can see that you're well, and that will put their minds at ease. Are you working here, now?"

"I will be," said Conner. "Norah is to find Nolan and I work here at the mill."

Finn nodded, but he wasn't looking at his brother. Norah was watching him carefully, and Finn couldn't make himself look away. She didn't look happy—he could see the corner of her pretty mouth twitching down. He tried not to let his mind wander to a time when he had kissed the corner of that mouth. "That's kind of her," said Finn.

"Yes," said Conner, his voice suddenly full of amusement. "Norah's always kind, you know."

"Yes," Finn agreed. He could feel his ears burning and blessed the sun for the fact that no one would notice. Finn blinked and sent both Conner and Nolan a brief smile. "Will you be heading to Canada, do you think?"

Conner shook his head slowly. "Not yet. But perhaps soon. I hope soon."

Finn hummed in understanding. "Well, now that I know you're sorted and not eaten by wolves, I can head home and let the family know."

He placed his cap back on his head.

"So soon?" Norah asked, speaking to him for the first time since Finn had arrived. He couldn't account for the effect two small words from her beautiful mouth had on him. "You've only just arrived. You should rest first."

"Yes," agreed Conner. "Rest up, and you can head home tomorrow. Unless you'd like to run away as well?"

Finn knew his brother was teasing, so he didn't bother responding to the last comment. "Where are you and Nolan staying?" he asked.

"We're renting a room in town," said Conner. "Until we run out of money or can find something better with our wages. You're welcome to stay with us for the night."

Not relishing the idea of another nine or ten hours of walking, Finn agreed, and they started back the way they had come. Conner seemed to find something incredibly amusing because he kept snorting. From beside him, Nolan only smiled vaguely. For all the teasing Finn had received for being so quiet, Conner had chosen one of the quietest lads to make friends with.

When they arrived at Norah's boardinghouse, the men stood back while she climbed the stairs alone. She turned around for a moment before opening the door to mumble, "See you tomorrow, like," and then she slipped inside. When the door clicked behind her, Conner let out a guffaw so loud Finn was sure Norah would have heard it. He hurried to shush his younger brother, feeling his ears burn again. He wasn't sure what Conner was laughing about, but he had a fairly good idea.

"You should have seen your faces," said Conner. "The both of you!"

Finn growled, but Conner easily moved away from his brother and hurried on down the path that led back over the river and to the heart of the city.

"He's not wrong," Nolan mumbled as he hurried past Finn to catch up with Conner.

"You don't know what you're talking about," said Finn, annoyed at having to keep pace with his younger brother while said brother continued to tease him.

"I know a lot more than you think," said Conner, as he strode over the bridge connecting the mills to the city.

"Did Norah say something?" Finn asked, panting now.

Conner paused as he turned back to look at Finn. "She said a few things. But I don't think we're at liberty to repeat them, are we Nolan?"

Nolan shook his head of red curls. "Decidedly not."

"You're infuriating," said Finn, narrowing his eyes at them. "Both of you."

Conner and Nolan shared identical smiles, apparently much pleased with themselves. Finn couldn't bring himself to be quite as furious as he made himself out to be. After all, he couldn't recall the last time he had seen Conner smile, much less laugh. Finn hoped Lowell would be a good place for the lad. He deserved to be happy, after all. Finn ignored the little voice that told him that *he* deserved to be happy as well. It was becoming increasingly easier to do, and he wasn't sure if he should feel triumphant or concerned.

* * *

Norah was surprised to see Finn following behind Conner and Nolan as they approached her the following morning at the mill building they had agreed upon the day before. She had expected Finn to leave at first light, but there he stood, looking considerably less rumpled than the day before. He had even shaved, looking more like the Finn she had met in Liverpool. The one she had forced herself to keep at a distance.

Norah knew she had been staring a little too long because Finn raised his eyebrows at her with a little grin when she still hadn't spoken after they had all been standing before her for several moments. He had not smiled at all the day before, and she hadn't realized how much she had missed the sight of it.

"I don't have much time, like," said Norah, clearing her throat. "I'm on my breakfast break right now. But I've spoken with Mr. Cooper, and he's said you could both start today, so you'd better hop to it, like. You'll find him just inside that building."

She pointed to the tallest building to their right, and Conner and Nolan's eyes followed the motion. Finn's did not. He was still looking at her.

Conner turned back to his brother and embraced him quickly, clapping him on the back several times. "I'll see you next month, maybe," he said.

"Send my love to me mam?" Nolan muttered his request.

Finn said he would and waved them both off. Norah didn't know why she still stood there. If she had known what was good for her, she would have hurried back to her boardinghouse for breakfast or even back to the weaving room. Anything would have been better than standing opposite Finnegan Boyd, waiting for him to walk away again. He turned his gaze back to her and held it much longer than felt proper for two people who had shared so much but who couldn't quite say what they were to each other anymore.

"I wanted to see Conner off," said Finn. "Make sure the lad was fully settled. Thought it would be best to have some good news to bring home to everyone."

Norah could only move her head enough for a brusque nod. She was firmly rooted to the spot on the cobbled walkway, her body tense, poised for what, she didn't know.

"I suppose," said Finn slowly. "That this is goodbye then."

Goodbye? Of course it was. He had nothing to stay for—his life was back in Boston. Norah knew that, but the idea of yet another goodbye was too difficult to think on. It was why she had avoided the last farewell altogether. It seemed it would never get easier.

"You won't be coming back, like?" she found herself asking. Her face burned as she begged her mouth to stop. "To see Conner, that is?"

"I'm not sure," said Finn. His eyes looked troubled; he didn't want to come back. She couldn't blame him for it. After all, he had made it perfectly clear that there would be nothing between them moving forward. His return would only complicate things and make it more difficult to find a sense of normalcy. Wasn't that what she had been trying to achieve by leaving the Boyds in the first place? She had wanted to give them both the best chance at moving on.

No, Finn should not return to Lowell. Norah would make sure to encourage Conner to visit his family in Boston as often as possible so as to avoid this ever happening again.

Finn took a step towards her and then another before her mind had time to register the change. "Did you want me to?" His voice came out as a whisper, so close now that she could feel his breath on her face.

"No," she answered so quickly that Finn flinched and took a half step back, the hurt evident in his eyes.

"Yes," Norah amended, and Finn's eyes flashed back up to her face, causing her to panic. What did he want her to say? "No. I don't know."

Something in Finn's eyes changed then; where once she had seen confusion, she now saw defeat. And she wasn't sure what to make of it.

"*Go bhfóire Dia orainn!*" Finn muttered before moving to take her face in his hands.

Heaven help us.

Norah couldn't have agreed more. After months of his being the one to keep her at a distance, Finn had finally closed the space between them. He pressed his lips to hers, and, without thought, Norah moved into him, placing her hands on his shoulders and stepping closer. Finn did not seem to mind. His hands traveled slowly to her shoulders and down to her waist, where they held her to him gently. It was so incredibly like Finn—gentle and loving and everything she had come to know him to be. Everything she had wondered if she had imagined—everything she had missed about him.

He kissed her as if they weren't standing in the middle of the street, as if those passing by couldn't see them, as if there was nothing improper about kissing a lass who you had pretended was your sister only the day before. If any of those thoughts crossed through Finn's mind, Norah never would have known it. He smiled into her lips, a sigh of relief escaping him, which Norah felt to her very core. This was happiness; this was home. No matter how hard she had tried to move past it, it still rang true.

Finn pulled away far too soon, taking a step back and pulling his hands from her waist like he'd been burned or, more likely, had finally come to his senses. Or both. His eyes were already troubled. Guilt instantly settled in Norah's stomach, but she wasn't sure why. He had been the one to initiate the kiss, but he was not happy about it, though there was no denying that he had been only a moment before. She wasn't sure what had changed, but at least that was in line with the last few months. She couldn't make sense of anything he did anymore.

Norah had heard Finn's siblings complain about his reticence from time to time, but she hadn't been able to see it at first. He had always been quite talkative with her, always trying to get to know her better. Now she fully understood. He had become closed to her. And she would never know why.

Finn was nodding at the ground with sudden resolve. "I told you I wasn't very good at letting go. Goodbye, Norah."

There was a finality to the way that he said it that answered her previous question. He had no plans to ever return.

CHAPTER TWENTY-THREE

Since meeting Norah, Finn had believed himself to have begun a slow descent into madness. Now, it seemed, his decline was complete. Because he had just kissed her in broad daylight, after months apart, without so much as an explanation or an apology. Then he'd run away, attempting to put as much distance between them as he could.

Finn had been trying for so long to make himself stop and listen to the truth—that Norah was not free. She was not his to love but had pledged herself to another man, however unfair to her the union had been. The man was a scoundrel—wherever he was. Finn wished a curse upon him and immediately regretted the thought. This mess was not entirely Norah's husband's fault, though there was no denying he took much of the blame.

Norah was Finn's Bathsheba, his Delilah unawares—but he could never, would never have her. He was determined this time to stay away for good. He would resist temptation. Never mind that he had finally felt at peace, whole again with Norah in his arms. It shouldn't matter. It shouldn't. But it did, and that was why he had left.

The return trip to Boston took almost twice as long as it should have. Despite his resolve, Finn had difficulty putting more distance between himself and the city of Lowell. Perhaps, he had concluded, it would have been easier to board a ship at the docks and go to whatever distant shore it would take him. It would be easier to keep his promise and ignore the string's tugging.

"Here he is at last!" Catriona called, pulling Finn into an embrace when he arrived home well after dark. He felt weariness to his bones but was most weary of spirit. He had no soft smile to offer the family members who crowded around him, offering him portions of their meal and asking after the task he had taken on.

"Where is Conner?" asked Bridget, wringing her hands impatiently as she waited for Finn to answer.

"Calm yourself," said Finn with a humorless chuckle. "You'll harm the baby."

Finn received a shove to his shoulder and a scowl from his younger sister.

"All right," said Finn, putting his hands up to placate her. "I found him. He is working in Lowell."

There was a collective murmur of surprise and then—much to Finn's chagrin—pity.

"Was she very unhappy to see you?" Órla asked gently.

Finn was tempted to ask who Órla was referring to, but based on the looks everyone was giving him, no one would have been fooled by his feigned innocence.

"I don't know," said Finn with a sigh of defeat. "Though she didn't appear upset with Conner at all."

"Well, she isn't in love with Conner," said Torin matter-of-factly. "So I don't see how that's relevant."

Finn, who had just taken a bite of the stew Catriona had placed before him at their small table, inhaled his food in surprise. He coughed and sputtered while the knowing grins on his family's faces widened. As he struggled for breath, he hurried to form some response that would throw them all off the scent. But, not surprisingly, he could think of nothing eloquent to say.

"What?" he asked lamely. Torin and even Daniel laughed loudly.

"There's the *fear dearg*," Torin hooted, using the old nickname as he flicked the tip of Finn's red ear.

"I've had too much sun," said Finn, pushing his younger brother's hand away and standing up to his full height as a reminder of which of them was the older of the two.

"Sure, boyo," Torin said with a nod and a wink, unfazed by Finn's attempt to assert his dominance.

"What are you on about, anyway?" Finn asked.

"You mean the bit about Norah being in love with you?" Torin asked. "I didn't think I'd have to explain it to you—not after Conner said you were wearing the face off her—"

Torin's words were cut off as Finn shoved him hard. "You don't know what you're talking about," said Finn in a deadly whisper. "None of you do, though you all seem to think you know the whole of it based off a few words from Conner."

"And our own eyes," Daniel muttered. At Finn's dark look, Daniel took a step back, his hands up as he shook his head, making it clear that he had no intention of fighting his brother-in-law about it.

"And Ma," said Bridget, coming to stand in front of Finn, her arms folded across her chest. "She told these ruffians to keep their gobs shut and leave the both of you alone."

"A lot of good that did," Finn said for something to fill the air while he processed Bridget's words.

"They aren't the ones who went and messed it all up, Finnegan," said Bridget, her eyes narrowed with displeasure. "You've done that pretty well all on your own, I'd say."

"I haven't messed anything up," said Finn. He knew there were a great many things he had royally mucked up, but they were not exactly the ones his siblings were referring to. "As I said, you don't know the whole of it. She's *married*, Bridget."

Bridget's mouth snapped shut with a click, and the faces of those around her mirrored her surprise. Finn nodded as understanding dawned on them, though he had never felt such disappointment at having been right.

"Are you sure?" Órla asked when it was clear Bridget was not capable of asking the question everyone was thinking.

"She told me herself," said Finn. "She was married when she was seventeen."

Bridget shook her head in confusion and finally opened her mouth. "And they're still married?"

Finn hesitated, rubbing his neck as he considered how to answer the question. "Divorced. Or separated somehow."

"Divorced isn't married, you eejit," said Torin.

Silence followed this statement, and Finn looked around, waiting for someone to set his brother straight. When no one did, Finn was again forced to be the voice of reason amongst them. He took no pleasure in it—in fact, the words felt as if they might tear him apart.

"'Tis to God," he said hollowly. "Or have you forgotten that we are Catholic?"

Even if the Protestant church recognized the divorce as valid, a marriage between two Christians, especially two Christians of the same denomination, was considered sacramental, bound on earth in the sight of God. Sacred. Unbreakable.

"Listen to your brother," said Da for the first time from his place on the other end of the table. Finn had almost forgotten he was there with them. Da didn't clarify which brother should listen to the other, and Finn didn't bother waiting to find out. He moved to the door without another word, hoping that a bit of night air might clear his head and, if nothing else, communicate to his family what he couldn't seem to—that there was no use talking about it. It had been a hopeless situation from the start, and he had only been fooling himself for ever believing otherwise.

* * *

After begging not to be let go for missing a shift at the sugar factory the day before, Finn was ultimately reassigned to an area where workers were needed and quickly. It was more dangerous work fixing larger machines which Finn was not entirely familiar with, but work was work, and Finn threw himself into it with all he had. He focused on doing his job to the very best of his ability, staying later than his shifts until the work was completed. This often meant that he got home later than the rest of his family, which was just fine by him. He wanted to avoid their pitying looks.

He thought more than once about following Conner's example of striking out on his own but quickly felt guilty for even considering it. It would break Da's heart to lose yet another son, and Finn would miss sweet Roisin and the other children something fierce. No, there was nothing to be done except to press on. He had done it before, though, admittedly, this felt so different. He tried to convince himself that it was because it was new and raw, but Finn wasn't sure he believed that himself.

"You're home," a little voice whispered into the dark as Finn arrived home late one night in July. He recognized Roisin's voice immediately and hurried to hush her.

"You should have been asleep hours ago, my rose," said Finn, finding her hand in the dark and leading her back to the bed she shared with her brother and sister.

"So should you," said Roisin. "Ma says she's worried about you because you're never home anymore. And Aunt Órla says you're just like Granddad now, but she didn't tell me what she meant because she says those words weren't for my ears."

"Or for mine, I'm sure," said Finn.

"I think they just mean you're both quiet," said Roisin. "But I don't mind. I like quiet sometimes."

"You'd never know it with all the gabbing you're doing, child," Finn chuckled. "Now go back to sleep."

"Yes, off to bed, Roisin," another voice whispered in the dark, and Finn cringed. He'd been avoiding Bridget for a reason. He always tended to open up a little bit more than he had intended to with her, and the lass was too curious for her own good.

"I'll get you some dinner," said Bridget as she moved out from behind the blanket, acting as her and Daniel's bedroom wall. She made her way to the small stove in the corner and began stoking the embers within as she uncovered a loaf of bread and started cutting it. Her movements were quick and sharp, and it didn't take Finn long to realize that she was angry.

"What did I do now?" Finn whispered, sitting down at the chair nearest her and bracing himself for her answer. But Bridget ignored him until she set a plate of food before him and then sat across from him. He could barely see her with only the light from the stove, but what he could see confirmed his suspicions. She was positively fuming.

"Are you going to tell me what I've done," Finn asked. "Or would you like me to guess?"

"This isn't a joke, Finnegan," said Bridget, slapping a hand down on the table as softly as she could but loud enough to get her point across.

"I never said it was," said Finn, sitting back in surprise.

"Norah hasn't replied to any of the last three letters I've sent her," said Bridget. "Nevermind that each one takes ages to pen, as Daniel is still teaching me my writing. But I haven't heard a word from her since your little visit."

"Why did you say it like that?" Finn asked. "'Little visit.'"

"Because I've heard all about it from Conner," said Bridget. "How you barely said a word to her when you were there, but as soon as he'd turned his back, you were *kissing her in the square.*"

"I—well—" Finn had no response to that. She was right, of course. But it wasn't like it sounded, and he wasn't exactly sure how to explain himself.

"I'm so ashamed I can't even look at you," said Bridget. He saw the outline of her face turn away from him as if to prove her point.

"It's not like I knew she was married when this all started," said Finn. "I would never have . . . I would have kept my distance. I know I should have anyway. But there was just something about her that drew me in—"

"This has nothing to do with her being a married woman," said Bridget. "Though I can't deny the news surprises me. I'm sure there's more to that story than you've said. No, this has everything to do with you not listening to a word Ma told you."

Finn's eyebrows knit together in confusion. "I don't follow you."

"What did Ma always say when the boys went courting lasses?" Bridget asked, waiting expectantly for him to reply.

She had said a great many things, to be sure. But with Bridget's severe tone and the expectant way she was waiting for him to say something, Finn couldn't remember one single instance, let alone the one she obviously referred to.

"'Never string a heart along.' You've done a poor job of that, and no mistake."

The air in the room shifted. Finn slumped in his chair, once again rendered speechless. She was right—of course, she was. Finn had taken for granted the fact that Norah was a strong, determined woman when he, of all people, knew how she had been mistreated. He had betrayed her trust in him and used her ill, regardless of anything else.

When he'd thought her free, he had been ready to set aside all sensibility and marry her. However, the moment he had learned the truth, Finn had cast her aside, not wanting to further tangle his heart and repeat the mistakes he had made in the past. It hadn't been fair to her—she hadn't been the one to cause his heartache all those years ago.

But when had he spared a moment to think about why Norah had told him the truth about her past? She'd had nothing to gain and everything to lose, and she'd lost him the moment she had said those cursed words. "After I realized my marriage was over—" What? What happened after it was over? He would never know. But what he did know was that he owed Norah an apology. He had thought himself in love with her but had not given her the consideration and respect she deserved. He regretted it bitterly now.

"How do I fix this?" Finn breathed into the dark.

"I don't know," said Bridget, her tone gentler than before. "But you need to."

They could agree on that, at least.

* * *

25 July 1846, Lowell, Massachusetts

NORAH'S EARS RUNG FROM THE NOISE OF THE MACHINES, AND SHE was exhausted from her twelve-hour shift, but she had promised Esther that she would attend a lecture that evening. The lass had begged and begged, giving Norah every excuse and reminding her that the next day was Sunday, so she could rest if she needed.

"Just let me wash my face and fix my hair," Norah said as Esther reminded her of the time. The lass was bustling about their small room in such a rush that she almost knocked over the small writing desk they shared. Esther hurried to pick up the paper and ink which she had spilled, apologizing profusely to Norah.

"I think I've spoiled the letter you were working on," said Esther, shaking the paper in the air as though it would help matters any.

"Don't worry, like," said Norah, moving to take the letter from Esther before she dripped ink on the floor. "I wasn't ready to send that one anyway."

"Have you seen my bonnet?" asked Esther, already moving on. She was patting the pockets of the apron hanging over the back of the chair, and Norah almost laughed at the idea of Esther finding her bonnet there.

"It's on the bedside table here," said Norah indicating the place where the offending bonnet lay in plain sight. "What has you in such a state? Will there be a lad you know at this lecture?"

Esther nodded, blushing fiercely. "I want to hurry so we can get a good seat."

"You mean a seat near yer man?"

"I wouldn't say he's my man, exactly," said Esther, picking at the ribbons of her bonnet as she finished tying it on her head.

"But a lass can always hope," said Norah fondly. "Why don't you start off then? I'll catch you up shortly. You can save me a seat if you'd like."

Esther nodded enthusiastically and was out the door without another word. Norah moved back over to the writing desk to tidy up, collecting the pile of letters that had been knocked over. She let her fingers run over the direction on the front of the first letter. The writing was unfamiliar, very much unlike the loopy scroll she had come to know as Bridget's handwriting. Somehow Norah knew who the letter was from, though she hadn't yet been able to convince herself to open it. Perhaps she never would; it might have clouded their final goodbye, and she didn't want anything to do that, no matter how much pain now accompanied the memory.

Norah placed the letter down carefully, retrieved her bonnet, and set out into the evening to catch up with Esther. She hadn't made it very far down the walkway when she ran into Conner and Nolan.

"Just the lass I wanted to see," said Conner as he fell into step with her.

"Are you going to the lecture too?" Norah asked. Once she'd taken a moment to inspect them, she realized that couldn't be the case. Nolan had a bag slung over his shoulder, and Conner carried one at his hip.

"No," said Conner. "We're headed to Boston for the weekend to check on our families."

"Oh." Norah tried not to show any emotion, but it was several moments before she realized she had slowed her pace considerably.

"I was wondering if there were any letters or anything you wanted to send with me," said Conner. He said it in that insufferably knowing tone he had taken on whenever he mentioned his family.

"No," said Norah quickly. "No letters."

"A message, then?" Conner persisted.

Norah all but glared at the lad. "No, Conner. I'm afraid I have nothing for your family."

Conner paused and gave her a long sideways glance before nodding. "Suit yourself. We'll be back by Monday. Don't get into any trouble while we're away."

When they parted ways, Norah allowed herself to slow down once more. Conner was going to Boston. He was going to see his family. That news caused an aching in Norah's heart that she had not expected. She missed the Boyds more than she could have imagined. They had become her family and, because she hadn't been able to keep her feelings for Finnegan in check, she had lost them forever. She felt the loss keenly as she imagined sitting around the hearth with Alastar and Catriona's little ones, watching them play and listening to their laughter. She missed speaking with Bridget, Órla, and Mrs. Boyd. She missed the feeling of belonging they had given her by making her one of their own. Esther and even Helen and Abigail were sweet enough girls, she supposed, but there was not the same sense of community. They didn't understand Norah's Irish ways. Perhaps no one ever would again.

CHAPTER TWENTY-FOUR

26 July 1846, Boston, Massachusetts

Conner's arrival home shouldn't have surprised Finn. Bridget had mentioned it at least three or four times during the week after she had received a letter informing the family of his plans to return for a visit. Even so, seeing the lad stride into the Boyds' apartment early Sunday morning as if he were the prodigal son left Finn with a feeling of emptiness. Here they were, all the living Boyds, save Michael, reunited at last. But there was still something missing. If the other members of his family felt the same, they didn't let on. Catriona insisted on making a veritable feast to celebrate Conner's return, and there was singing and catching up to do. But no matter how hard he tried, Finn couldn't bring himself to feel truly present for any of it, despite sitting there in the midst of it all.

His mind kept turning to the letter he had sent more than two weeks earlier. He'd still had no word from Norah. Conner had come bearing no letters, though Bridget had specifically asked about her friend. She had sent an angry look Finn's way when Conner had admitted Norah specifically said she had nothing for them. No matter how hard Finn had tried to set things right or how long he had wrestled with that letter, it still wasn't enough. Finn had to accept that; he had no other choice but to do so.

He was lost in thought on the walk home from Mass to their neighborhood in East Boston, surrounded by his family yet feeling all alone. It had been many years since he had felt the same sense of loneliness. He had felt it acutely that summer when Michael and Niamh began courting and for a considerable time afterward. But this was different somehow. In the end, Niamh had not returned his affections, but Finn was positive Norah loved him, even now. And God knew he loved her.

"Finnegan," Da called from the front of the group. "C'mere to me, lad."

Finn started from his thoughts, surprised to hear his father address him. Finn hurried to his side, glancing at the faces of his family on his way. There were those knowing looks again.

"Yes, Da?" Finn asked, falling into step beside him.

"Just a story for you, lad," said Da quietly. "Do you remember Cian Doyle?"

"Vaguely," said Finn. "I remember he was married, but I don't remember what became of him. My, I haven't heard his name in years. Wasn't he a few years older than Alastar?"

Da nodded as he stared at the road ahead, busy with people coming to and from church. "He got married about the same time as Michael."

Ah. That would account for Finn only having a vague memory of what Da was referring to. Finn had been too preoccupied with his own troubles to worry about someone else's.

"Mary Kelly was a slight thing," Da continued. "Remember, she and Cian had met through a mutual friend. I don't think they knew each other very long before they married."

"All right," said Finn slowly, struggling to remember any of the details. He could have sworn Cian Doyle's wife's name was Sarah.

"They got an annulment if you'll recall," said Da. "There were dozens of rumors as to why, but Mary's family had some connections in the Church, and they were able to push it through somehow."

Finn's eyebrows rose as he waited for his father to either continue the story or explain the purpose behind it. But Da didn't say anything more, and both he and Finn settled into silence as the rest of the family chatted merrily behind them.

Daniel was recounting what he had learned at the latest free public lecture at the Lowell Institute in Boston. Such a concept as a free lecture was still new to Finn, as his own education had been limited and brief. In that way, America had not disappointed. If one had time outside of work, there were often lectures or events one could attend, either for free or for a few pennies. Daniel had even told the Boyds of a plan he had heard about to create a library open to the public.

Finn had never worried too much about bettering himself when he had been destined to help run the Boyd farm, but there were so many more possibilities available to him now. Especially with Daniel's nightly lessons in reading and writing, which he offered to any member of the family who was interested. The lad would make a fair teacher yet. Finn, on the other hand, had no immediate plans for his future beyond working to make a life for himself and his family. But he couldn't deny that interest had been sparked in knowing *more* than he did now about how the world worked. Boston, he hoped, was a good place for that.

Boston's Irish community was larger than any Finn had been a part of before, save back home in actual Ireland. All the Irish here banded together against those who would rather they go back to their own country. It eased the tension by degrees and gave Finn hope that even the Americans would eventually recognize the Irish as their own.

"You should open your nightly lessons to some of the neighbors," Bridget said to Daniel as they walked hand-in-hand. "It would be good practice for you."

"But then how would Torin and the rest be able to ask their millions of questions?" Órla asked with an innocent smile.

"I don't ask a million questions," said Torin indifferently.

"Well, it's certainly more than a few," said Bridget. "But at least you ask them so I don't have to."

"See," said Torin, turning to Órla with a laugh. "I'm right helpful."

Everyone hurried to help make the midday meal after services so that Conner could begin his journey back to Lowell Mills long before dark. He had a shift in the morning, for which he was determined to be there. Torin had already tried to convince the lad to ask for his job back at the sugar refinery, but Conner was resolved.

"I'm going to try to strike out on my own for a time," Conner had said. He had given no further explanation, but Bridget had quickly shooed Torin away, insisting on a few moments alone to talk to Conner while he helped her cut vegetables. Finn told himself he didn't care what they were talking about and tried to find distraction by playing with the children. But even Oona's giggles proved insufficient to keep his eyes from wandering over to where Bridget and Conner's heads were bent together as they whispered conspiratorially.

"Uncle Finn," said Oona. "I've been teaching Cuán how to say words."

"Have you now?" Finn asked, focusing very hard on the lass.

"Yes," said Oona. "I've been teaching him everyone's names and all."

"And how is your pupil progressing?"

Oona giggled at Finn's serious tone. "Not well at all. He still calls me 'Nuh!'"

Finn's eyes flitted up to Bridget. To his surprise, both Bridget and Conner were looking at him. And Conner looked angry. The lad turned back to Bridget and whispered something harshly to her. Finn could only make out his own name being said before their voices lowered even more, making eavesdropping impossible. A moment later, Conner stood up from where he had been working with Bridget and stalked towards Finn, who could only guess as to what had caused such a fierce look in his brother's eyes.

"A word," said Conner, pulling roughly on Finn's arm. They were out the door of the apartment a moment later. Conner continued to hold Finn's arm as he pulled him down the stairs and out into the afternoon sun.

"What are you about, lad?" Finn asked, yanking at his arm and successfully freeing it at last. Finn rubbed at the place where his brother's vice-like grip had been only a moment before. He had to work very hard not to let his anger get the better of him and outright shove Conner in retaliation.

"What's all this nonsense I hear about you and Norah?" Conner stood with his feet planted firmly, his arms folded across his chest as he waited expectantly for Finn's reply.

"I don't know what you mean," said Finn slowly. He tried to think of what Bridget could have told Conner that the lad didn't already know. Finn had been under the impression that Conner knew more than anyone about what had passed between Norah and himself. But for the life of him, Finn could think of no reason why his little brother should be so worked up about it.

"Sure you do," said Conner. "What's this nonsense about Norah and divorce and things never working out between the two of you?"

"I don't know what Bridget said to you, but—"

"Torin was right," said Conner, not allowing Finn to finish his thought. "You are an idiot."

Finn bristled. "Did we come out here so you could berate me? Because I'd much rather do that inside and out of this sun if you don't mind."

Conner placed a hand on Finn's chest to stop him from escaping.

"I don't understand why you're so angry," said Finn. "'Tisn't like there is anything I can do about any of this, Conner. It's out of my hands."

"You're a coward if you think that's true," said Conner. "There's nothing I can do right now to be with Gráinne, nothing I can do to bring Ma or Alastar or Gran or Aunt Aileen back." His voice got higher and louder with each finger he ticked off to represent the names of their lost family members. Conner's breath was coming fast. Finn had just begun to wonder if the lad would pass out when his younger brother took a calming breath before continuing.

"But Norah is alive, Finn. She's living and breathing mere hours from here with a story you clearly didn't hear the end of, and you're sitting here moping."

"I'm not moping," Finn countered, but even he could hear how weak the argument was.

"She's right there," said Conner. "'Tisn't my place to tell her story, but she deserves for you to hear it. I think it would change quite a few things."

Conner's breathing was finally calming down, and the lad had relaxed a little, letting his arm fall from Finn's chest.

"But not from you?" Finn asked.

"I won't betray Norah's trust," said Conner loyally. "I think we both know enough to know that she is owed more than that. It's certainly more than she got from you."

Finn wished his family would stop reminding him of what a fool he had been. He had been doing a fine job of it himself. But what was he supposed to do now? Norah wouldn't reply to his letter. Should he send another, asking for the rest of her history, as Conner suggested? For some reason, the very idea left Finn feeling empty.

You're sitting here moping.

Why was it that his siblings kept making so much sense? Wasn't he supposed to be the reasonable one among them? Like a light opening from the heavens, like dark clouds dissipating after a storm, something inside Finn's mind shifted. The clouds parted, as it were, and all of the weeks and months of self-loathing and the years of hopeless pining gave way to something else entirely.

Finn had promised himself to live with no regrets, yet that was all he had been doing for years. He had been making himself miserable, first by convincing himself he could never love again and then by being sure that there was no possible way that he and Norah could ever be together. Everyone—even young Conner—seemed to be able to see something Finn couldn't, and he was beginning to think that he wasn't half so sensible as he had once thought.

But no more.

He would beg Norah for forgiveness for being the fool he was and ask her to finish her story. If there was any way forward, he would find it. They would find it together if she would let him. The only question was, would she be able to forgive him for betraying her trust? How he hoped the answer was yes.

"I'm coming with you," said Finn, just as surprised as Conner was by the exclamation.

"Sure you are," said Conner. A slow smile broke across his face, and he clapped a hand across his older brother's shoulder. "About time, too."

"How did you get so wise, Conner?" Finn asked, mussing up his brother's dark hair until Conner turned away with mock indignation.

"Certainly not by example, and no mistake," said Conner.

"Too right, lad," said Finn. "I hope to be better in the future."

CHAPTER TWENTY-FIVE

27 July 1846, Lowell, Massachusetts

Norah,

I beg you to allow me to apologize. I should have done it when I saw you last, but I was weak and didn't understand the full extent of my sins. As I think back on the time since we met, I am filled with regret at my actions.

Norah carefully refolded the paper, trying to forget the words she had just read. It had been a mistake to open the letter in the first place. She had waited as long as she could stand, but in a moment of loneliness and weakness, she had longed for a bit of familiarity. In all honesty, she had missed Finn and had hoped that his letter would indicate that he felt the same. But he stated that he regretted his actions and their time together. How could she have possibly misinterpreted that? His rejection of her after she had told him of her past had hurt like none before. She had known he was trouble from the very beginning—but she had only herself to blame. There must be something wrong with her, she had concluded; something she couldn't see or didn't fully understand about herself, but which was somehow made obvious to others. She was almost sure of it now.

With a sigh, Norah opened the letter once more. It was better to know the worst of it than to conjure up images of all the possibilities all day long, making it impossible to focus on her work.

Despite all of the betrayals you have endured, you allowed me to be your friend. You allowed me to bare my soul to you, to tell you the secrets I have long kept in my heart. But the moment you asked me to be the keeper of your secrets, I betrayed your trust. I was so consumed with my own sorrows that I did not stop to think or listen to what you needed. I have long considered myself the most sensible of the Boyds, but I have recently discovered that I am nothing more than a fool. Forgive me, Norah, for not loving you and cherishing our friendship the way you deserved. I beg you to forgive me for not trusting in you enough to listen to the rest of your story. If I could take anything back in this life, it would be that. Though it feels hopeless in this life, in my heart, I will always be

Yours,

Finn

Hers? After all that had passed between them, all the sorrow and the hurt and misunderstanding, he couldn't possibly mean it the way it sounded. Norah clawed desperately at the hope which rose within her, doing her best to keep it locked away deep in the recesses of her heart. It would do her no good on this new journey, this new life she was attempting to create for herself. Her childhood happiness in Sligo, the sorrows of Cork, and then the resurgence of hope in Liverpool would now be only points on a map in her heart. America was her new journey, and she intended to make the most of it.

"Are you finally reading that letter?" Esther asked quietly as she dressed for the day by candlelight. Helen and Abigail still lay in their bed, waiting until the last possible moment to leave the comfort of their blankets. Norah smiled faintly as she folded her letter once more and stuck it into the pocket of her apron.

"I thought 'twas time," said Norah. Esther had seen Norah eyeing the letter often enough, trying to decide if it would be worth reopening too-fresh wounds to read it. The answer, now that she had read it, was both yes and no. She was left with a feeling of bittersweetness. But at least now she knew all of it and could work to move beyond it.

"Are you still not going to tell me who it is from?" Esther asked. The lass was unable to hide her curiosity. "I bet it's from that 'brother' of yours."

"Conner?" Norah asked, confused by Esther's emphasis on the word "brother."

"No," said Esther with a knowing smile. "The one Helen said she saw you kissing. The ginger one."

Norah bit her lip to keep from grimacing. She should have known it would only be a matter of time before someone mentioned seeing her and Finn locked in an intimate embrace in broad daylight. Luckily, no one had said anything to the matron yet. Norah prayed that they never would, as she was already scrutinized closer than the other girls, what with her being Irish and all.

"It *is* from him!" said Esther with an excited squeal.

Both Helen and Abigail hushed her, covering their heads with their pillows. Esther ignored them and continued to press Norah for more details.

"Helen said he was very handsome," said Esther teasingly.

"I never said '*very* handsome,'" Helen's muffled voice called from under her pillow.

"Close enough," said Esther. She bounced back and forth on the balls of her feet, unable to contain her excitement. "Are you going to marry him, Norah?"

"Things are not as easy as that," said Norah. "But come, we have work to do. You'd best get Helen and Abigail up, like, before they're late."

Already ready for the day, Norah moved from the room into the dimly lit hallway. Several girls were milling about, chatting, and making their way out of the boardinghouse and to their respective buildings for the beginning of their shifts. Unlike Helen and Abigail, Norah had quickly grown accustomed to the early hours necessary to run a mill. As it was only a little after four in the morning, it was still dark out. Norah followed the other girls down the cobbled street lined by gas lamps, stifling a yawn as she went. She may be able to wake up on time, but that didn't mean she relished being awake hours before the sun.

"Morning, Norah," said a familiar voice as two figures hurried past, darting across the street to the building opposite her. Norah might not have recognized them in the dark had it not been for Nolan's bright red hair.

"Back already, is it?" Norah called after their retreating forms.

Conner turned around to look at her as he continued to walk backward towards his assigned mill. "I told you we had a shift this morning," said Conner with a barely distinguishable grin. "I'm nothing if not responsible."

Norah barked a laugh. She'd heard plenty of stories from his siblings to the contrary, but she had always known Conner to at least try his best.

"I'll stop by your boardinghouse around dinner, yeah?" Conner asked, hurrying after Nolan again and not waiting for Norah's reply. Norah turned back to rush down the street once more but stopped short. There, by the side of the building that Conner and Nolan had just disappeared into—

No. It had been a trick of the light, or the dark, rather. She was still tired, still trying to wake herself up. At least, that's what she wanted to convince herself of, and she fervently prayed that she was correct. Heaven knew there was only so much more she could handle without divine intervention. Being haunted by her past would definitely warrant that, to be sure, and Norah absently wondered if it was time to talk to Father MacGill.

* * *

By the time Norah's shift ended, she was almost positive she had either seen a ghostly apparition or the spitting image of Finnegan Boyd at least three times throughout the course of the day. The second instance took place when she hurried back to her boardinghouse with Esther for their short breakfast break. The third had been when Norah had finally finished her shift and began her meandering walk back to her boardinghouse. Her fingers were sore from running them over the length of moving fabric for hours on end, and, as usual, she had a pounding in her ears that never seemed to go away anymore.

240

In her current state, it was easy to attribute her hallucinations to fatigue. After all, there was no way that he could be leaning against the wall of her boardinghouse, his eyes on his shoes and his arms folded across his chest. It was far too natural an image to be a reality, and if Norah had learned any lesson in life, it was that if something appeared too good to be true, it probably was.

But hallucinations didn't often tip their caps as lasses passed by them and offer a word of greeting to individuals *not* experiencing the hallucinations. At least, Norah didn't think they did. But there was no mistaking that slow, soft smile that spread across Finnegan's face when he looked up and met Norah's eyes. Norah's heart knew that smile as well as it knew the feel of its own beating, and she felt herself answering in kind, though she fought hard not to.

The next moment her smile disappeared as she tried to make sense of his presence there. He had given her every impression—both from their last encounter and his letter—that things were finally settled and finished between them. And she was sure she had never met a more confusing person in all of her days.

"I thought I was going mad, like," Norah managed to mutter, maintaining several feet of distance between them.

"That's a fine how-do-you-do," said Finn quietly.

Norah frowned at his casual reply. What exactly did he mean by showing up like this, unannounced and, frankly, unwelcomed? "What are you doing here, Finnegan?"

He winced, and Norah fought the urge to feel guilty about it. This was her home, her attempt at starting over. As much as she had missed him, she didn't need this. She didn't need to apologize for wanting to defend her own survival.

"Back to Finnegan, is it?" he asked. He uncrossed his arms and stood up straight, but he did not approach her, for which Norah was grateful. It was taking all of her energy and resolve to force her heart to remain untouched by the dejected look he was giving her.

"It has been for some time, like," said Norah. Her words came out hard as she worked to close off her heart. They were back to the beginning once more.

"I suppose I deserve that."

Norah had no reply. After what felt like an eternity of Finn's steady gaze on her face, she moved to continue on her way into the boardinghouse. If he had nothing more to say willingly, she wasn't going to force it from him.

"Wait, please," he said, his voice strained. He moved to step behind her but didn't stop her from going. "May I speak with you?"

"You're finally ready to talk?" Norah asked. The words were biting, and all of the hurt she had hidden deep inside her threatened to spill over. She raised her chin and clenched her teeth together, refusing to show how hard-fought her strong exterior really was.

Finn only nodded, his eyes never leaving hers. "If you're willing. I thought perhaps we might go walk down by the canal."

Norah appeared to study him when in reality, she was testing her own mettle. Could she handle whatever it was that Finnegan had to say at last, after months of silence broken only by the most confusing letter she had ever received? She nodded once, hoping she wasn't remiss in thinking that she was strong enough.

They walked the short distance to the canal in silence. Finn held his hands clasped behind his back, his lips in a thin line, and his brows furrowed together, deep in thought. When they had walked for several minutes in silence, the flowing of water beside them the only sound, Norah finally stopped walking. Finn was so lost in his thoughts that he continued on for several paces alone before realizing it.

"You said you wanted to talk," said Norah, rubbing her palms on her skirts. They were sweaty and sticky in the summer heat, and she wished she'd had a moment to wash up. It might have made the whole ordeal easier to bear.

"Actually," said Finn slowly as he turned back to face her. "I was hoping you would do the talking for now."

Norah scoffed at that. "I have nothing to say, like," said Norah lamely when Finn continued to wait.

He nodded in understanding and took a deep breath. "It has been brought to my attention that I didn't hear you out all those months ago when you were telling me about your past."

"Not for lack of my trying," said Norah harshly. "You made it clear you had no interest in hearing the rest of my story."

"I was hurt," said Finn, lifting his shoulders and arms and dropping them in defeat. "I wasn't—haven't been thinking clearly for some time now."

"Is that your excuse, then?" she asked, shaking her head in disbelief. "Is the only reason you spent any time with me aboard the *Rosemary* because your brain had been addled?"

"I thought so at the time," said Finn so fervently that Norah's next cutting remark died on her lips. "But I think that might have been the sanest I've been in ages. Or so certain people have strongly suggested of late."

"Have you been talking to Conner?" Norah asked, her eyes narrowing.

"Yes," said Finn. "But the lad was infuriatingly vague. He only said I needed to talk to you. I should have come to you and asked you the questions that have been plaguing my heart instead of making assumptions that have hurt us both."

He took a step forward and then another. Slowly he reached for her hand. When she didn't immediately pull away, he claimed her other hand until both of hers lay gently within his rough but warm grasp. Norah cursed herself for being so weak, but still, she didn't move away.

"I believe you were telling me a story," said Finn, looking at their hands with the smallest of smiles. "You left off on the part about how your marriage ended—your divorce, I've assumed."

Norah started and looked up at him sharply. Finn looked so startled by the movement that he almost stepped away but seemed quickly to think better of it.

A dozen questions raced through Norah's mind at his words. Had he thought she was divorced? Was that what had upset him? With him standing so close, she couldn't make sense of it. She needed him to move away, to stop holding her hands so tenderly that coherent thought was impossible.

"I didn't get a divorce," said Norah with effort.

Finn blinked, waiting.

This was feeling eerily familiar—her divulging the secrets of her past and him standing in utter silence. Would he walk away once more when she had finished the whole of it?

"I left," Norah quickly said before she could lose her nerve. "After I realized the full extent that my husband was capable of, I walked away and intended to never look back."

"Did you?" Finn swallowed thickly as he waited for her answer. She could tell it took a great deal of effort to speak even those two words.

"Not in the way you might be thinking. I had never intended to have any contact with that man again, but about six months after I began working at the dyebaths, I received a letter from my husband's solicitor requesting my presence at the reading of my husband's will. He had died quite suddenly, you see—a disease of the liver, I was told. That was no great surprise as he drank himself sick more often than not. I felt wicked for wishing just such a fate on him more than once . . .and even more guilty once his solicitor read me his will. He left me all his moveable property, you see. My inheritance."

Silence followed her words, and Finn's mouth opened and closed several times before he was able to speak again. "That's where you got the money. Not from your parents, but your husband. You're a . . .widow?"

She nodded, wondering how this news could have been so shocking to him. Had he truly thought that she would have allowed him to kiss her, that she would have kissed *him* if she had still been married? She had more respect for herself than that, no matter how much of a counterfeit her marriage had felt. But he had thought her divorced, not still married.

Realization dawned as she recalled a significant difference between the Catholic and Protestant faith. Catholics believed marriage ended only in death. In Finn's eyes, she *had* been married this entire time. It had been his worst fear realized all over again—loving someone he could never have. Again.

Norah was caught between pitying Finn and continuing on in her anger. If he had just *asked*—!

"What did you come here expecting me to say, like?"

"I don't know," said Finn. "Not that."

He hadn't let go of her hands. He was looking at her as if seeing her for the first time, and Norah couldn't help feeling a bit unnerved.

The heat began to creep up her neck, and she hoped he wouldn't notice the way his gaze affected her the same way it always had.

"Then what did you come here for, Finn?" the nickname slipped out, and Norah regretted it on the instant.

A grin spread across his face. "Honestly?" he asked. "I came here to ask you to run away with me. I had this big speech prepared, asking you to either pursue an annulment to your husband or—or"

"Or what?" Norah breathed, oscillating once more between fury that he would assume her so weak and elation that there might be such a simple solution to months of sorrow.

"I was going to offer to convert for you," said Finn with a sheepish smile and a shrug. "We could move to New York, or you could come with me to Boston if you prefer. It doesn't really matter to me—wherever you are is home. I could settle quite happily here if that made *you* happy."

Norah shook her head vehemently. "I couldn't ask you to do that," she said. "Your religion defines who you are—you and your family. I couldn't. I can't take you from them. Not after all they've given up and lost. I won't do it."

Finn nodded, his eyes falling to her hands again. He had that look about him that told her he was struggling to find words, so she hurried to further qualify her statement.

"I made a promise to God that fateful night on that blasted ship," Norah said. "The night I watched over Roisin when I wasn't sure if any of you would live or die. I promised Him that if He would spare Roisin and your life, that I would try harder to see Him. You don't know how much I've wished I'd made the bargain for all of you . . . I've been attending church again for the first time in five years or more. I started off with some of the Episcopal congregations in town, like."

She had the fleeting thought that she should stop there—that she didn't owe him an explanation. But, as ever, she had difficulty censoring herself once she had begun. "I have even been to St. Patrick's. It's different than I thought it would be . . . I can't explain it. The closest I've come is that there's something familiar about it. I think Conner about had a heart attack when he volunteered to come with me to church after he first arrived in town, and he followed me into a Catholic church."

The words kept flowing from her mouth, and she couldn't stop them, but Finn was making no effort to add to the conversation. It was maddening not to know what he was thinking and feeling while she stood there, a bundle of nerves and uncertainty, pouring her innermost thoughts for Finn to see and judge.

Suddenly, Finn stepped away, dropping her hands and turning his back to her. He ran a hand through his hair, and when he was done, it was left sticking up in odd places. Norah had to resist the urge to reach out and flatten it again. It was obvious that Finn was distraught. Not so obvious was *why*.

"What is it?" Norah asked with exasperation when Finn did not turn back around.

"I'm kicking myself, is all," he finally answered, still turned away from her. "You've been alone here for months, thinking the worst of me—not that I deserved any better—whilst I've been trying not to think about you at all because I thought you were a married woman. I thought I was doing the proper thing. And all this time—"

He stopped abruptly, shaking his head and blowing out a sigh. Slowly, he turned back around and reluctantly met her eyes.

"Can you ever forgive me for hurting you?" he asked, his face full of remorse. "And for the heartache and wasted time?"

Norah didn't answer at first. Despite his revelation and supposed willingness to lose everything for her, she still held so much hurt close to her heart. For a fleeting moment aboard the *Rosemary*, he had convinced her that she was truly worthy of love, only to dash her hopes and leave her grappling in the darkness of self-doubt.

But there was no denying the truth. She still loved him. And it was only fair that Norah fully considered his question and its implications. But how could she do that when he was looking at her as if she held his salvation in her hands? How easy it would be to just say "yes." Then he would hold her in his arms and make her feel whole once more. Knowing Finn, he was very likely to kiss her as well. She closed her eyes against the image, shaking her head slowly to dislodge the distracting thoughts that filled her mind.

"No?" Finn asked, his voice farther away. Norah opened her eyes to see that he had taken a step back. His face formed into a neutral expression as he waited for her answer, but there was something not quite right about his eyes. He was in pain, and Norah fought against the continued desire to reach out and take it away. Not this time. She couldn't be strong enough for them both. She had given too much of herself for too long that she had no excess to give.

"I'm not sure yet," she said at last. "I think . . .I think I need some time to think about it, like. Before I can give you an answer."

Finn nodded, the wrinkles about his eyes becoming more defined until Norah had to look away.

"After all the mistakes I've made, 'tis only fair," he said, his voice unsteady. "I need to head back to Boston soon. I'll need to start looking for new employment, as I've pressed my luck coming up here twice now, and I doubt any overseer has the patience for that. But I'd like to write you, if you'll allow it."

Norah nodded once, keeping her eyes fixed on their feet, still not trusting herself beyond that.

A movement caught her eye as Finn seemed not to know what to do with his hands. He reached out for just a second as if he would move to embrace her but thought better of it, clasping his hands in front of him and then quickly putting them behind his back.

"Shall I walk you back to your boardinghouse?" he asked quietly.

Norah shook her head, looking out at the canal. "I think I'd like to walk here for a time," she said. "To collect my thoughts."

She could hear him inhale deeply then let out his breath, long and slow. "I suppose this is goodbye, then."

Norah nodded to her feet. "Are you heading back this evening?"

Finn shook his head. "Tomorrow morning," he said. "I walked all last night to get here, and I'm not sure I have it in me to do it again."

"Perhaps you could—" She stopped herself, second-guessing the request. What difference would an evening make if she needed to examine her heart and, more than likely, the most painful parts of her in order to answer his question truthfully? But, hang it all, she *wanted* to see him again, though it had the potential to bring even more pain. That had to mean something, surely. "Perhaps you could come and say goodbye before you go."

She chanced a glance at his face as she spoke, and she almost couldn't fight an answering smile, as Finn's was so wide and full of hope.

"I'd like that," he said.

Norah nodded silently, and Finn tipped his cap, bidding her farewell until the morrow, leaving her wondering if that glimmer of hope she had given them both would spark into a flame or die out completely with the setting of the sun.

CHAPTER TWENTY-SIX

Conner looked surprised to find Finn pacing just inside the door of his and Nolan's small, rented room when they both returned from their shift at the mill later that evening.

"I thought you'd be with Norah," said Conner, taking off his cap and moving to wash his hands at the small basin beneath the window.

Finn laughed derisively. "You overestimate my ability to woo a lass, brother."

Conner turned to Finn, placing his still-damp hands on his hips. He shook his head slowly at his older brother, only serving to irritate Finn.

"Let's hear it," Finn said, holding up a hand to indicate he was ready for his brother's ridicule. "Might as well have it out."

"I just don't understand why the two of you complicate things so," said Conner. "Don't you love each other?"

"I can't speak for Norah," said Finn. "I should think I'd made that mistake often enough already. It's why I'm in this mess to begin with—putting words in her mouth and making false assumptions."

Finn eased himself onto Conner's cot in the corner of the tiny room. He placed his head in his hands, staring hard at the wooden floorboards as his mind continued racing through all of the things he wished he had or hadn't said since meeting Norah.

"Tell me what to do, Conner," said Finn through his hands.

From somewhere nearby, Conner barked a laugh. "You know I'm only just seventeen, right?"

"I know," said Finn, looking up at his brother glumly. "But I'm beginning to wonder if you aren't the wisest of us."

Conner stood a little taller at that. "The good book does say, 'Out of the mouth of babes,'" he said with a laugh.

"You're well onto being a man, Conner," said Finn with a touch of pride.

Conner was positively beaming now. "About time someone saw it, too. But enough of your flattery. What seems to be the trouble?"

Finn's smile at his brother's antics disappeared quicker than a day of fine weather back home in Ireland. "Norah isn't sure she can forgive me."

Conner's expression immediately darkened, and he quickly folded his arms across his chest as if restraining himself from avenging the lass. "What did you do?" he asked evenly.

Finn almost laughed at the picture of the protective brother Conner created. But, in truth, Finn probably deserved the punch Conner looked ready to give. "Nothing more than you already know. I assumed she was still married—which I suppose meant that she'd been unfaithful to the blaggard of a husband she'd told me about. You saw the mess I made of everything with that assumption. I was . . .less than kind when I assumed she had led me to believe she was free. I said things I should never have even thought, let alone spoken aloud, and I blamed her for something completely out of her control. I caused her more pain—I, who she'd given her trust to, turned around and betrayed her."

Silence filled the room, and even Nolan looked uncomfortable with the abrupt change. He fidgeted, scuffing his feet against the floorboard and clearing his throat while throwing Conner a meaningful look.

"But do you love her?" asked Conner, looking back at Finn. He asked with such ease as if the answer to the question might solve all of Finn's problems.

Finn couldn't help but look at his brother in disbelief. Did the lad really think Finn would be so distraught if the answer was no? "Of course I do!"

"Does she know that?"

Did she? Had he ever spelled it out to her in as many words? His actions had certainly been confusing enough that there was little wonder she doubted him now. Resolve burned inside Finn's chest. He would tell her before he left. He had to. It wouldn't fix everything between them, but Norah deserved to hear it. She deserved to hear the words spoken again and again until they began to fill up the void of silence and loveless years she had endured from those who should have loved her best. Finn swore to himself that she would not doubt his sincerity no matter what her answer was. Never again.

Conner tsked. "You really are daft, aren't you?"

"I think you're getting a little too much enjoyment out of this," Finn grumbled. "Your time will come soon enough."

"Ah, but you forget," said Conner with an air of superiority. He patted Finn on the shoulder as he moved to sit down beside him. "The lasses actually like me. And I intend to keep it that way."

"Good luck with that, lad," said Finn. "Enjoy your high and mightiness now. You'll likely need more luck than you think before all is settled and done."

Conner chuckled and moved to join Nolan in the preparation of an evening meal, leaving Finn to wrestle with his thoughts. How could he possibly convince Norah of his feelings? But more importantly, was it possible to convince her to forgive him?

* * *

"That's the tenth time you've turned over in the past few minutes," Esther sighed, the bed creaking under her as she turned to face Norah in the dark. "At this rate, I'll never be able to fall asleep. You'd better just tell me what's bothering you so we can both get some rest."

"'Tis nothing, like," Norah said, her voice muffled into her pillow.

"Nothing doesn't cause restlessness," said Esther. "Is it about your Irishman?"

"He isn't mine," said Norah, turning over to face Esther more fully.

"Why not?" asked Esther. "Don't you want him to be? Does he want to be?"

"He as good as asked me to marry him," Norah admitted.

"Oh, that's wonderful!" Esther whispered excitedly into the dark. "What did you say?"

Norah didn't answer. At seventeen, Esther still believed that marriage was the solution to all her problems, and Norah hoped for the lass's sake that she was right. But it was not the reality for everyone, as Norah knew all too well.

"Not all marriages are happy ones, Esther."

Images of a life Norah had spent the last six years or more trying to forget came unbidden to her mind. Her naive anticipation of being able to call herself someone's wife and the added pride and sentiment of being a doctor's wife, like her own mother, was painful to recall. The abrupt crumbling of all of her hopes and dreams the first time Niall had shown his true colors to her only compounded on the anguish the recollections carried with them.

Esther's question broke through the gloom, and Norah was grateful for a distraction.

"But would this one be?"

That was the question, wasn't it? Would—*could* Norah and Finn be truly happy together? There were so many ways in which they were different, from the ways they were raised to the hardships they had endured. But they had a good many things in common, as well. Finn had a strong desire to help others, and he was fiercely loyal. He was gentle—he was sure. But would he remain so, when trials came, as they inevitably would?

Norah couldn't pretend this was the same situation as her first marriage. She had barely known Niall, except by reputation. But she was scared—far too scared—based on the way Finn had suddenly turned on her when things had become difficult, that Finn would not be all he appeared to be. Norah was reminded of Órla's declaration that every man had the capability of being good or evil if he chose it. What was Finn most likely to choose when it came to it?

"It's impossible to know," Norah concluded.

"Is he not a good man?" Esther asked.

"I think he is," said Norah. "That is, I hope he is. But how can you really know a person?"

"My ma always tells me to look at how he treats those in his life, especially his ma and those beneath him. Is he kind to them? Does he pass over anyone? I, for one, would like a man who likes children. I plan to have a whole lot of them, you see, so he'd need to like them well enough . . ."

As Esther continued listing the merits her future husband should possess, Norah considered the lass's advice. From almost everything she had seen, Finn had always been the model son, brother, and uncle, excepting that still mysterious incident of having pushed Conner into a stream.

Yes, he had hurt Norah immeasurably and quite unnecessarily, it seemed, by not allowing her to finish telling him about her past. But he had been, if appearances were to be believed, truly repentant and contrite. Why, the man had even offered to run away with her, to say goodbye to his family and religion, if it would make her happy. Which it most decidedly would not have done. But he had been willing to do it. For her. To make it up to her. To show her . . .that he loved her?

Esther nudged Norah's arm lightly, and Norah realized that the lass had asked her a question. "What are you going to do, Norah?" she repeated.

"I don't rightly know," said Norah.

"Well, you'd better figure it out quick," said Esther through a yawn. "I'd love to get a decent night's sleep again."

Norah nodded absently, realizing with a snort that Esther couldn't see her in the dark. "I'll try."

She did her best not to toss and turn, but sleep did not come easily. Round and round, the scenarios played out in Norah's head as to whether forgiving Finn and allowing him back into her heart would be the right thing to do. Because it definitely *wouldn't* be the safe thing to do. Opening herself up had been what got them into this mess in the first place. But would she be a fool to turn him away, simply because he *might* hurt her again? It was a war between heart and mind that she feared she would never win. Then she would have no one to blame but herself for her own misery or success. Isn't that what she had wanted? To never be beholden to anyone ever again?

As she recalled the oath she'd sworn to herself long ago, the answer came, slowly and softly at first, but settling into her heart with a burning she could not deny. Allowing herself to be friends with Bridget Boyd had brought with it heartache and pain, but gone was the loneliness Norah had forced herself to endure. For each obstacle and trial she had faced since then, there had been a Boyd close by to offer aid and support if only she would accept it. Sorrows could not be avoided—they were a natural part of life, as Norah knew only too well. But wasn't it better to face the trials hand in hand with someone than to do so alone?

It was still hours before sleep finally took Norah, but when it did, there was a smile on her lips and the seedling of faith in her heart.

* * *

FINN WAS WAITING FOR NORAH IN FRONT OF HER BOARDINGHOUSE when she hurried across the buildings for her breakfast break the next morning.

"Sorry I wasn't here earlier," he said with a tip of his cap as Norah drew near. "But I didn't think you'd have time to really say goodbye before you started work. And I . . .wanted to see your face in the light of day, if I could."

Norah felt a genuine smile spread across her face for the first time in far too long, and she quickly worked on rearranging the muscles in her face to show a bit more solemnity. Late-night revelations had led to an inkling of hope that might give way to just enough faith, if she could find a way to abate her fears.

"You asked if I could forgive you," said Norah, bypassing a greeting.

Finn's eyebrows rose in surprise, and Norah could only guess that he hadn't expected her to broach the subject so soon.

"I've given it quite a bit of thought," Norah continued.

Finn nodded, swallowing thickly as he waited for her to go on. Norah waited as he took in several deep breaths in anticipation of her words, perhaps relishing a little too much how her continued silence caused him to hold his breath altogether.

Norah took a step forward, and Finn's quick intake of breath was enough to pull a laugh from her lips. "I imagine that I can," said

Norah. "As I'm sure you figured out ages ago, like, I have quite the soft spot for handsome men who fall at my feet."

Finn let out a surprised laugh and reached for her, his hands pausing mid-air near her arms as he waited to see if his embrace would be welcomed. Norah stepped into him and wrapped her arms about him as she buried her face in his chest. She could feel Finn breathing in deeply, and she wished she'd had a moment to freshen up. But Finn only pulled her closer to him, running a hand up and down her back and up again into her hair, his fingers playing with the whisps that had already come undone from her bun, made all the more unruly by the humid summer air.

When Norah finally pulled away to look at him, Finn's eyes were burning with resolve, and some emotion that made Norah feel so incredibly wanted that she felt tears spring to her eyes before she could stop them.

"Have I mentioned how beautiful you look when you blush?" Finn asked, clearly unaware of the way his fingers in her hair were causing gooseflesh to appear on her skin. Nor the curious looks they were getting from the girls filing out of the boardinghouse on their way back to their respective buildings. With a glance in their direction, Finn gently led Norah around the side of the building and out of sight of the giggling girls who had been knowingly watching their exchange.

"No," said Norah when they had stopped around the corner. "But I've often thought the same about you, like."

At her words, the tips of his ears began to redden, and Norah didn't even try to quell her laughter at the sight of his suddenly flustered expression. Not, that is, until Finn bent down, bringing his face so close to hers that the tips of their noses brushed against each other. Norah reached up to place a hand on his stubbled cheek, savoring the feeling of him being near.

"Last time I kissed you, my sister about had my head for using you ill and stringing you along," he said. "I'm doing my best not to kiss you unawares again."

Norah smiled at how tortured Finn looked at the thought. "Ah, but you forget the old saying. 'You can't kiss an Irish girl unexpectedly—'"

"'—You can only kiss her sooner than she thought you would,'" he finished with a chuckle. "Even so, you've not been given a choice on too many things in your life, Norah. I don't want to be just another to add to your list."

"Are you trying to say goodbye again, Finnegan Boyd?" She pulled back enough to look him square in the eye. It only took a moment before he winced under her scrutiny.

"Not even close," he said, his expression solemn. "I was hoping that, very soon, at least, you would agree to never say goodbye again."

"You'd better say what you mean, like," said Norah. "I'll have no more dancing around, like, and leaving the other to guess a word's meaning."

"I love you, *mo ghrá geal*. I want to marry you," he said with a laugh. "I want to spend all of my days by your side. I want the pleasure of admiring your tender, giving heart and helping you however I can. Now you know what I want, but it doesn't mean a thing if none of that will make you happy. Because that's all I really want, *mo stóirín*."

"And you won't change your mind if things prove difficult? If your family disapproves?"

"I'm beginning to believe my family would be more disapproving if I *didn't* ask you to marry me," he said. "But no, I have no intention of ever changing my mind or heart. You have my love and devotion—unconditionally, from this moment forward."

It wasn't enough to erase all the past hurts, but it was a start to the healing Norah now believed would take place. With time and hard work, which they were both quite accustomed to, she had every reason to believe that there could be a future for them. So, when Finn leaned down once more and begged permission to seal his promise with a kiss, Norah was more than relieved to surrender her fears for the promise of love and a brighter future.

To know that they would both be given a second chance at their own happy ending was enough to cause Norah to pull away from Finn's lips with a laugh of pure delight. He followed her not long after in what she hoped was the first of many moments of joy to be shared. Together.

EPILOGUE

"Aren't you going to open the door?" Norah whispered expectantly when Finn stopped just short of the doorway leading to the Boyd's apartment.

"I wasn't planning on it, no," Finn whispered back, turning to Norah and slowly pulling her into his arms.

"Finnegan Boyd," said Norah chidingly, though she couldn't bring herself to be truly angry with him. "What would your family think if they found us out here like this?"

"Hm," Finn hummed thoughtfully into Norah's temple. "I should think, 'Tis about time.' Besides, you know as soon as we walk in there, there won't be another opportunity like this one. I wanted to offer you a proper welcome home."

Norah couldn't argue with that, especially when Finn leaned in to claim her lips with his own. The beginnings of his whiskers tickled Norah's nose and chin. Instead of finding it irritating as she once thought she might, Norah found something comforting and familiar about the sensation. Finn held Norah close enough that she could feel the steady rise and fall of his chest, and it was several moments after the door had opened and Bridget's gasp of joyous surprise filled the air that Finn reluctantly let his arms fall from about Norah's waist.

"What did I say?" Finn muttered from behind Norah as Bridget excitedly pulled her into the apartment.

"I told you," Daniel laughed from where he sat at the table in the center of the room. He held out his hand expectantly, a wry smile on his face.

"Did you know?" Torin asked accusingly. Digging a hand into his pockets, he pulled out a penny and begrudgingly placed it in his brother-in-law's open palm. Then, turning to his sister, "Did you tell him something? Was there a letter I wasn't informed of?"

Bridget's laugh mirrored her husband's. She was still holding onto Norah's arm as she led her into the room. "There was no letter, Torin. Just intuition."

"That's all some of us need," said Órla cheekily as she placed little Colum in her husband's lap and moved to embrace Norah.

A moment later, Finn reclaimed Norah from the womenfolk. He took her hand in his own, and Norah saw him searching about the crowded room until his eyes settled on his father. Mr. Boyd was sitting quietly beside the empty fireplace, watching the hustle and bustle of his family with a small yet contented smile.

The Boyds all followed Finn's gaze and quieted as they made room for him to approach Mr. Boyd, pulling Norah along with him.

Norah had always admired Mr. Boyd. He was a hardworking man who only wanted what was best for his family. But she couldn't help feeling nervous that this—that *she*—was not quite what he'd had in mind for his son.

"Your ma would be happy for you, lad," said Mr. Boyd with a nod.

Quiet murmurs of agreement filled the crowded space.

"They all would," Catriona said, wiping a tear from her eye as she held Cuán a little closer in her arms. The lad wrapped his arms around his mother's neck and gave her a beaming smile that looked like the spitting image of his father.

"Are you going to marry Aunt Norah after all?" Roisin asked, breaking the silence of the room and sending all of the adults into fits of laughter.

"Well, someone should, don't you think?" Finn laughed. "And I did think Conner was a little young yet."

"Oh, Norah!" Bridget said, pulling Norah away from Finn once more as the family gathered around the table for the evening meal. "We ought to make you a new dress for the wedding. Órla and I will do it, though I don't promise it will be as lovely as the one you made for me."

"I'm sure it will be perfect," said Norah. Her cheeks already hurt from all the smiling she had done since Finn had shown up in Lowell and convinced her to come back with him. "As long as you don't send Finnegan to buy the material."

Finn guffawed goodnaturedly as he sat down beside her and quickly took her hand beneath the table. Bridget, who sat on Norah's other side, took Norah's other hand.

"We missed you," she whispered with a watery smile. "Welcome back."

Finn squeezed Norah's hand to pull her attention back to him before leaning forward and unashamedly placing a chaste kiss on her lips right there at the dinner table for all his family to see. He lingered for a moment, his eyes steadily fixed on her. "Welcome *home*."

Home, indeed.

TRANSLATION AND PRONUNCIATIONS

Please note the pronunciations in Irish vary, as there are three distinct dialects. The Boyds would have spoken Munster Irish.

Aoifa – EE-fuh

Catriona – kat-REE-un-ah

Cian – kee-an

Cuán – COO-an

Gráinne – GRAWN-ya

Niamh – neev or nee-uv

Oona – OO-nah

Órla – OR-lah

Roisin – roe-SHEEN

céilí/céilithe – KAY-lee/KAY-li-huh – Irish, meaning a social gathering, usually involving music, dancing, and food

Éire – Ay-rah – Irish, meaning "Ireland"

fear dearg –fayr darrig –a mischievous faerie in Irish mythology, known for going about dressed all in red

go bhfóire Dia orainn—go FOR-ay jee-ah O-ran—Irish, essentially meaning "heaven help us" or "God help us"

mo chroí – muh KHREE – Irish, meaning "my heart"

mo ghrá geal – muh GRAW gyAL – Irish, meaning "my bright love"

mo leanbh – muh lawn-uhv – Irish, meaning "my child"

mo stóirín – muh stor-EEN – Irish, meaning "my sweetheart"

slán – slawn – Irish, meaning "farewell"

tá mé i ngrá leat – taw may ih ngraw lyat – Irish, meaning "I'm in love with you"

wean – a slang term used in some parts of the north of Ireland (where Norah is from) or Scotland, meaning "child" or "wee one."

la's – "lads" in Scouse/Liverpool slang

ta' – "thank you" in Scouse/Liverpool slang

paddy – a derogatory term used to refer to the Irish

AUTHOR'S NOTES

I have included the 1912 translation of the Middle Irish song, *Be Thou My Vision,* because it is closer to what would have been sung in Irish at the time than the Old Irish version. I have included the first, third, and sixth verses of the song.

I have shown only a glimpse of the conditions the Irish would have endured in "coffin ships," the ships carrying Irish immigrants, so named because of the abhorrent conditions that were essentially death sentences to many passengers. As the Boyd family were to have traveled in early 1846, the assumption would be that conditions would not have been quite as grave as in coffin ships that sailed later in the year and the proceeding years during the Great Hunger. When illness broke out aboard coffin ships, it was not unusual to see mortality rates in the 20-30% range. Some ships saw up to 50% of their passengers and crew members die before disembarking.

Because of government regulations in the United States charging ships more to make port there, it was not unusual for immigrants to be told they were traveling to the United States and then to be dropped off in Canada instead. There were hospitals and quarantine sheds set up on the islands in the St. Lawrence river, but unfortunately, some sick Irish didn't make it that far and ended up perishing on the beaches.

St. Patrick's in Lowell, Massachusetts, was not actually built until 1853, but the predominately Irish Catholic population established the parish itself in 1831.

ABOUT THE AUTHOR

R achel Nickle's two main ambitions as a child were to be a teacher and an author. With the publication of her *Hearts of Eire* series, she is now fortunate enough to claim both titles. Rachel graduated from Utah Valley University with a bachelor's degree in English education.

When Rachel isn't teaching or writing, her passions include going on adventures with her family and dabbling in various hobbies, including painting and attempting to learn new languages.

Rachel lives in Utah with her husband and their children.

Norah McGowan has kept Finnegan Boyd at a distance since the moment they met, intent on keeping her past behind her. Unfortunately for Norah, she is an enigma the normally reserved Finn is determined to figure out. Although she is closed about her past, she is also kind and caring—to everyone except Finn.

Both get more than they bargained for when his family and Norah must travel to America in the wake of the Great Famine and troubles with the law in Liverpool. Flung together aboard a ship bound for new opportunities and a better life, Finn and Norah grow closer, no longer able to deny the draw they feel to one another. Amidst sorrow and loss, secrets from the past threaten to make a future together impossible. They must navigate beyond the chasm of misunderstanding and their seemingly insurmountable differences to win a chance at love and belonging.

ALSO AVAILABLE AS AN EBOOK

SWEETWATER BOOKS

CEDAR FORT
Publishing & Media

AN IMPRINT OF CEDAR FORT, INC.

ISBN 978-1-4621-4290-3   USA $16.99

9 781462 142903   51699